THERE IS NO LIGHT IN DARKNESS

I love you to the moon & back.
xo,

THERE IS NO LIGHT IN DARKNESS

Darkness Series #1

Claire Contreras

THERE IS NO LIGHT IN DARKNESS

Darkness Series #1

Claire Contreras

To the most eloquent writer and avid reader I've had the pleasure of knowing.

The person who gave me one of the greatest gifts a dreamer can ask for: the love of reading.

I know that wherever you are, you're smiling.

I miss you, Papi.

Cover design by Sarah Hansen of www.OkayCreations.net

Photo credit: Aleshyn Andrei

Edited by Jovana Shirley of Unforeseen Editing

Kerri Williams

Formatting done by Theresa Wegand Proofreading & Editing

"Don't believe in everything you see.

Because what you want might not be what you need.

Hold your breath, jump with me, and we'll survive."

—Phillip Phillips

Tell Me a Story

PROLOGUE

Screams coming from downstairs wake me up. I rub my eyes and look at the pink My Little Pony alarm clock my daddy put on my nightstand. It reads: 3:30. I know it's not afternoon because there is no light shining through my windows. I throw off my covers and run to the door, opening it quietly. I look down the hall and see that mommy and daddy's bedroom door is open. That's when I hear the loud noises. *Bang. Bang. Bang.* Three. That's how many I hear. I try to make myself scream, but I can't. I've heard that noise before; it's the noise that happens when my daddy's gun goes off. That's the noise that happens before the deer stops blinking.

But there are no deer here.

I run downstairs and pass the pink *Happy Birthday* banner daddy was putting up for me before bedtime. When I get to the kitchen, I see a man walking to the door, carrying someone over his shoulder. The person he's carrying is wearing my daddy's PJs, but his head is covered. I gasp loudly when I look at the floor and see my mommy.

"Mommy!" I shriek. "Mommy!" but she doesn't look up from the pool of red water she's laying in. The smell makes my tummy ache. I kneel down beside her and start shaking her as I crinkle my nose. I look up when I hear footsteps and see a man that I don't know. He has one blue eye and one shiny eye. I don't like him. He's giving me a mean look. Behind him there's a boy I've seen before. We look at each other for a long time; he looks blurry through my tears, but I can make out his big green eyes. The shiny-eyed man yanks him by his arm and leaves. He yells something, but the noise in my ears doesn't let me hear it. I keep shaking mommy until another man comes in, a nice-looking man with yellow hair like mine and pretty sky blue eyes. He touches my face lightly as tears stream down his face. "Close your eyes, baby girl," he whispers. And I do. I open them back up when he pinches my arm. He lifts me in his arms, and I realize he's taking me away from mommy. "Mommy!" I shout as I try to squirm away, but he hugs me tighter. My eyes are starting to feel heavy. I try to keep them open to search for light, but I know I'll never find it.

CHAPTER ONE

Present

I open my eyes to the dark and shoot up into a sitting position. My chest is heaving, and my body is dripping in sweat. I put my hands over my heart in hopes of getting it to slow down as I gulp deep breaths in between heavy pants.

I hope I didn't scream. I hope I didn't scream.

I listen for footsteps, but the only sounds I hear are coming from the torrential downpour outside my window. I try to get my eyes to focus on my surroundings, but I can only make out the little red numbers illuminated on the black alarm clock on my dresser. 3:30. That number haunts me.

I take a deep breath again and plop my body back down on the bed. I've been having the same nightmare for the past twenty-one years. My new therapist prescribed a sleeping pill that's been helping me sleep dreamlessly. Tonight, it isn't enough though—not that anything ever will be. If the nightmare was just that—a nightmare—it wouldn't hurt so much. If I could understand it, maybe it would hurt less—maybe more, who knows. No amount of counseling is ever going to make me feel safe anywhere. I can't sleep without my bedroom door locked and double-bolted. I can't go anywhere without a wooden baseball bat in my car and a can of pepper spray in my purse. I don't feel safe anywhere—not even in my dreams.

A minute later I hear him pounding on my door. This is the issue with having a roommate. I sigh, getting up to open it.

"Are you okay, Cowboy? I heard you scream," Aubry asks as his concerned blue eyes search my face.

"I'm good, Aub. Go back to sleep; it's still early," I reply with a weak smile, hoping that appeases him enough.

He takes a deep breath and runs a hand through his shaggy dirty-blond hair. "I'd feel better if you'd let me stay here. Besides, Cole would kill me if I leave you alone right now."

I roll my eyes at that. "Aubry, Cole's in New York, and he's nobody to kill you over leaving me alone."

He shakes his head dismissively and pushes past me to step into my room. Aubry and I have been best friends since we met thirteen years ago when I moved into Maggie's house. She is Aubry's adoptive mother and my guardian. Both of us attended The University of Chicago, so it was only natural that we would room together. That was seven years ago, and we've been living together ever since. He now works for an up-and-coming advertising agency, and I'm a third-year law student at Loyola University.

"Where's Haley?" I ask as I walk back to bed.

"She left. We broke up. Long story. We'll talk about it later," he replies as he looks around my room, probably trying to locate my extra comforter.

I sigh. "Aub, really, I'm fine now. I'll get a glass of water, and I'll be fine. Promise."

He stops and searches my face again before sighing and shaking his head. "Alright, Blake, you know where to find me. If it happens again, though—"

"I know. Here," I interrupt as I give him the key to my room. He gives me a kiss on the head before closing the door and locking it behind him.

I switch on the television while yawning and stretching my back. I should find reruns of SportsCenter on right now, which is exactly what I need. When I find the channel, I smile at the sight of Cole in his sharp navy suit and tie. I let his smooth voice soothe me as I drift back to sleep. Later, I feel my bed sink and wake with a start. What is Aubry doing? I turn to see Cole grinning widely as he shows me the key I'd given Aubry earlier. After a couple of minutes of staring at him, I realize I'm not dreaming and launch myself at him, sobbing uncontrollably.

"It's okay, baby. I'm here now. Everything's okay," he coos as he caresses my back.

I climb on top of his lap and let him cocoon me in his protective arms.

I hate crying. It makes me feel weak. Unfortunately for him, I only let myself cry in front of Cole. Lately my nightmares have gotten more detailed, and my lack of sleep is starting to affect my life. Most days I feel like a walking zombie. I've been living on a 5-Hour Energy diet for the past month. I'm not even sure if I'm remembering things or making them up as I go. I feel like my reality and my nightmares are meshing together, and it's only a matter of time before I drive myself crazy with all of it.

"This one was so real, Cole," I say in between sobs.

He continues to stroke my hair. He doesn't have to say anything to me; he's been dealing with my nightmares for a long time.

"I know, baby. Go to sleep. I'm here now; nobody will hurt you," Cole says softly into my hair.

It isn't until I wake up a third time and feel an arm wrapped around my body that I register that Cole's sleeping with me. I turn sideways in his death grip so I can watch him sleep for a little while. Watching him sleep is an old favorite pastime of mine. When we were younger, I used to do it all the time if I had trouble going back to sleep.

I study the way his long brown eyelashes fan his golden cheeks. His defined jaw and twice-broken nose accents his features perfectly. The short chestnut brown hair I used to love to run my hands through. His full pink lips are slightly parted. My eyes drift down from his face to his toned muscular arms down his naked chest to his taut stomach that he works so hard to maintain, and they land on the V that leads to his masculinity, where my fingers itch to touch him.

As if on cue, Aubry barges through my bedroom door. "Russell is here," he pants, covering his face with his left arm.

I crinkle my eyebrows. "Did you open the door with the key, or did Cole leave it unlocked again?"

Aubry takes a deep breath. "He left it unlocked. Did you hear what I said?" he asks in an annoyed tone.

"Take your arm down," I say with a laugh. "We're dressed. Well, I am anyway. I'm not sure how Cole looks under these sheets."

"Well, as I said, Russell is here. I haven't let him in yet, but I don't think he's going to be happy that there's a guy in your bed. Actually, I know he'll be pissed that *Cole* is in your bed," Aubry specifies, pointing at Cole's sleeping form.

I groan. He's right. My boyfriend will be upset. Russell already has his speculations about Cole, and I don't want to add fuel to the fire. I've never let Russell stay the night, and if he finds Cole in my bed, it'll be the breaking point of our relationship. The last time Cole was here, he *accidentally* mentioned that I had the most comfortable bed in the apartment. Russell asked Cole how he would know that, and Cole answered that he slept in it all the time. That turned into a huge fight between Russell and me. I almost broke up with him over it because the last thing I need is somebody telling me what to do—but I need Russell in my life right now.

I sit on my knees and start shoving Cole's body with both hands. "Cole, you have to get up. Cole, wake up."

Cole's lips form a slow smile, showing off the dimple on his right cheek. "Hmm ... Blake ..."

I look back at Aubry with pleading eyes, but he just stands there laughing and shaking his head. *Idiot.*

I glare at him. "Aubry, can you go open the door for Russell and entertain him?" I hiss.

He shrugs. "Whatever. Don't be pissed at me when the British invasion catches you off guard," he mutters, walking back to the living room. I shake my head at his lame words as I continue to shake Cole roughly.

"Cole, wake up!" I say loudly.

His green eyes pop open, and he sits up startled. "What?" he asks confused. "I was just having the best dream."

I roll my eyes. "Russell is here. You have to get up and go to the guest room ... please," I beg. He narrows his eyes at me for a couple of seconds before muttering a curse and uncovering himself roughly as he stands. He stretches his arms above his head, giving me full view of all of his toned back muscles and that gorgeous firm ass of his that's covered by tight black boxer briefs. I close my eyes and squeeze my fists together to resist the urge to squeeze it. *Damn, it sucks to have to depend on people.*

Russell's stepfather is the Morris in Lewis, Smith, and Morris Law Firm—one of Chicago's biggest firms. I learned this two years ago, when we first met in law school. I started getting closer to him because of it. We were friends for a while before we became a couple earlier this year. The fact that he's smart, charming, good looking, and has a sexy-as-hell British accent, makes being with him painless. I do like him, though. He's a fun guy, he's nice, and he doesn't annoy me. As long as he doesn't try to push me to talk about my past, we should be fine for a while. The only people I trust can be counted on one hand. Unfortunately for Russell, my hand only has five fingers, and they're all taken by a trustworthy person, so he won't be making the cut.

Cole looks back at me with a smirk on his face, and I know I've been caught ogling. I shrug and he chuckles.

"We can make him leave, you know?" he says huskily with a mischievous twinkle in his eyes. My treacherous heart speeds up, and the butterflies in my stomach awaken.

"No, Cole. We can't," I sigh, trying to keep my composure. "Just go over there. I'll see you later," I say as I wave him off in the direction of the bathroom. "Thank you for last night."

I don't even bother to ask him what he's doing here. I already know the answer to that. Today is my twenty-fifth birthday. It's also a day that I do not, under any circumstance, celebrate. I don't accept presents. I don't accept phone calls. Nothing. My birthday is a reminder of the day everything was taken from me.

It's a reminder of death.

"Sure thing, baby. I'll always be here for you," he says with sad eyes and a grave seriousness in his tone. "Always."

He walks through the Jack-and-Jill bathroom and to the guest room on the other side before I can say a word. Russell knocks lightly before pushing the door open as I'm getting out of bed. I can feel the color drain from my face. They missed each other by a hair. *What is it with these guys barging in my room today?*

"Hey, what are you doing here?" I ask with a smile, trying to mask my discomfort.

"It's your ... Well, I found out today is your day—the one you don't like celebrating."

Hearing his flustered explanation melts away my apprehension of him being here. Bless his soul; he doesn't want to say the b-word. I think I might actually enjoy him saying the damn word. Everything sounds so nice coming out of his mouth. I blame it on the accent.

"Who told you?" I ask in a small voice.

"Aimee did. I hope you don't get angry with her," he replies in a sheepish tone as he shuffles his feet.

I smile at the sight of him as I try to think of ways that I'm going to kick Aimee's ass. Aimee is one of my good friends in law school. In the beginning, I wanted to get close to her because of her godfather. He's Mark Lewis from Lewis, Smith, and Morris. He also happens to be my attorney. I can't shake the feeling that somehow he's connected to my past, but I've never met him. The more I got to know Aimee, the more I liked her, so I eased up on my Inspector Gadget bit and just became friends with her.

I keep telling her that I want to go to her parents' house, using the excuse that I want to see where the mayor lives. Her father is the mayor of Chicago—something that she hates for people to know. She says she hates going home because she says it's too depressing. None of those things matter to me; I really want to go to see if I can find any dirt on Mark Lewis.

"It's fine—as long as you didn't get me anything. It's complicated," I say, not wanting to explain myself.

"It's okay. I didn't bring you a present or a cake or anything. I would like to take you to dinner, but not to celebrate today—just to celebrate us. Is that okay?"

I close my eyes. "Russell, that's still a celebration," I mumble under my breath.

"You have to eat, Blake. It's just a meal."

"I usually don't eat today," I reply quietly as I walk to the bathroom to brush my teeth. I do not want to have this conversation right now—or ever. "Can you wait for me in the living room? I'm going to take a quick shower."

He comes over to me and wraps me in his arms. "Sure, but think about dinner, please," he pleads before giving me a quick kiss and walking out of my room.

I let out a deep breath once he closes the door behind him. I skip to the door and lock it. I never leave my bedroom door unlocked when I shower. I'm startled when I turn back around and see Cole standing in the doorway between the bathroom and my bedroom.

"What?" I whisper harshly, making my way over.

"Nothing. You locked it," he smirks as he nods in the direction of the door.

"I always do, but you already knew that," I snap.

"Not when I'm here, you don't," he snaps back.

I tilt my head back and let out something that sounds like a growl of frustration. Cole laughs.

"What now?"

"You're cute when you're frustrated," he says as his green eyes dance in amusement.

"Give me space, please," I say as I push his chest with both hands. His chuckle vibrates against my arms, sending a shiver through my body. The sound of his laugh is one of the sexiest things I've heard—aside from Russell's accent, of course.

I roll my eyes. "Cole, just hurry up in here. I need to pee and shower."

"So do it. You've done worse things in front of me," he counters with a raised eyebrow.

"Will you hurry up? We can't both be in here at the same time; it'll look bad."

He closes the gap between us and examines me slowly, from my feet to my face, making me feel naked. His tongue coaxes his bottom lip, slowly soothing it, and I feel it affecting the aching parts of my body. If I could form coherent words, I would ask him why he's doing this, but I can only focus on his shirtless chest.

"We can both be in here," he says, inching closer to me until I can feel his breath on the side of my face. "I'm still sleeping. Need help undressing?" he murmurs as he runs the pads of his fingers down the sides of my arms, making my breath quicken.

I try my best to keep my composure as the air between us crackles with desire.

"Cole, please," I whimper.

"Please what, baby?" he asks huskily as he pushes a strand of hair behind my left ear and caresses my earlobe. His smoldering eyes dart from mine to my lips when I bite down on it, trying to contain a lustful sound from escaping my lips. He moans softly at the sight of it, and his own breathing becomes labored. I throw my head back with a frustrated groan and let out a gasp when I feel his lips press softly against my neck.

"Cole," I plead, panting. "Please don't. Please."

He stills and exhales sharply against my neck, giving me chills. "Fine. I'll go back to my room," he says gruffly, his blazing eyes boring into mine. "Just know that I'll be thinking very naughty thoughts and doing very naughty things to myself while I picture you naked and wet."

I squeeze my eyes shut and clamp my legs together tightly as he laughs and walks back to the guest bedroom. *Damn him.*

As I take a very cold shower, I begin to recall my nightmare and the day that my mind has been willing me to forget for the past twenty-one years.

CHAPTER TWO

Past

"Mommy!" I screamed. "Mommy!" But she didn't look up.

I knelt down in the pool of blood that surrounded her and started shaking her. I was still shaking and calling her name when a man walked in. He had one blue eye and one dark shiny eye that looked as though it could have been made out of glass. As much as I hated looking at his glass eye—because it was taunting me, looking everywhere but at me—I couldn't seem to stop staring. The eye was brown; his real eye was blue. He was bald, had a thick blond beard on his face, and was very big. I thought he looked like a monster in a scary movie. He walked into the kitchen and looked around, screaming something that I didn't understand. I trembled at the thought of what it might be. I looked around while he paced and saw the bloodied party hats and the cupcakes I had helped Mommy frost before bedtime.

When he turned around to go back outside, I saw Nathan hovering by the kitchen door. He was the little boy that I used to play with on the farm, and he looked like he'd been crying. I wanted to blink my tears away and ask him what he was doing in my house, but I was frozen. Nathan and I stared at each other until the man with the glass eye yanked him by the arm and yelled something. I wished I could have stopped the drumming in my ears so that I could make out what he was saying. When Nathan left, I wanted to get my knees off the floor and run to him; he made me feel safe.

I remembered the time at the farm when I fell out of a tree we loved to climb and Nathan jumped off to help me. He kissed my scraped knees and elbows and walked me to my dad.

A familiar-looking man stepped into the kitchen. He was young and had sky-blue eyes that looked tired. His eyes looked tired like daddy's when he came home from work. He had short blond hair. I'd seen him on the farm, too, I think. He reminded me of somebody, but I was too frazzled to think about it.

He held on to his chest, and tears formed in his eyes when he noticed my mom. He walked out after a minute of staring at her. He was wiping his face when he walked back in and turned to me saying, "Close your eyes, baby girl."

I saw another man walk in—a dark man. He looked around the kitchen, and I noticed his eyes widen when he saw my mother. He looked scared, which made me feel even more scared. This man was a grown up. How could he be scared, too?

I did as I was told, and Blue Eyes pinched me with something before lifting me in his arms. I tried to open my eyes again, but I couldn't. Suddenly, I felt very tired.

I crinkled my nose at the foul odor around me; it smelled like a mix of blood and gasoline station. I wanted to look around, but my eyes didn't want to open, even though I was begging them to. I needed to see Mommy. I needed to see Daddy. I needed to see Nathan. I needed to wake up from the terrible nightmare. I had something in my dry mouth that was keeping it open yet closed. I stuck my tongue out and tasted it. It was hard and stiff; it was fabric. When my eyes finally cooperated, I saw the black floor before I was jerked abruptly against a hard wall. I whimpered at the impact.

"Shit. Slow the fuck down. You're going to get them hurt," a man yelled. I recognized his voice as Blue Eyes.

"What does it matter? We're going to kill them anyway," the other man replied.

"Fine. Pull over right up there," the young man said.

We're in a car? I'm in a car? I started breathing heavily as I looked around. It was dark, but as the car slowed, we passed a street light, so I could make things out. I was in a van, like the one Daddy used to move boxes in. I twisted my body so I wasn't facing the wall, but my sticky clothes didn't let me move much. When I turned, I saw Nathan facing me. He was wrapped up in rope and had fabric in his mouth, too. His green eyes were wide, and he looked as scared as I felt. He had tears running down his face, and I heard myself sniffle back my own. My heart started beating faster when I heard the men step out of the car and slam their doors. I couldn't see anything beyond Nathan. I didn't want to see anything beyond Nathan. I heard the men screaming outside, the doors open again, and then I felt the van sink when they got into their seats and slammed the doors.

"Okay, so where are you taking them?" one man asked.

"Don't worry about it. I told you—you don't need to know."

"Like hell, what if Jamie asks me? I can't lie," he replied, sounding desperate.

"You will, though. Remember, I'm getting you that plane ticket tonight. You'll leave with your family. Just stay the fuck away. I'll have people watching you. If you step near Jamie or any of his guys, I'll start stripping off your family one by one."

"I didn't want to get involved in this shit anyway. Glass took it too far. Nobody was supposed to die—least of all her. What was he thinking? How could he do that?" I could hear sniffling coming from their direction, and one of them kept apologizing to the other. What is he sorry for?

The car stopped, and I instinctively scooted as fast as I could toward Nathan. We huddled together until the door in the back opened, and we were met by a pair of sky-blue eyes. I wasn't sure why, but he made me feel somewhat safe. I was glad it wasn't anybody else. Maybe it was because I could see the sadness in his eyes. Still, the longer he stood there, the worse the feeling in the pit of my stomach got. I moved as close as I could to Nathan, and he did the same until we were shoulder to shoulder.

"I'm sorry. I'm so sorry," Blue Eyes whispered. "I have to separate you. You'll both be safer this way. Everything is okay now."

He leaned in and grabbed Nathan, who let out a muffled scream, mimicking my own. Blue Eyes put Nathan over his shoulder and turned around. Nathan stopped screaming and turned up his head so that I could see him. I knew he was trying to be brave. My brave friend. My chest was heaving in sobs as I watched him get taken away from me. As I drowned in my tears, the other man started to speak.

"I'm sorry, little girl. This wasn't supposed to happen," he said in a broken voice. "I know you don't understand this, but I'm truly sorry."

I wished people would stop saying that to me.

Blue Eyes came back and closed the back door again before going to his seat. "I'm going to take you to a good home now, Baby Girl. You'll be with your Aunt Shelley. She's going to take real good care of you."

I fell asleep crying, wondering where we left Nathan. I hoped he was back home with his family. The next time I woke up, I was lying in a bed, untied, and a woman with blond hair and kind blue eyes was watching me. I made her cry when I asked her where my mommy was.

"You're mommy is an angel now, Doll," Aunt Shelley said as tears swam in her blue eyes. "She'll always be with you."

"Do you know my mommy?" I asked quietly.

"I do. I know your mommy very well," she replied hoarsely.

"Do you know where my daddy is?" I replied as I slumped my shoulders.

"No, baby, I don't," she said as she ran her fingers through my hair.

I asked her for my parents every day for months. One day I woke up with no hope and stopped asking.

Aunt Shelley tried to make me feel comfortable and never gave up on me. She started taking me to a therapist when I wouldn't stop drawing pictures of women with blonde hair lying in red puddles. The therapist asked me a lot of questions, and one day Aunt Shelley stopped taking me. She homeschooled me until I was ten and she got diagnosed with breast cancer. She had a double mastectomy and survived the cancer but still enrolled me in the local elementary school, where some of my friends from dance classes went. The school gave her the option to let me skip a grade since I was advanced, but she decided against it. She said that adapting to school was a big enough deal and that I didn't need middle school to be my first school experience.

When I was twelve, Aunt Shelley was diagnosed with lymphoma and was given four months to live. She never told me she was dying.

"I'm sick, Cupcake," she said one night over dinner.

I frowned. “Sick how?”

“I have cancer,” she said in a wavering voice. I gasped. I knew a couple of kids in school that had family members die of cancer.

“Are you gonna die?” I ask quietly.

Tears filled her eyes. “God needs another angel to help him, but I don’t know when he’ll need me.”

She told me she loved me and I would be with people that would take care of me. She said her neighbor, Phoebe, would take me to a good lady named Maggie Parker. She asked me to promise her that I would behave, continue to study, and follow my dreams. I promised her everything. I would have given her the world if I could.

One night after dance class, I lay in bed with Aunt Shelley as she was hooked up to uncomfortable monitors. She squeezed me to her side and held me close. We had a live-in nurse with us, which led me to believe that things were going very bad. Aunt Shelley refused to stay in the hospital and leave me alone. As I lay with her and talked about math and science, she asked me what I wanted to be when I grew up. I told her that I wanted to put bad guys in jail. She suggested I become a lawyer because I had guts or a police officer because I was selfless.

I looked at her with a smile on my face. “I love you, Aunt Shelley.”

Tears formed in her eyes, and I wished I hadn’t said anything. I didn’t know what came over me. I just had to say it though. It was the first time I’d ever told her that I loved her, not because I hadn’t always loved her, but I couldn’t say the words before then.

“I love you, too, Blakey,” she replied.

We fell asleep hand in hand. She passed away the next day. For the second time in my life, I felt alone, lost, and hurt. Thankfully, I only felt that way for a week—until I was taken to Maggie's house. That was where I met the people that I considered my real family. The ones I adored, would die for, and kept me going. The same ones I would shut out in order to protect from getting hurt by me.

CHAPTER THREE

Present

"So, did you have a nice weekend?" Cole asks, breaking the comfortable silence we had as I drive him to the airport.

I roll my eyes but can't keep myself from smiling. "You were here all weekend; you should know that I did."

"Did you like that I was here all weekend?" he asks as he jabs me in the ribs playfully.

I squeal and shimmy a little. "It was alright," I say with a shrug.

His chuckle makes me grip the steering wheel a little tighter. When we get to the next red light, I turn my body to face him. Whatever I was thinking about bringing up vanishes when our eyes lock and I see a mix of sadness and longing in his eyes that reflect my own. Honking cars startle us out of our trance, and I clear my throat as I turn my body to continue driving. I park in front of O'Hare International Airport and watch as he gets down and opens the back seat. He puts on a navy sports jacket before reaching in for his bag. I turn in my seat to face forward when he closes the back door.

"I guess I'll see you ... Thanks for coming," I say quietly, looking straight ahead. I've always been horrible with goodbyes, and goodbyes with Cole aren't my favorite thing in the world. I hear him sigh loudly and I tilt my head when I feel him get back in the car.

He leans in and my heart goes into overdrive when he picks up the hand I have resting on the gear. "You don't have to thank me," he says. "See you soon, baby," he murmurs softly as he grazes the top of my hand with his lips, liquefying my insides.

I'm not sure how long I sit there staring at the door that Cole walked through before my brain starts functioning again. I shake my head to clear my thoughts and notice a little black velvet box on the passenger seat. My first thought is: Shit. He left something. My stomach turns at the size of the box. *It could be a ring. Oh my God, is he going to propose?* I can't even think about that, but damn it, I'm reaching over and picking it up anyway. I don't know why I love to torture myself like this. I clutch on to the little box with shaky hands before I take in a deep breath and open it. I let out the breath when I see a necklace with a silver skeleton key on it. It's amazing. I don't analyze it too much before I snap the box closed and toss it back on the passenger seat before driving home.

When I get home, I start sorting through the mail and find a letter from the Lewis, Smith, and Morris Law Firm. According to the letter, there are things that I need to take care of in Mark's office. I can't understand what else he could possibly have for me. When I turned eighteen, I inherited my Aunt Shelley's estate, which made me $530,000 richer. I already had money that I'd gotten over the years when I was living in Maggie's house. I used some of that money to get Aubry and me the apartment we're currently renting. Before he got a decent job, Aubry helped pay the bills while I paid the rent. We now split the rent and utilities because Aubry said that he refused to be a charity case.

After reading the letter, I immediately call Cole and leave him a message asking if he's received a similar letter. I also mention the damn box. Cole had a bank account set up for him by his dad when he was dropped off at Maggie's house. According to Maggie, his father said that he could no longer watch him and begged her to keep him. He left her the bank account information to give to him when he turned eighteen. Cole hired a man to track down the money, hoping he'd find his dad, but he hit dead ends. I know his situation is different because—unlike Cole—I've always known why I have an inheritance and who it's from. Still, there are a lot of things about my past that I don't understand. I wonder if we will ever get the answers we want. I call the attorney's office and request for Mark Lewis to be present when I go in, but an hour later I get a call to inform me that he's going out of town.

As I'm opening the door for Aimee, my phone chirps in my hand. I look down and find a text message from Cole.

No letter, baby. Keep me posted. The box is yours.

I purse my lips before my mouth goes into a wide smile. I can feel Aimee's eyes on me, but I'm too concentrated on my phone to pay attention to her right now.

It's beautiful.

A second later I get his reply.

So are you ;)

The combination of his words and the little wink smiley face makes me smile like a teenager as I stuff my phone into my back pocket.

"Hey, gorgeous," Aimee says when she sees me. We kiss on both cheeks, like the Europeans we aren't, and make our way to the kitchen. She sits down on a barstool around the island that surrounds my stove.

"Are you hungry?" I ask Aimee as I pour her a glass of red wine. I always ask if people are hungry as if their answer is going to deter me from wining and dining them. I got my love for cooking from Maggie. She's a much better cook than I am, but I try to stay on her level regardless. My favorite part about cooking is drinking red wine while I do it.

"You know I'll eat anything you make as long as you keep pouring that wine," Aimee replies with a sly smile. "So ... anything new you want to tell me about?" she asks with a raised eyebrow as she eyes the shorts I'm wearing.

"Not really. It was just Cole being Cole."

She shakes her head. "I have got to meet that guy soon."

I laugh lightly. "Oh, before I forget, by any chance, do you know if Mark will be in town this week?" I ask nonchalantly.

"Hmm ... He should be. I heard my dad talking about a big trial coming up next week. He probably has a lot to do to prepare for it. Why?"

"Just wondering. I have to go by there this week, and I wanted to meet him. So I figured if he was here, maybe I'd request to see him."

"I still don't understand why he would be your attorney. I think you must be mistaken. He doesn't practice estate; he only takes on criminal cases. The one who dabbles in estate law is Morris. You should speak to Russell about it."

I don't know why Shelley took her business to Mark, but I know that I'm not mistaken. He's the one that signs off on everything. I'm only allowed to meet with Mark's assistant, Veronica Stein, about my estate. I know this because I have asked to meet with Daniel Morris in the past and my attorney has stepped in and declined the request. I asked Daniel about it one day when Russell took me to his house for dinner, and he said that Mark liked to deal with his clients personally. I didn't mention to him that I'd never even seen Mark in person.

"You're probably right. I'll ask Russell," I reply quietly as I serve our angel-hair pasta with vodka sauce. As we eat sitting around the dining room table, we discuss the usual—school, fashion, and boys. Aimee has had a crush on Aubry since they met last year, but Aubry had a girlfriend.

"So Aubry and that Haley girl finally broke up," she says, smiling over her wine glass.

I stare at her for a moment. "Is that why you came over looking like you were going on a hot date?"

She gasps and puts her hand over her heart. "Blake Brennan! I would never!"

We both break out in a fit of laughter before we continue eating.

"Aimee, I love Aubry like a brother. Hell, that's what he is to me—a brother. He's an amazing guy, but he always goes for the bad girls. You know the ones who step all over his heart just for fun. Well, yeah, that's what Haley did to him. He's taking the break up better than I expected, but still. I just don't want either of you getting hurt."

Aubry is a hopeless romantic, but it's as if he enjoys getting hurt. I wish Aubry and Aimee would get together though. Aubry needs someone stable in his life. They would make an adorable couple, too. I just don't think Aimee is crazy enough for Aubry.

Aimee leans into the table and places her hand on mine. "I know, Blake. I get that, but I really like him. He's funny, and he's sweet. Just don't worry about him ... or me," she adds in a soft voice. I search her face for a while before nodding slightly.

I don't know if it's a wine or food coma that I'm slowly seeping into as I sit here pretending to listen to Aimee ramble about God knows what. My eyes are locked on her fingers drumming against the table, and the strangest feeling washes over me. I'm still lost in the familiarity of the drumming fingers when Aubry comes in and interrupts my train of thought.

"Hey, Aimee. Blakey," Aubry says, smiling. "Is there any food leftover? I'm starving."

"Do you even have to ask?" I smirk. "You know I won't let you starve. Aimee, is it okay if I leave you with Aubry for a little while? I'm not feeling so good. I think I may have over done it with the wine," I say as I get up to clear the plates. It sounds like a lame excuse, and I hope neither of them calls me out on it.

"You overdid it with the drinking? No way," Aubry deadpans. He's such a dick sometimes.

"Yeah, whatever. Just be a gentleman and take care of Aimee while I lie down for a little while. Aimee, is that okay? I'm sorry to leave you hanging," I say, even though I know she's elated that I'm leaving them alone.

"No, it's totally fine. Go. I hope you feel better," she replies quickly. I see Aubry raise an eyebrow at her quick response. I fail to stifle my laughter as I walk toward my room, leaving them chatting.

After I lock my bedroom door behind me, I run to the desk on the other side of the room and open the envelope from the attorney's office again. Sure enough, it's signed Mark Lewis. I need to meet this man in person. I try to shake away the thoughts I keep having about Aimee and the drumming of her fingers. It is a total coincidence I tell myself repeatedly. Total coincidence—except I don't believe in coincidences.

I lie down with the black velvet box in my hand until Aimee knocks on my door to let me know she's leaving. I toss the box under my pillow and open the door to her smiling face. I laugh and link arms with her as I walk her to the door.

"I'll call you tomorrow," she says as she hugs me goodbye. "Thank you!" she whispers loudly.

"Don't thank me yet," I reply as we air kiss on both cheeks.

When I walk back to the living room, I see that Aubry's door is half open, so I peek in.

"Aub?" I call out.

"Come in," he shouts from his in-suite bathroom.

I walk in and look around at his messy room before I plop down on his comfortable bed. Aubry's room is bigger than mine, but the view from mine is much nicer, and I have a small balcony, which I love since I have a little set up for my organic vegetables there.

"So what'd you guys talk about?" I ask as I bite down on my lip to keep from smiling.

"Oh, you know, nothing of importance. We set up a sex date for next week. Other than that, not much," he says in a serious tone.

I wrinkle my nose as I sit up. "What?" I ask as I turn to face him.

He breaks out in laughter. "Just kidding, Blake, damn. I told her I'd call her next week so we can go have dinner."

"Why next week?" I ask confused.

He exhales harshly. "I don't know, Blake. I just need time to think about shit. She seems like a nice girl, and she's hot as fuck. I don't wanna fuck it up with her."

I walk over to him and give him a hug. "Good. I think you guys would be good together."

He kisses the top of my head. "I love you, Cowboy. Thank you."

I smile up at him and go back to my room. Once I'm lying down, I call Cole's phone.

"Hello?" answers a female voice.

I bite down on my tongue to suppress the urge to growl at her. "Hey, Erin. It's Blake. Is Cole available?" I say as politely as I can. *Why is she answering his phone?*

Erin Kelley is a Sports Illustrated model. She's landed the cover—twice. I hate her. I hate her perfectly non-frizzy wavy platinum blond hair. I hate her skinny, tall, gorgeous body. I hate her lively blue eyes. Most of all, I hate that she has him.

"Hey, Blake," she replies cheerfully. "He's in the shower right now. Do you want to leave a message, or do I tell him to call you back? I haven't seen you in a while. I heard you had a relaxing weekend."

Oh yeah, and I hate that she's so damn nice to me.

"Yup. My weekend was pretty uneventful, which I was glad for. Just have him call me back. It's not that important though. Thanks."

"I'll let him know, but I'm sure he'll call you back anyway," she replies kindly.

Ugh. Why can't she be a bitch? It would be so easy to wish bad things on her if she was a bitch. I know why I hate her. I hate her for the same reason Cole hates Russell. The thought of Cole hating Russell makes me smile.

"Thanks again, Erin. Good night," I reply, smiling into the line. Not that she can see it, but I know she'll hear it.

I hang up and sit Indian-style in bed, trying to get the image of Erin and Cole out of my head. I'm still clutching my phone in my hand and trying to figure out whether or not

I watered my tomato tree today when it starts vibrating. *Cole.* I smile—a showing-all-my-teeth, ridiculously goofy, "I feel like I'm fucking fifteen again" smile.

"Hey," I answer.

"Hey, baby, what's up?" Cole says hushed.

I always loved that he called me that. Now I wonder if he calls her that. My stomach drops at the thought, and suddenly, I hate it.

"Do you call her that?" I ask a little rougher than I intended.

He laughs—a full-out belly laugh. I hate him. "Why? Would it bother you if I did?"

"No," I lie as I bite down on the inside of my cheek.

"Yes, it would. If it didn't, you wouldn't be asking me," he replies, and I can hear him smiling. I want to scratch his eyes out.

"Whatever. Don't answer me. I don't want to know," I say annoyed. "I called to ask you if you've heard anything from that P.I. of yours."

Cole doesn't remember how he ended up in foster care. Maggie said his dad dropped him off when he was a toddler. He only remembers a couple of things before his dad dropped him off, though. One being an episode of *Transformers* that he watched—very helpful. I spoke to my therapist about it once, and she says it could be Cole's way of blocking out the pain of being abandoned.

He exhales into the line, and I shudder at the chill that goes down my spine. I can almost feel his breath against my ear. "No, I don't. Why? Did you find something?" he asks, and I can hear the exhaustion in his voice. His P.I. has gotten nowhere on the hunt for his father. I've been helping him search, but we always draw a blank. We can't even find a birth certificate with his name on it.

"No, sorry. Not really. I'm not sure. Maybe," I say before letting out a frustrated groan. I'm so confused that I can't even think straight anymore and I don't want to tell him anything yet. I don't even know if there's anything to tell. I'm going on a gut feeling here.

"I'm going to see the lawyer again on Thursday. I had to schedule the meeting with his assistant again. My friend, Aimee, says he's here, but when I requested him, they told me he was out of town."

"Damn. That's so weird, Blake. Let me know what happens when you go." I hear noise in the background, and Erin starts saying something to him, but thankfully I can't make out what it is. "I have to go, Cowboy. Call me after your meeting. Lo—" I shut my eyes tightly and hold my breath. "Later," he finishes and I exhale.

"Yeah, good night. Thank you for the necklace. It's really beautiful."

"You're very welcome. I've had it for a while."

"Well, thanks. I'll talk to you later, then."

"Oh, Blake?" he calls out before I press End.

"Yeah?"

"Only you." With that, he hangs up.

I smile to myself because now I know I'm the only one he calls that stupid belittling nickname. And I love it. Yeah, I'm an idiot.

CHAPTER FOUR

Past

I couldn't even bring myself to cry during Aunt Shelley's funeral. I sat through the services with a blank stare on my face, feeling desolate. I knew there were a lot of people around me paying their respects as I kept my head down. I didn't see anybody—just darkness. The only thing going through my mind—*why does everybody that I love leave me?* My answer was the same every time—*it's me ... It must be me.*

After her casket was lowered to the ground, I sat in front of the gaping hole, thinking about how much it reminded me of my heart. Phoebe—the nosy neighbor I was staying with until I packed up—told me to take as long as I needed. I couldn't find my voice to tell her that it wasn't going to be long enough. I sat staring at that hole with a rose in my hand for hours. When Phoebe got up, a man sat in her place.

"I'm sorry for your loss," he said gruffly, his own voice full of agony.

I remember wishing I could meet his gaze, even for one second, so he could know I heard him. I couldn't though. I couldn't let him see the emptiness in my eyes. I'd just lost the last person I had left in my life, and I couldn't even cry for her. *What did that say about me?* I wondered. Instead, I sat staring at his shiny black shoes.

"Thanks," I whispered. He sat there a little while longer, and then I saw his black shiny shoes get up and walk away.

A couple of days after the funeral, Phoebe drove me to Mrs. Parker's house. That was the longest car trip of my life. I was headed to yet another unknown home. I felt like a bag of hand-me-downs being tossed from one home to the next. I saw a sign that read: "Welcome to Peoria" and I knew we were there. Phoebe pulled into the driveway of a large two-story home with a two-car garage. The neighboring houses all had the same look. They were brick with manicured topiaries, and I couldn't help but wonder what a foster home would be doing in the middle of this neighborhood.

I was expecting an ugly gray house. That seemed more fitting. I hesitated for a while before I unbuckled my seat belt and stepped out of the car. I walked over to the trunk and waited for Phoebe to open it. Phoebe owned an old wooden-paneled station wagon—the ones that used to be popular in the late seventies or early eighties. I was pretty sure she got the car when it first came out. I was impatiently tapping my foot as I waited for her. She was a heavy-set white-haired woman, and it took her an hour to walk from the driver's seat to her trunk.

"Hey, you Blake?" a male voice asked behind me.

I tilted my head to one side and instantly got a crick in my neck. I cringed and began to massage it as I looked at the guy standing in front of me. He was probably about my age—thirteen—but much taller than me. He had dirty-blond hair and a lanky, long body. I craned my neck as best as I could to look into his hazel eyes. He reminded me of one of the kids that was in my class last year.

"Yeah, and you are?" I asked, raising an eyebrow. I wasn't in the mood for small talk today. I just wanted to get in the house and lock myself in my new room.

"Aubry," he said, extending his hand to me so I could shake it. I looked at his long thin fingers for a beat before I slid my hand in his and shook once.

"You live here, too?" *Screw it. Might as well be polite to the kid.*

"Yeah, it'll be three of us now," he shrugged. He had really big shoulders, but they were hollow looking. It looked like Mrs. Parker didn't feed the boy enough.

"Do you eat?" I asked, scrunching my eyebrows together and pursing my lips.

Aubry laughed, and when he did, the creases around his mouth showed. He looked like he laughed a lot. He was cute. He seemed genuine. I liked him. I'd become an expert at reading people. Well, at least I thought I had.

"I eat a lot. Momma says if it weren't for my metabolism and swimming, I'd be a cow."

I nodded my head and forced a polite smile.

"Mrs. Parker is your mom?" I asked, confused. Phoebe told me that Mrs. Parker fostered kids, but I didn't expect them to be that close to her.

"Yeah," he replied, looking at me like I was an idiot.

"Cool," I replied with a shrug.

Phoebe finally made it to the trunk and put her key in. As she greeted Aubry, I got my suitcases out and started lugging them toward the front door when Aubry stopped me and picked two up for me. Before we made it all the way to the door, another boy stepped outside. He was dark; his skin looked like smooth chocolate. He was tall—the same height as Aubry—but his build was muscular. He had big almond-shaped brown eyes, and his black hair was low on his head. He smiled brightly at me, and I was almost blinded by his perfect white teeth.

"Hey," he said as he eyed me up and down and made his way outside. I replied by nodding. "I'm Greg." He stood in front of me and grabbed the suitcase out of my hand.

"Thanks. Blake. Nice to meet you," I replied. He waved off my thanks as no big deal and turned back to the house.

"So he's the other guy?" I whispered to Aubry who was now walking next to me.

"Nah, he lives a couple of houses down," Aubry stated. "He goes out with my cousin Becky, and she's always here, so he's always here. Cool dude."

We headed inside and a round fair-skinned woman with short brown curly hair up to her shoulders walked toward us with a huge smile on her face. I let out a breath when her kind brown eyes found mine.

"Oh, aren't you the prettiest little thing?" she cooed before wrapping her arms around me. "I'm sorry for your loss, honey. God has a plan for all of us. I'll make sure you're happy here." She whispered the last part so that only I could hear. I wondered which loss she was sorry for. I wondered if she even knew about my many losses. I nodded against her shoulder but didn't reply.

"Thank you, Mrs. Parker. I'll be sure to stay out of your way. You won't even know I'm here," I said quietly once she let me go.

"Nonsense," she said loudly. "You will do no such thing. You will bother me as much as you can, and you will call me Maggie. None of that Mrs. Parker thing around here."

I gave her a small smile and looked around. The wooden stairs were to the right, directly in front of the front door. To the left, there was a sitting room with a large burgundy cloth couch and a white coffee table. Mrs. Parker laughed when she saw me crinkle my nose as I looked at the room.

"The couch is temporary. Cole opened up a bottle of pop on the white couch that was there two weeks ago and managed to stain everything. I had to get rid of it, but I didn't want to leave it bare, so I made him and the boys bring up this couch from the basement. They had strict rules not to go near the sitting area with food or drinks, but Cole is a bit of a rule breaker. He's grounded until Friday. No football, no girls, no video games. Since those are his three favorite things, he's been suffering for two weeks. He's probably moping around in his room, doing homework right now. You'll meet him at dinner time." Maggie had a soothing voice, and even as she told me the story—which she was obviously upset about—she sounded as if she was talking to me about cute little puppies in a pet shop. I could tell that she truly loved these boys, and it made me feel warm inside. *Maybe this place wouldn't be so bad after all.*

After giving me a tour of the downstairs area, Greg and Aubry helped me take my stuff upstairs and showed me to my room. Greg knocked on the first door to the right of the stairs.

"This is your room. Becky's in there now, cleaning it. She stays here when she comes over," he explained.

A girl with a wide smile, fiery red hair, and bright blue eyes opened the door. I'd never seen anybody with such red hair before.

"Hi," she cheered joyfully after looking at me up and down a few times. "I'm Becky—your best friend and sometimes roommate," she said before pulling me in for a hug.

When she let go, I looked at her and crinkled my forehead. "What makes you think I want a best friend?" I asked curiously.

"Oh, I can tell. You need one. You're wearing a sweater that's two sizes too big for your body, you have on sweats, and your boots make you look like you're going to work in construction. Trust me. You need me as a best friend," Becky said matter-of-factly.

To my surprise, I laughed. A real laugh. The sound was so foreign to my own ears that I scared myself. From the looks on Greg, Aubry, and Becky's faces, I could tell I surprised them as well.

"If you say so," I said with a smile as I shrugged.

The boys left us alone, and Becky helped me unpack all my clothes and put them into the drawers that she emptied out for me.

"So do you want to play dress-up?" Becky asked excitedly. I bit down on my lip. I was scared of playing anything that had to do with her dressing me up. I might go downstairs looking like a Moulin Rouge dancer.

"How old are you?" I asked curiously.

"I'll be fourteen next week. How old are you?"

"I'll be fourteen next month. So why would we play dress-up?"

"Pfff, you don't have to be five to play dress-up, Blake," she said laughing.

"Umm ... Well, I've never actually played dress-up. I just know that only little kids do it," I whispered, staring down at my hands.

She gasped. "You've never played dress-up?"

I shook my head and suddenly regretted telling Becky because I realized that I had given her permission to dress me up. Becky plucked my eyebrows, straightened my loose curls with a hair iron—something I'd never even seen before—filed and painted my nails, and applied makeup on me. I told her about living with Aunt Shelley and how she died a week ago. About how I don't really remember my parents because they died when I was little. I didn't go into detail about how or when. I'd never had anybody to talk to, and it felt good to confide in Becky. Not that there was much to tell. I'd had friends growing up, but they were mostly from dance class and school. It was going to be weird actually living with kids my age.

"Do you live close by?" I asked Becky curiously.

"Yeah," she replied distractedly. "A block over. I ride my bike here every day. Sometimes my mom works nights on the weekends, so I stay with Aunt Mags. I like staying here better anyway."

Becky gave me a plethora of information on everybody. I found out that Aubry was Maggie's adoptive son. She saw him in an orphanage one Christmas and knew he was meant to live with her. He was just shy of two years old and had been left there by his teenage mother. Two years later, Cole was dropped off by his father, who couldn't care for him any longer. Greg stays over when things in his house are going bad. He lives with his alcoholic mother and whatever boyfriend she lets move in with them. Maggie is good friends with his grandmother, but she lives a couple of towns over, so Maggie took to watching him for her.

"His mother's a bitch," Becky whispered loudly.

My eyes widened and my mouth popped opened.

Becky shrugged nonchalantly at my reaction. "She is. I'd rather not have one than end up with her as mine," she said, shaking her head. "Poor Greg," she added sadly. I could tell Becky really cared for Greg.

"At least he has Maggie and you guys," I said with a reassuring smile.

"Yeah," she sighed. "I just wish he could move here. He stays over a lot because he's Cole and Aubry's best friend, but still ..."

An hour later I was looking at myself in the mirror and was surprised to see that I didn't look like a flapper or the annoying lady from *The Drew Carey Show,* Aunt Shelley loved to watch. I looked ... older. My long dirty-blonde hair was brushed and straightened perfectly; my lifeless gray eyes were brightened by black eyeliner and light gold eye shadow. My already golden skin had bronzer, making it look like I tanned. I was wearing tight jeans and a tight periwinkle sweater that covered my growing chest and low furry charcoal-colored boots.

"You look sexy," Becky said as she jumped around me, clapping her hands. "Like a woman. I knew you had curves under all that funk you were wearing."

"I don't want to look *sexy*, Becky. Maybe I should wear other jeans or something. I don't want Maggie to think I'm slutty," I pleaded.

"Nope," Becky replied, shaking her head. "Aunt Maggie doesn't judge a book by its cover. She already met you wearing that hideous thing you came in wearing. She'll know I put you up to this. Trust me. I've worn way skimpier things. Your top doesn't even show off your boobs. You're wearing a sweater," she replied exasperated.

"Fine," I sighed.

We went downstairs and met Mrs. Parker in the kitchen.

"Aunt Mags, look at Blake's *transfermation,*" Becky announced triumphantly.

"Trans*for*mation, Becky," Mrs. Parker corrected as she turned around and looked at me with kind brown eyes. "Blake, you look lovely, not that you didn't already. I don't think you need all that makeup though."

"Oh, Aunt Mags, it's only for dinner. She's not going to wear it to school," Becky said, rolling her eyes. "Besides, she'd never played dress-up before."

Maggie gave me a sad smile before turning back to put the food on serving plates.

"May I help you?" I asked politely. I always used to set the table at Aunt Shelley's house. I felt like it was the least I could do.

"Sure, Blake, will you set the table for me, please?" Mrs. Parker asked kindly. "Becky, show her where everything is, please."

As Becky and I set the table, she continued to feed me gossip. She told me that she and Greg were a couple, but all they've done was hold hands. Apparently, the kids in school were already kissing—with tongue! *Gross*. The thought made me want to go brush my teeth.

"Why would you want to touch someone's tongue with your own anyway?" I asked half disgusted—and half curious.

"I don't know, but I think I'm going to try it with Greg at some point. I'll let you know how it feels," she replied wistfully.

I cringed. I couldn't believe she was even considering that.

Once we set the table and got the drinks, Mrs. Parker asked us to get the boys.

"Do Aubry and the other kid share a room?" I asked Becky as we made our way upstairs.

"Nah, they each have their own rooms. The house has five rooms. Maggie gets the big one at the end of the hall, Aubry sleeps in the one next to her, and Cole sleeps in the one across the hall from Aubry's. Then there's your room, which I use when I come over, and there's a guest room. Greg stays in there sometimes, but most of the time they do a big sleepover," she explained. I had already used the bathroom, which was across from our room, so I made a map in my head as to where their rooms were.

"A big sleepover?" I asked confused.

Becky laughed. "We set up sleeping bags downstairs when we watch scary movies at night, and we all sleep there."

I nodded, but didn't reply. I didn't like the thought of sleeping outside of a room, so I made a mental note to pretend illness on the days they did that.

"Why don't you get Cole since you haven't met him yet?" she said mischievously. "His jaw is going to drop when he sees you. He's a bit of a playboy, though. I'm warning you right now." She leaned over and whispered, "He's gotten to second base with like three girls from school already."

I laughed and was suddenly curious to see this Cole character. I walked to the room she pointed at—right next to the bathroom and diagonal to ours. I lightly knocked once. Becky started to laugh and told me I had to pound the door down in order to wake Cole up if he was sleeping. I knocked harder and then twice more. Still no answer. I pressed my ear to the door to see if I could hear anything.

Finally, after three more loud knocks, I opened the door a little and peeked in. I looked over my shoulder and saw Aubry's door open. Becky must've still been in there. I opened Cole's door wider.

"Cole?" I called out tentatively. His room was dark. The light of the television and hallway helped me see him lying on his bed. I made my way around and got a closer look at him. He looked so peaceful. He had brown hair and really long eyelashes. I could barely make out his features in the dim light, but that half of his face looked very cute.

"Cole?" I said in a hushed whisper. Nothing. My heart started racing, and I felt the blood draining from my body. *Why isn't he answering? Why isn't he waking up?* I started to shove him roughly.

"Cole," I said loudly as I shoved him. "Wake up, Cole!" I was practically panting when he groggily opened his eyes and looked at me as if I were crazy. Becky walked into the room and switched the lights on before walking away laughing. I looked into Cole's deep green eyes, and I felt the air swoosh out of my body as my heart dropped to my feet.

I was terrified. A little less so now that he was awake and I knew he wasn't dead. He sat up and turned his body toward me in one swift quick move. He looked as terrified as I felt.

"Do I know you?" he asked, wiping his face with both hands roughly.

"Umm ... no, I'm Blake," I replied slowly.

He got up and put his hands on his hips. He was much taller than me. *Why are these guys so tall? Or is it that I'm so short?* I looked at his naked chest and saw the defined lines on his abs. Cole was thin—not lanky like Aubry and not muscular like Greg—just average. He was tall like them though. He was wearing basketball shorts, and I was horrified to see that there was a tent in them. I looked back to his face quickly and saw him smirking at me. He looked down at his awakened crotch and looked at me with a sheepish grin.

"Morning wood," he explained with a shrug.

I crinkled my nose. "Eww," I replied, completely disgusted. "I just came to tell you that the food is on the table. I'll be downstairs."

I turned to leave and heard him blow out a low whistling sound. I turned back around and saw his eyes staring at my butt. I shook my head and rolled my eyes. *Unbelievable.*

CHAPTER FIVE

Present

I'm leaving work early to meet with Veronica, Mark's assistant, about the letter they sent me. I'm making it a point to get there ten minutes before 12:00 in hopes of catching Mr. Lewis before he goes to lunch. I'm interning in a law firm for the summer, and it's a block away from Lewis, Smith, and Morris. So far, all I've done is file papers and answer phone calls, but I'll take what I can to get my foot in the door. I call my boss, Gina, ten minutes before clocking out to remind her that I'm leaving early. At 11:30, I grab my purse from the bottom drawer of my desk, get up, and clock out. I run to the elevator and catch it right before it closes.

"Hey, Blake, you look rushed."

I look back and see Martin, a new attorney that started working here recently. He's one of those guys that won't shut up once he starts talking. I made the mistake of starting a conversation over the coffee pot in the break room last week. My entire lunch hour was spent with him yapping away about bad coffee and his break-up with an ex that refused to drink coffee. I ended up having a granola bar for lunch that day. Needless to say, I was grouchy and have since decided to keep my discussions with Martin to a minimum.

"Yup, I have somewhere to be," I reply in a rush before turning around and facing the doors in front of me. Maybe he won't talk too much since this elevator is jam packed.

"Oh, really? Where you headed?" he asks.

I make a conscious effort not to groan out loud or roll my eyes even though he can't see my face.

"I'm meeting someone for lunch," I half lie since I am meeting someone, and this is technically my lunch break. He doesn't need to know that I'm only working a half day.

When the doors open, I bolt through the lobby and out the doors. I've never been more thankful to be wearing flats.

I make it to Lewis's building in record time. I look at my gold watch and see that it's 11:45. Perfect. I make my way inside the busy lobby where everyone is bustling out of the building, ready for lunch. I skip over to the bathroom on the left side of the lobby and switch my flats for my heels. Once my flats are tucked away in my purse, I eye myself in the mirror. I fix the flyaways in my hair and clean up some smudged eye liner from under my eye before walking out. As I walk toward the elevators, I hear a man to my right shout "Mark" loudly. I turn my head in that direction and catch a blond man looking at me. When our eyes meet, I stumble back a step from the impact.

We stare at each other for what feels like an eternity, but it's really only half a second. Mark's blue eyes are looking at me in wide panic, and I can feel my heart pounding wildly against my chest. He turns around to greet an older man as I feel an unhealthy supply of blood rushing to my head and hear a loud ringing in my ear. I haven't been able to peel my eyes off of him, so I catch him when he looks back at me.

The surprise in his eyes has been replaced by sadness, and for some stupid reason, it tugs at my heart.

I let out a weak breath and wish I wasn't so stubborn. I wish I could turn back the last twenty minutes, go back to the elevator with Martin, and let him have his stupid conversation with me. I wish I didn't have this strong urge to uncover my past because with this urge comes devastation and sorrow that I'm not sure I'm strong enough to relive. Even though I have the memories from my nightmares, I'm not sure I want to experience them in the light. They're more real in the light. I should have kept them buried in the darkness, but it's too late for that. Mark's sky-blue eyes bring back a flood of nightmares that I wish were just that.

I catch my breath and quickly step into the waiting elevator. I furiously press down the Close Door button and shift from one foot to the other as I silently pray that Mark is leaving the building. When I step out of the elevator on the twentieth floor, I am greeted by a carbon-copy Barbie named Tanner. I had a slight altercation with her kid sister, Skipper, the last time I was here. I take a deep breath and inform Barbie that I'm here to see Veronica Stein. She plasters her fake smile, showing me her expensive veneers, and asks me to take a seat. I know I should sit, but I feel like a gassed-up bottle of pop that's just been shaken. Instead, I pace the waiting area while nervously smoothing out my long wavy hair.

"Blake," Veronica says, smiling when she spots me. "Come to my office, please."

Veronica is in her late forties and has short brown hair that tucks into her chin. She has skin so fair that it's almost translucent and sharp brown eyes. She's always impeccably dressed in what I can only assume are custom-tailored skirt suits.

Once we step into her spacious office, I take a seat in one of the leather chairs across from her desk. Veronica starts to shuffle papers on her desk until she finds a large manila envelope that has my name on it. She puts on her designer reading glasses and unclasps the envelope. She takes out some papers and skims through them with a raised eyebrow.

"Well, happy belated birthday. I have some papers from your aunt's will that we need to go over. It seems that Shelley wanted to give you half of her things on your eighteenth birthday and the rest on your twenty-fifth. A lot of people are doing that now," Veronica explains.

I sigh. "Veronica, I don't mean to be rude, but can we just go over the papers? I just want to get this over with."

She laughs. "Oh, Blake, I wish you'd come intern for us. You're my kind of girl." Her brown eyes search my face before continuing. "Your aunt left you a key to a safety deposit box as well as two more properties. These are plots of land. She also left you more money; I assume to cover the taxes for the land for a while. You just have to sign off on everything, and you can be on your way."

I'm totally dumbfounded. Shelley and I lived such a frugal life. I would have never known she had so much money.

"Are you okay?" Veronica asks, seeing my blank stare.

"Yes, I just ... I would have never known that Shelley had so much money," I reply honestly.

"Yeah, well, some people don't like to flaunt what they have. I personally think if you've got it, use it while you're alive. It's no good to you once you're dead—especially if you don't have kids to hand it down to. Thankfully, your aunt had you to leave it for."

I smile weakly and start signing the deed to the land. She hands me the safety deposit key in an envelope, and I thank her as I leave. As I wait for the elevator, I open the envelope in my hands. There's a letter from Aunt Shelley along with a key.

Blake,

This is going to be a lot to take in, so you may want to sit down to read this.

When the elevators open, I snap the letter shut and look up. My heart drops when I find the sky-blue eyes that terrorize my nights watching me intently. I take a moment to assess his face again, slowly this time. He looks about forty years old, give or take. His blond hair is slicked back; he has light blond hair that sprinkles his jaw. His nose is long and straight and his eyes—those sky-blue eyes... I've dreamed of finding him and asking him questions for so long, but now that I have him in front of me, I don't think I can bear to know the answers.

"Mr. Lewis," I say as I extend a shaky hand to greet him. "I'm Blake Brennan. I'm a friend of Aimee's."

I watch as his eyes widen before he finally sticks his hand in mine. I feel as if he's reaching into my heart and turning the knife that's been there for the past twenty-one years.

"It's about time we formally meet, Blake," he replies as he examines every inch of my face. "Would you like to step into my office? I have a couple of minutes to kill."

My eyes widen at his choice of words, but I nod in agreement.

I pull out my phone as we reach his office door and send Cole a text message that says I'm thinking about him. If I die, I want him to know that. I wish I could have sent him one that said I love you, but I'm not *that* positive that I'm going to die.

Mark's office is massive. He has a huge cherry wood desk in the middle of the room, a bookshelf to the left, a bar to the right with barstools, and an amazing view of the river and city behind him. The decor screams *grandeur*.

"Have a seat, Blake," he says as he shrugs off his jacket and tosses it on a barstool. He misses it by a long shot, so it lands on the floor. I suppress the urge to pick it up and place it on a seat in front of his desk. He goes over to the bar and asks me if I want a drink. I shake my head no and watch as he pours himself some single malt scotch. *Maybe I should have said yes.*

"How are you?" he asks, searching my face.

I'm not sure my vocal cords will cooperate and reply.

I open my mouth a couple of times and finally clear my throat. "I'm ... fine. How are you?" I ask in a confused tone.

"Good. How's law school?" he asks, watching me intently.

This would be a good time to use my poker face. I take a deep breath and pray that I have a poker face to play with.

"How'd you know I was in law school?" I ask evenly.

"You said you're a friend of Aimee's. I assume you know her from school. That girl doesn't have a social life outside of school. I'm assuming you have some questions for me?" he asks, raising an eyebrow.

I take a deep breath as he takes a sip of his drink and can no longer wait to ask him the one question that's been tormenting me for the past thirteen years. "Did you kill my father?" I ask quietly.

He chokes on his drink and coughs a couple of times. "Wha ... What? I meant questions about your estates. What are you talking about?" he sputters.

"Sorry," I say as my phone starts ringing. I look down and see Cole's name on my screen before I send it to voicemail. "That was an awkward thing to ask, but I know who you are."

He clears his throat. "No, Blake. You don't know who I am. If you did, you would not ask me a question like that. My job is to put criminals behind bars. Why would I kill someone?"

I feel the walls of my throat starting to close in, and I urge any stupid tears to stay away. "Can you tell me what happened to him?" I whisper brokenly.

The question makes his face crumble. He recovers his composure quickly, and I know that if I wasn't looking for a thousand truths in his eyes, I would have missed it.

"I don't know what you mean, Blake. Who is your father?" he asked, surely in the voice he uses on his clients.

"Mr. Lewis, I know you're the man that took me from my house when I was little. I don't know why you did it, but I'm sick of not knowing who I am. Did you kill him or not?" I ask boldly.

"I already told you that I don't kill people," he spits angrily before getting up to pace his office. "I don't have any information for you, Blake. I suggest you save your energy and stop poking your nose around in places. You may find something that you don't like. Trust me, I learned the hard way."

I tilt my head to scrutinize him. "What are you talking about? You're one of the best attorneys in Chicago."

"Yes, I am. That doesn't mean I'm not paying for my past. Please—just let it go. You've done well for yourself."

"You say that as if it's easy," I mutter under my breath before I realize what he just told me. "How do you know what kind of life I've lived? Have you been watching me?" I ask horrified.

"I've been keeping an eye on you, yes," he sighs. "It's for your own good. Can I trust you to keep this to yourself,

Blake? I have a meeting in five minutes and one hell of a week in front of me. I can't have this weighing on my mind right now."

I laugh sarcastically. "I would hate to be a burden on your conscience, Mark. Your secret is safe with me. I still have questions, though."

"Blake, do you know the saying, 'curiosity killed the cat?'" he asks and waits for me to nod. "In this case, curiosity kills everybody except the cat. Trust me, it hurts more that way. For the sake of the people you love, let it go."

"Well, Mark, lucky for me, I don't love anybody," I huff.

He looks at me with a raised eyebrow. "Sure about that, Blake?"

His response makes my breath falter. I do love somebody, I love five somebodies, and I'm scared as hell to lose them. I turn and open the door to let myself out. I have to get out of here before I choke this man. He freaking knows what happened, and he thinks it's a joke. I feel tears of anger pooling my eyes, but I won't let him see them. I close the door quietly behind me, and I don't stop walking until I'm back in the parking garage of my building. I turn on my car, and as I pull out of the parking garage to go home, Coldplay's "Fix You" comes on the radio.

When you lose something you can't replace.

When you love someone, but it goes to waste.

Could it be worse?

Cue the goddamn tears. Damn Chris Martin and his ability to make me cry every time he opens his damn mouth.

When I get to my apartment, I call out for Aubry, but he's not home. I go straight to my room and take out my cell phone. Ten missed calls. Three from Russell, five from Cole, one from Becky, and one from Aubry. I sort through my text messages and see one from Aimee and one from Cole.

Aimee's is to ask me how it went with Mark. I reply quickly saying it went well. Cole's message simply says: **I'm always thinking about you.** I get butterflies and smile at my screen before calling Russell.

"Hey, babe," he says with his sexy accent.

"Hey, sorry I didn't call back earlier."

"No, that's fine. How did your meeting go?"

"It went well. I think I'm coming down with something, though. I don't feel well at all," I groan.

"Oh? Do you want me to come over and bring you some soup?" he asks concerned.

"No, thank you. I think I'm just going to sleep it off. I'll call you in the morning."

I text message Aubry and Becky. I let Aubry know I'm home and going to take a nap. I tell Becky I'll call her back tomorrow because I'm not feeling well. This should buy me enough time to read the letter from Shelley. I call Cole back because he won't accept a simple text message, and I really need to hear his voice right now.

"Hello?" he answers on the second ring. He sounds like he's out of breath.

"Hey, were you working out?" I ask.

"Uh ... no, what's up?" he replies clearing his throat. I hear a woman say something to him in the background that I can't make out. "Hold on a sec," he says to me and puts the phone down. I hear his muffled voice, talking to who I assume must be Erin. He sounds like he's trying to calm her down. Then I hear her scream, "You picked up the phone in the middle of fucking me! Who the fuck are you talking to?" That's when I hang up and run to the bathroom to throw up my breakfast, since that's all I've eaten all day. I was already feeling a little queasy from the mixture of not eating, Shelley's letter, and my encounter with Mark, but Cole answering the phone in the middle of ... Oh my god, I feel sick again. I sit on the cold tile next to the toilet, clutching my stomach for a few minutes.

I try to reason that he wasn't thinking when he answered the phone. It's normal for us to drop everything and tend to one another. He didn't mean to let me know what he was doing. I'm thinking all of this, but none of it makes me feel any better about the situation. The visual is already there, silently plaguing me. Now all I can think about is his hands holding her face as he kisses her softly. His lips on her skin. His body rocking against hers as he whispers how beautiful she is. I shut my eyes tightly and cover my ears with my hands. I can't deal with the thought. I can't. I can't think about him with somebody else anymore. I know I have no right to feel this way, but I can't help it. The thought of him with another woman has been bothering the hell out of me lately.

I get up and press my palms to the counter. I look at my reflection, and I realize I look the way I feel—like death. My white frilly blouse is half tucked out of my navy blue pencil skirt. My clothes are wrinkled, my makeup is running, and my eyes are red. I have little freckles around my eyes from my convulsive vomit.

I laugh at myself. I can't believe it took *that* to make me vomit. *Why would he answer the phone in the middle of sex?* I groan. The thought alone makes me hover over the toilet seat again. I need to hold it together. *This is stupid*, I tell myself repeatedly as I brush my teeth. When I finally get in the shower, I turn on the water and sit on the floor sobbing as I let the water wash away my sorrows. All the memories that usually haunt my nights have been brought to light, and I'm not sure where to go from here. I see three missed calls from Cole and decide to send him a text saying I'll talk to him tomorrow and apologize for calling. I quickly turn off my phone and toss it aside before opening the letter from Shelley.

Blake,

This is going to be a lot to take in, so you may want to sit down to read this. I'm sorry that I couldn't give you any of the answers you needed when you were with me. You were so young, and I couldn't for many reasons that you wouldn't understand. There is a lot more to your life than you realize. You will find out some things—if you haven't already—that will make you doubt everything. Please doubt everything—just don't let those things define you. You must be careful whom you trust. I just want the best for you. I know you're doing great things. I always knew you would make a difference in this world. This last part is very difficult for me to tell you even though I am no longer physically present. It may be harder because of that since I cannot defend my actions. I know you will hate me for this. I just hope you can find it in your heart to forgive me one day. If not, know that I'm very sorry and that I've always loved you very much.

Here I go ... I'm not your aunt. Your mother and I spoke every day, and she sent me photos of you all the time. Sometimes, she would even bring you to visit me. I loved you with all my heart from the time you were born. The things I left for you in the safety deposit box are yours to do with as you please. I use Mark as your attorney for a reason; please do not question that. Mark is a good man and has your best interests at heart. If you ever need anything, he'll be there for you. Maggie—Mrs. Parker—was also a friend of mine and your mother's. I knew she would take good care of you.

I know she did an amazing job with you. I'm sure you haven't been able to find out much about your past—if you've looked. Not many people know the truth about what happened that night. I never knew the full story.

The name your parents gave you is Catherine Blake Brennan. I'm only giving you this bit of information so that you can continue your search for the truth. I hope I'm not hurting you more than I am helping you. Please don't use that name—trust me on that. Burn this letter when you're finished reading it.

I love you, Blake. Please don't forget that.

Love,

Shelley

I sit stunned for a few seconds until the letter drops from my shaking hands. I try to fill my lungs with air, but I feel as though whatever air they had left vanished with my identity. I gasp for air a couple of times and bring my face between my knees until I calm myself down. I look at the time. 4:23. I wipe my face and take a couple of deep breaths before turning my phone back on.

I don't check to see who the voice messages I have are from. I call my boss, Gina, and request the week off. I need time to think, and if I'm going to find out what is in that box, I need this week off. I'm sure she heard my broken voice because she didn't bother sounding upset about my being away for a week. Not that I mattered there; I'm just a measly intern.

I'm not sure if I should stay here or book a trip and go somewhere—far away from all of this madness. I don't even know where to go, though. Maybe I'll call Becky and Greg and pay them a visit. There are three loud knocks on my door. The code.

"Blake?" Aubry shouts. "Are you sleeping?"

I cleared my throat. "Yes," I shout back.

"Let me in," Aubry says firmly.

"Go away, Aub."

"Cole's on the phone. He needs to speak to you."

"Tell him to go fuck himself," I say brokenly. "Or Erin," I mutter under my breath. I try for angry because I should be angry that he answered the phone like that. He should have known how much it would hurt me, but I'm too lost to feel anger.

"He says he's sorry. He's begging you to talk to him. Blake, I don't have all day. I have a date. I can't be playing messenger."

"Don't then. Tell him I'll call him tomorrow. I need to be alone right now. Please."

I hear Aubry relay my message to Cole as he walks away. I hear him walk back to my door a couple of seconds later, and he knocks again. This time I get up and let him in. When he looks at me, his face falls. He wraps his arms around me and holds me as I slowly let myself fall.

"What happened? Is it because of whatever Cole is apologizing for? Or did you have a nightmare while you were napping?" he asks concerned.

"No, it's not him. I had a nightmare while I was awake," I say, sniffling back my snot.

"Oh. You mean you're remembering things?"

"No, I mean I'm living them," I say with a trembling chin as I wipe my tears. "I went to the attorney's office today, and I found out some things I can't talk about. On top of that, Shelley left me a key to a safety deposit box, more money, more land, and a letter. I haven't been to the box, but the letter pretty much says that my life is a lie. She wasn't even my aunt," I choke out the last words and Aubry pulls me into a tight hug.

"Shit. That's ... fuck ... I'm sorry."

"I'm so scared, Aubry," I say hoarsely.

"You'll be okay, Cowboy. I'm with you. We're all with you," he says, kissing my cheek lightly.

"That's what scares me," I whisper.

CHAPTER SIX

Past

I was doing well my first year of high school. I had joined the cheerleading squad; it was the closest thing to dance that the school had. I had been dancing since I was five when Aunt Shelley started taking me to classes, and I missed it. Becky was also part of the squad, so I was glad that we had something to bond over. I liked my new home with Maggie, Aubry, and Cole. They made me feel like I belonged. Becky had already warned me about Cole and his womanizing ways—as if I needed a warning about that. Anybody that stepped within five feet of Cole could smell it on him. He may as well have a scent made named Gigolo. I'd lived with him for three months, and although he stopped hitting on me after the first month, I'd witnessed twelve girls walk through the doors of the house. Twelve. That was one for each week that I'd been here.

In the beginning, it really bothered me. I wasn't sure if it was because it meant that I no longer had his attention or because the girls he hooked up with annoyed me. It was probably both. The worst part was I wasn't even interested in him. Well, that was a lie—I may have been a little interested in him. As hard as I tried to fight it, it was hard not to be drawn to him. He was magnetic. When he was in a room with you, he consumed you. When he left the room, you mourned the loss of his presence. I knew I wasn't the only person that felt this way. I had him in a couple of my classes in school, and when he got in trouble and was sent to the principal's office, everybody acted like they lost a pet. The girls pouted and whined, which annoyed the shit out of me. The guys complained to the teacher and slumped their shoulders.

It was an odd thing—Cole's presence. As much as I would have loved to avoid him, he was like a pneumonic plague. My lungs didn't fully function when he was too close to me, and I think he knew it. I'd never been to an actual school before this year. I thought it would be scary, but the things I learned through Becky and the guys helped me get over my fear. I knew there were a "cool" crowd, a "nerdy" crowd, an "outsider" crowd, and a "theater" crowd. It seemed like there was a crowd to label everyone.

I didn't even know what crowd I was in really. Becky, Greg, Aubry, and Cole hung out on their own but were also in the cool crowd, so I guess by default I ended up there. I didn't fit in that crowd at all though. I was more comfortable with the nerdy or outsider crowd. I didn't like the people in the cool crowd because sometimes they treated some of the kids in other crowds like shit.

Homecoming was around the corner, and everybody started asking their dates. I was putting my books in my locker for the day when I saw someone lean against the locker beside me. I looked up and noticed Justin's blue eyes watching me as he hitched his red backpack higher on his right shoulder.

"Hey, Justin, what's up?" I asked as I continued to figure out what books I needed to take home.

"You going to the dance this weekend?" he asked as he reached over and stilled my hands with his.

I stopped putting my books away and tilted my head toward him, giving him a tentative smile. Justin was one of the most popular kids in school. He was your typical all-American boy next door, a senior, and played two sports. No doubt he had a date to the dance already.

"I'm not sure," I mumbled, trying not to give away the fact that nobody had asked me to go.

"Will you go with me?" he asked. I looked at our hands when Justin squeezed them slightly.

"Umm ... sure," I replied, smiling hesitantly.

"Great, I'll pick you up on Saturday then," he smiled, showing me his perfectly straight white teeth.

"Okay," I smiled back brightly. When Justin walked away, I looked back into my locker and bit down on my lip to stop from giggling like a maniac. I couldn't wait to tell Becky about this.

When I got to cheerleading practice that day, all the girls on the squad were acting like he had proposed to me. Sasha—one of the cheerleaders in my grade—kept going on and on about how she had gotten to second base with him already and what big hands he had. I tried my best not to pay attention to that. For some reason, it made me panic a little. I hadn't even kissed a guy—let alone run through any bases with them. I hoped Justin wasn't expecting me to do anything with him. I didn't mind kissing him, but I wasn't interested in doing anything more.

When I told Aubry about going to the dance with Justin, he told me I needed to be careful. Greg said the same thing and told me he'd heard some bad rumors about him. Cole begged me not to go as Justin's date. He said—and I quote—

"You can be my date. I already told Cindy I'd go with her, but we can all go together if you want." *What a jerk. Really, who says that?* I rolled my eyes and resisted the urge to slap him.

I had on a sheath silver dress that stopped a little bit above my knee. Becky applied minimal makeup on me and fixed my hair so it was down yet out of my face. I was examining myself in the mirror one last time when I heard the doorbell ring. I let out an excited squeal, yelled goodbye, and flew down the stairs. I opened the door and smiled brightly at Justin, who was wearing a tuxedo. He gave me a once over before handing me a lilac gladiola.

When we stopped at a red light, Justin slightly turned his body to me. "So have you thought about college yet?"

His question took me aback, and I wondered if I should remind him that I was a freshman. "Umm ... not really."

"Oh, well, I'm going to the University of Florida next year. Maybe you can visit me sometime," he said with a wink. I smiled back politely. "I want to study business management and hopefully take over some of my father's franchise restaurants around town."

"That sounds great," I said.

I liked Justin, but something about him made me feel uncomfortable. His hand brushed my leg a couple of times when he switched gears, and it was obvious that it was on purpose. He told me that I was the prettiest girl in school and about the guys that would like to be in his place right now.

I was beaming at the statement until he mentioned the six or seven girls he turned down. I caught myself wanting to roll my eyes a few times. Hanging out with a group of guys had made me immune to a lot of bullshit. Guys will say anything to get in a girl's pants—I learned that from Cole. Guys will promise you the moon and the stars if it means they might get a blow job—I learned that from Aubry. Guys will treat you like a queen and do "bitch work" around the house if it means the girl will stop rehashing old arguments—I learned that from Greg.

At the dance, we mingled with everybody. Justin introduced me to more guys on the football team. I'd met a few already since Greg and Cole also played football. The girls on the cheerleading squad flocked to us when we went to get drinks. Really, they flocked to Justin and pretended to play nice with me since I was there, too. Secretly, they were all thinking, "*Lucky bitch. I wish he was my date*," while they left their poor dates nursing their purses and cold chairs.

We spoke to Becky and Greg when they arrived. Aubry and his date Sandra got there, and we all hung out in a group for a while. When Cole stepped in with his date, my breath caught in my throat. I saw Cole checking me out a couple of times, but every time his eyes met mine, he gave me an icy look. I didn't understand him at all. It was pointless to even try. Becky leaned into my ear and told me that Cole hadn't taken his eyes off me the entire night. I rolled my eyes at her because she knew damn well I would have been his date if he'd asked me properly. I looked toward him anyway though and caught him watching me.

I danced with Justin, but after he stepped on my toes for the tenth time, I told him that I wanted to sit down. Justin agreed and apologized for torturing me with his moves. I laughed along with him, but I didn't correct him because dancing with him really was torture. A couple of times he asked me if I wanted a drink. He had snuck in a flask and had been spiking his drinks the entire night. I declined because I didn't think I liked the taste of alcohol. I'd never tried it, but if it tasted as bad as it smelled, I knew I would hate it.

At some point, Justin leaned over and whispered that he was bored. He pulled me up from my chair, and I cringed, thinking he was taking me back to the dance floor. When he pushed through the gym doors that led out to the hallway, my heart started to race.

"Where are we going?" I asked when we reached the end of the hall by the locker rooms.

"I just wanted to get you alone for a while," he slurred as he swayed into me, pushing my back gently into the lockers. He lifted my chin, and I found myself meeting his intense deep blue eyes. "You look so beautiful tonight, Blake," he said, making my stomach do somersaults.

I smelled the repulsive stench of vodka on him as he inched closer to my face and squeezed my eyes shut right before his lips touched mine. I'd never been kissed before, unless you count the pop kiss I shared with Aubry when we played spin the bottle that time. I wasn't sure what to expect from a real kiss, though. His lips felt rough against my own, and I gasped when he slipped his tongue between my lips. I wasn't sure what I was supposed to do with it once it invaded my mouth. It felt slimy and bumpy and gross against my own. I pushed it with mine a couple of times, following his lead. Suddenly, I felt his hands cup my breasts, and I jerked away from him, breaking the kiss. The hard look in his eyes made a sudden coldness wash through my core. He barked out a laugh at the look on my face and roughly pulled my face back to his as he slammed me into the lockers behind me, giving me no room to move.

I felt my breathing become heavier, and for a moment, I couldn't breathe. I tried to push him off, but he wouldn't budge. He started walking sideways, dragging me tightly against him, his lips painfully planted on mine. I started to panic when I realized that we were now in the guy's locker room. He let go of me—just slightly—but continued to tell me how much he wanted me and how he was dying to know what I felt like. My eyes darted around the room as I searched for something I could grab to use as a weapon.

"Justin," I said in a shaky voice. "Let's go back to the dance."

"You're such a cock tease, Blake," he spewed, disgust dripping in his voice. "Nobody will ever know."

He pushed me against the wall, and I cringed at the impact. He pressed himself against me and slid his hand up my thigh.

"Please, Justin," I begged. "Please don't do this to me."

He laughed and forced his hands into my panties in one swift move, making me whimper. I clamped my legs tighter together so that his drunken fingers couldn't open them. His mouth took mine again, and I bit down on his tongue—hard. A growl escaped him, and he grabbed both of my shoulders and threw me down to the ground. I yelped when I landed awkwardly on my side—my panties not letting me take control of my legs. He pushed me down hard and grabbed me by the neck.

"You like to play rough? I'm going to show you what that feels like," he said harshly. He bit down on my lip so hard that I instantly tasted the blood in my mouth. I screamed for help. "Shut up," he ordered as he jammed his finger inside me.

A painful screech escaped me as he continued to violently push his fingers inside of me.

"Please ... Please stop ..." I wailed below him, but it just made him push harder and faster. I stilled when I felt him get off of me slightly—and then heard him unzip his pants.

"No! Please no! Please, oh God, please ..." I begged in between sobs.

I heard the door open with a bang and felt Justin's body lift off of mine. I scrambled my legs together and pushed myself to the wall. I tightly wrapped my arms around my legs, trying to soothe the excruciatingly raw pain I felt between my legs. Through tears, I watched Cole punch Justin repeatedly in the face. The door opened again, and I saw Aubry run up to Cole.

"What the fuck are you doing?" Aubry yelled loudly.

"He was fucking raping her!" Cole yelled back, slamming his fist in Justin's face.

"What?" Aubry screamed as he looked around for me.

When he saw me huddled in the corner, he ran up to me.

"She liked it, Cole," Justin shouted. "She was begging for me to put my dick inside her."

I whimpered loudly through my sobs and shook my head. I couldn't say anything.

"Shut the fuck up," Cole screamed loudly. I could see his nostrils flaring as his body shook. I'd never seen him that angry.

Greg also appeared, and before I knew it, Becky was beside me, holding my face to her chest. Aubry carried me out of the school and sat me down in the car. Nobody said a word on the way home. All I could do was cry. I cried more than I'd cried in eleven years. I cried because the only thing I had left that was *mine* was almost taken from me. I cried because I couldn't believe I was stupid enough to trust a random guy. I cried because I believed that Justin was good, and I cried because I didn't know what else to do.

Becky stood outside of the shower as I washed off, still weeping. By the time I turned off the water, I was done crying. I dried, dressed myself, and somberly walked to my bed. At some point in the night, I was startled awake when I felt my bed sink beneath me. I sat up in a panic and almost screamed, but then I noticed it was Cole.

"What are you doing?" I asked wearily as I fiddled with my ivory comforter.

"I just want to make sure you're okay," he whispered.

"I'm fine. Can you please get out of my bed?" I whispered back, meeting his eyes.

He sighed and shook his head. “Okay.”

A mix of disappointment and relief spread through me when he left the room. Before I could contemplate asking him to come back, he walked back in carrying his pillow and a couple of blankets.

“What are you doing?” I shrieked a little too loudly as I sat up.

“Keep it down,” he hissed as he set up a makeshift bed with the blankets and tossed his pillow on the floor. “Gonna sleep on the floor.”

“Why?” I asked in a whisper.

“Because you won’t let me sleep in your bed, and I need to make sure you’re okay,” he said, taking a deep breath.

“I already told you that I am,” I replied with sheer annoyance.

His sad green eyes searched my face for a couple of seconds.

“Maybe I’m the one that’s not okay. I’m staying here. Just deal with it and go to sleep,” he said angrily as he lay down.

“Why?” I asked equally as angry. I hated having extra people in my room. I learned to deal with Becky when she stayed over, but that was it. Besides, he didn’t even lock the door. *Ugh.*

“Because if I go to my room, then I won’t sleep at all. I’ll be too busy thinking about you,” he huffed.

“Why don’t you sleep in Becky’s bed?” I asked a little nicer.

“Because. Just go to sleep.”

“Just sleep in Becky’s bed,” I repeated. “She won’t mind!”

He groaned. “Blake, just shut up and go to sleep.”

I shuffled out of my blankets and stood over him with my arms crossed. He looked up at me with a raised eyebrow and a devilish smirk.

"Are you really going to stay here the whole night?" I asked.

"Yes!" he shouted as he dragged his hand through his hair and plopped down on his pillow.

I walked over to the door and locked it before walking back to where he was. I snatched up his blankets and threw them on Becky's bed before I climbed back into my own.

"You're such a fucking pain in the ass, Blake," he spat irritably as he got up to get his blankets and lay back down on the floor.

"I just think you'd be more comfortable on a mattress," I said quietly.

"Yeah—maybe I would be—but maybe I'd rather be closer to you," he replied grumpily.

I was thankful the room was dark and he couldn't see my shocked smile from where he was lying. I'd never tell him, but Cole made me feel safe.

Justin didn't go back to school the following week. Because of his broken arm, he was replaced by Cole as starting quarterback. I inwardly smiled at all of this, thinking that my friend karma was a real bitch and she got Justin good.

The guys made me swear that I would tell them if Justin ever spoke to me again. He did speak to me again—he apologized for what he *almost* did to me. I couldn't even look him in the eyes as he spoke. For a while, the only male eyes I looked into were Greg's, Aubry's, and Cole's. I trusted them. I loved them. And that scared me more than almost getting raped ever could.

CHAPTER SEVEN

Present

Aubry skipped out on his date and comforted me with ice cream. He watched *Home Alone* with me before he made me watch the Cubs game. He insisted on sleeping on the floor next to my bed. When I woke up, I called Russell and asked him to come over. The first thing I need to do is break up with him. I hate doing this but knowing that I've been watched my entire life—and that those around me could be in potential danger—freaks me out. I know that I'm stuck with Cole, Becky, Greg, and Aubry, so I don't even try to isolate myself from them. Russell has nothing to do with this, though. Besides, as nice as he is, our relationship is going nowhere fast. I haven't been able to stop thinking about—

"Hey, beautiful," Russell says interrupting my thoughts before giving me a sweet kiss on the lips.

"Hey, Russ, do you want some tea?"

I hate tea, but Russell loves it, so I bought a kettle shortly after we started dating.

"Sure. How are you feeling today?" he asks as he runs the back of his hand down my face softly.

"Fine, I guess," I reply with a shrug.

We sit on the barstools around my kitchen island, and I can feel his eyes on me as he sips his tea. I'm chipping my nail polish, trying to figure out how to start this conversation. My previous breakups were easy. Boyfriends start getting possessive or too opinionated, and I cut them off. Russell is sweet though. He's laid back, he's honest, and he's nice. *Too nice for me.*

I take a deep breath and turn in my seat to face him. "Russ, I think we should take a break."

He sets his mug down and blinks at me rapidly. "What are you talking about? A break between us? Aren't you happy?"

The mix of confusion and hurt in his voice makes me cringe. I should've never gotten involved with this one—he's too ... nice.

I smile sadly. "I am, Russell. It's not you—"

"Oh, don't give me that rubbish," he snaps. "It's not you; it's me. I don't want that. Tell me what's going on."

I bite down on my lip to keep from smiling because angry Russell is kind of hot and very funny. "Really, Russ, I know it sounds cliché, but it's not you. It *is* me. I need to be alone right now. I'm lost, and I need time to myself."

He takes a deep breath and stands in front of me. He holds both of my hands in his and presses them to his lips while he looks at me intently with his hazel eyes. "I can help you find yourself. Let me help you, babe. I can make you happy."

I close my eyes because I can't stand to see the hope in his. "Russell—"

He takes my mouth with a possession he's never used before. He explores my mouth with his tongue as if he's searching for the part of me he thinks he has lost. He doesn't realize he never had it to begin with. When he breaks the kiss, he looks at me again. His eyes are desperate.

"Take a week. We'll take a short break. I'll call you next week, and we'll talk about this again."

"Russell, I can't. There's no point," I say slowly.

"Please, Blake," he says as he walks to the door. "Just think about it."

"Russell—" I say, but he walks out before I can finish my sentence.

That did not just happen.

I take a minute to process what just went down before calling Becky.

"Oh my God, and he just left? Just like that?" she asks amused.

"Yeah, crazy, right?" I say with a nervous laugh.

"That is the funniest thing I've heard in a while. I guess it's nice that he doesn't want to give up on you, though. Who knows? Maybe he's the one," she says quietly as she contemplates the idea.

I laugh at that. "He's too nice for me. He's such a great guy, though. It wasn't fair for me to use him like that to begin with."

"Well, you didn't need him anymore anyway. You already knew that his stepfather wouldn't be able to help you crack your attorney," she replies.

I groan. "Becky! I didn't *stay* with him because of his stepfather. I really do like him!"

"Sure, Blakey. Keep telling yourself that. You like him *so much* that you broke up with him. Was the idea that he might actually help you forget a certain someone scaring you?" she presses.

I frown. I'd never considered that. "No ... I never felt anything like that for Russell, but I did like him."

"I know, babe. You liked him, but he wasn't Cole."

"Becky," I groan. "It has nothing to do with Cole."

"Of course not," she replies sweetly. "So when are you moving over here?"

I smile at the change in topic and tell her how jealous Aubry is of her job location.

"I told him I could get him a job here, but he refuses to leave you behind," she says.

Her idea sounds fabulous, but she knows I wouldn't do it. Until I uncover the truths in my life full of lies, I'm stuck in Chicago.

"Why don't you meet us in New York this weekend?" she asks.

"What are you going there for?"

"Greg has a scrimmage game against the Giants," she says, yawning.

Greg is a running back for the San Diego Chargers. I usually see them when he comes to the East Coast for games, so I know she's already expecting me to agree.

"Sure, I'll meet you there then," I reply with a smile.

"Awesome! I'm so excited now," she squeals. "I can't wait to tell Greg that his cowboy will be meeting us there. Tell Aubry!"

"Obviously," I laugh. "You think he's going to let me rub it in his face that I saw you and went to a game without him?"

After Becky and I hang up, I scroll through my phone. I don't want to call Cole yet. Maybe I'll call him next week when I'm back in business. I doubt he'll let me get away with that. Knowing him, he'll show up here and demand to know why I haven't called. What's worse is that Greg will probably tell him that I'm going to New York.

We've gone long periods of time without speaking. While we were both working on our undergrad, we barely said a word to each other. We kept in touch through our friends and saw each other on holidays but didn't directly communicate with each other.

As I try to shake away thoughts of him with other girls, I pour myself some Lucky Charms and milk in a plastic cup. I switch on the TV and watch a rerun of *Saved by the Bell: The College Years.* I hate those episodes, but it's better than the alternative shows that are on. Thoughts of Cole and Erin seep back into my memory. Her angry voice after he answered the phone during sex repeats itself in my head. I let out a breath and feel my stomach churn. When I look back down at my now-soggy Lucky Charms, I'm no longer hungry.

I try to sleep but give up after an hour of relentless turning. *Maybe counting sheep only works at night.* My cell phone rings a couple of times, but I don't bother to get up and look at it. When the house phone rings, I sit up in bed. I look over at the cordless phone next to my bed and see Cole's name light up on the caller ID. I groan and sink back in bed.

I hate the fact that we even have a house phone. We rarely use it anyway, and it's just another way for people to have more places to contact us. When we installed our alarm system, we were told we needed one. The alarm system was my idea. Everybody thought it was dumb since we live in a condominium—an expensive one with a doorman—but I need to feel safe. When someone opens the front door or balcony doors, the little chime beeps. It annoys me sometimes, but it's worth it.

I hear Cole's deep velvety voice fill the emptiness in my room, and the butterflies in my stomach awaken. "Blake, Aubry told me you were home. Pick up the phone please. We need to talk. I'm sorry I couldn't be there for you when you called yesterday. I ..." he pauses and I hear rustling. "I'm sorry. I know you heard and I'm sorry. Please talk to me. It kills me when you shut me out. Call me—" The machine cut him off. *Good.*

After four years of not saying much to one another, when Cole and I started to speak again, we promised not to shut each other out again. Regardless of the girlfriends or boyfriends in our lives, we promised we'd be there for each other. We always put each other above everyone else in our lives. I feel bad for Erin because she is a sweet girl—even in times that I wouldn't be. She seems to have as much patience as Cole does, which irks me. I would love to say I'm happy that Cole has such a great girl in his life—and deep, deep, deep inside I am. He's my best friend. I want him to be happy. He deserves it, but still ...

He calls again, and I let the machine pick it up.

"Blake, please answer the phone. Please, baby," he pleads hoarsely. My heart drops at the sound of his voice and I feel the tears I was holding back run down my face. I finally roll over on my stomach and pick up the phone.

"Hello?" I answer in a cracked voice before I clear my throat.

"Baby, what's wrong?" he asks in a worried tone.

"Don't call me that," I whisper harshly. "Nothing's wrong."

"Bullshit, Blake. What happened yesterday?"

"Nothing. I don't want to talk about it."

My heart starts racing as I look at the phone base and start recalling all those movies I've seen where the phones are being tapped. The thought of people watching Cole makes me want to wrap him up in cling wrap and tuck him into a corner of my underwear drawer. It hurts me to think of my loved ones being harmed, and Cole has been through enough. We all have, but I can take the pain.

"Cole, I need to call you back. I can't be on the phone. I ... I'll talk to you tomorrow or another day," I say in a rush.

"What?" he exclaims. "What do you mean tomorrow or *another day*?" he emphasizes, growling the last two words.

"I gotta go, Cole," I say quickly.

"Why? Talk to me, damn it," he shouts angrily.

"There's nothing to talk about," I reply evenly.

"I know you've been crying, Blake."

"Yeah, well, I'm always crying," I sigh.

"No, you're not. You never cry during the day."

I laugh—a real laugh. *That's such a stupid thing to say. As if there's a right time to cry.*

"You're an idiot. I'll talk to you tomorrow. Thanks for making me laugh," I say with a smile as I shake my head in disbelief.

"You know what I mean," he replies quickly, and I can picture him stopping in the middle of his pace wherever he is. "We're not done talking, Blake. I need you to forgive me," he whispers. My heart drops when he says that, and I close my eyes to stop fresh tears from flowing out.

"There's nothing to forgive. I'm not the one you should be apologizing to," I reply quietly.

He exhales into the phone. "You're the only one that matters, baby."

"Stop calling me that," I say in a shaky voice. "I have to go."

I hang up before he can say anything else. I make a mental note not to speak to him on the phone through the landline. *I need to find out if people can tap cell phones.* I look outside and smile at the cloudless day. I figure I might as well enjoy the warm weather while it's here, so I decide to go to the park for a while before I head to the grocery store.

I walk around Grant Park and fill my insides with warm fresh air. I snap some photos for a couple of tourists and pick a spot to sit in. Herds of people are walking toward the river in their beach gear. It makes me wish I would have brought my bathing suit. I could use a tan. A couple of teenage boys are throwing their football around me. It makes me laugh, and I remember my teenage days and how no teenage boy would dare to get near me. *Oh, Cole, you were such a dick back then. Still are.*

When I get up, I saunter over a couple of steps to where the ball landed. I bend over, pick it up, and look up in time to see four ogling eyes. I laugh quietly and throw it back over to them. I'm not sure what they're more impressed about—that I threw it back or that a pretty girl can throw a football. Either way, loud cheers, laughter, and a couple of "Tommy, she's got a better arm than you!" break out all at once. I laugh loudly and tell them to have a good day as I walk away.

I head down the stairs of the train station and through the long hallway to wait for it. As I stand around listening to groups of teenagers talk about their summer adventures, I can't help but wish I were their age again. I'd do anything to be young and naive. I would love to go back and slap myself for all the times I spent on Google and other sites trying to find out who my parents were—instead of enjoying my careless life. I look around and see a couple of homeless people, the same ones that are usually in this station. It makes me sad to think that they have nobody. I know I'm an orphan, but I have a family: Maggie, Greg, Becky, Aubry, and Cole. They're my family, and they're a damn good family. I wouldn't trade them for the world.

I'm grateful that I have them in my life. I know I could be a totally messed up, angry, and depressed individual because of the cards I was dealt. Instead, Shelley helped shape me into a positive person, and Maggie continued to help me grow from there. I get sad sometimes. It makes me angry that I have nightmares. It makes me angry that someone took my family away from me without giving me a chance to enjoy them. I can't imagine what it must have felt like for them though. I didn't know what was happening—they did.

My wounds have somewhat healed, but it doesn't mean I'm less frightened. I am scared of the unknown. I am scared to be alone. I am scared to not be alone. I am scared to have people love me, and I am scared to have nobody love me. I live my life in a constant state of fear and need for control. I try not to be obvious about any of my feelings. I put a smile on my face every morning and pretend that I'm as normal as everybody else—even though I know I'm not.

As I wait for the train, I replay Shelley's letter in my head. *My name is Catherine. Holy shit!* By the time the train arrives, I feel like I'm going to be sick on it. I cram myself between a group of tourists and take the last empty seat. When I look up, I find an elderly woman in front of me, standing and holding on to the rail. *Of course.* I stand up and offer her my seat. She gladly accepts it, and I take her place holding the rail.

The Jamaican man that always sits in the corner is there. He's always playing his Bob Marley a tad too loud on his iPod. Even with the bustle on the bus, I can make out "Don't Worry, Be Happy" coming through his old school earphones. I roll my eyes for what seems to be the tenth time today and hope that I make it to the supermarket before the afternoon crowd does.

As I'm standing in line to pay for the few things I'm buying, I spot Cole and Erin in a magazine I'm flipping through. Erin has her arm draped around his waist, and he's on his cell phone, smiling. I love seeing him shine, but I hate seeing him in magazines with his different women. I should be used to it by now, but it still bothers me. Not that it should. I know I could be with him if I wanted to. I just feel like he needs to get things out of his system. And we wouldn't be living in the same city anyway, so what's the point? I can't ask him to give up the job he loves so much for me.

When I walk in the door, the alarm doesn't go off, so I know Aubry is home.

"Hey, Cowboy," he greets as he walks toward me in his work clothes. I smile at him. He is so good looking, my Aubry. He grew out of his lankiness and into a fit swimmer's body. He still swims every morning and most nights in our building's pool.

"Hey, Aub. You talk to Greg today?" I ask even though I already know the answer.

Greg was the one that started calling me cowboy. He told me the name Blake is a boy's name. I told him I was supposed to be a boy—not that I really knew this. He then went on to say that Blake was a cowboy name. The boys laughed, and the nickname stuck.

"I did. Did Becky tell you they're going to New York next weekend?" he asks, and I hear the hopefulness in his voice.

"She did. She said Greg has a game there. You should go," I say with a small smile.

His face falls. "I was hoping we'd go together. Take a break, you know?"

"Well, I did take the week off. I guess I'll go," I say, smiling. I was planning on going anyway. I haven't seen Becky in so long.

Aubry laughs and continued talking about his job and his new clients while I put the groceries away.

"So what's up with Aimee?" I ask as I'm rinsing off dishes after dinner.

I laugh as I watch a slow flush cover Aubry's face.

"She's an interesting girl," he says smirking.

"That she is. Please be careful with her. I know she's not your usual type, but she's a good girl."

"You know me, Blake," he says looking confused. "I treat my women with respect."

"So where do you want to stay?" I ask gladly getting off the subject.

He looks at me with furrowed eyebrows, and I already know what he's going to say. Before he can reply, I put my hands up.

"No, absolutely not. If you want to stay there, fine. I'm staying in a hotel."

"Blake, he's going to be mad. Cole has enough room. What would we tell him?" he groans.

"I'll tell him that I like my privacy or that I'm planning on taking Russell with me. Trust me, he won't mind letting me stay at a hotel," I reply with a smile.

He laughs. "It won't work. He even said you could bring Russell if you wanted."

The cup that I'm washing slips out of my hands, and I grip the sink to steady my weak knees. That doesn't sound like Cole at all. *Maybe he really is happy with Erin. Maybe she's the one.* The thought leaves a bitter taste in my mouth. As I'm trying to swallow past the lump forming in my throat, Aubry starts laughing.

"I'm just kidding, Blake. He didn't say that. I wouldn't put it past him though if it meant having us stay in his house," Aubry says, looking amused.

I pick up the dishrag and throw it at his face. "You're an asshole! I'm going to shower, and then we'll book our flight and my hotel room. Let me know if you want to join me, so I can book double beds."

While I'm in the shower, I hear my phone ring at least three times. I rinse the shampoo out of my hair quickly and dry myself on my way over to it. *Cole. Jesus Christ, what the heck does he want now?*

"Aubry!" I scream at the top of my lungs as I wrap the towel tightly around myself.

I open the door and take a startled step back when I find him standing in front of me with his phone to his ear and a smug look on his face.

"She's standing right in front of me, dripping wet with nothing but a tiny white towel on. I'm pretty sure I can see her nipples. Let me take a closer look," he says into the phone. I hear Cole screaming at him that he's going to kill him before he hands the phone over to me, snickering. I laugh and take it before I glare at him and close my door.

"Hey," I say as I rest the phone on my shoulder.

"Are you really dripping wet and wearing a tiny white towel?" he asks in a raspy low voice.

"Yes, I just got out of the shower."

"Good," he exhales into the line. "At least I don't have this raging hard-on for no reason."

My mouth dries and my insides flip as I feel my body reacting to his words. My nipples are hardening and the insides of my legs are pooling with warm anticipation. I let out a low moan and curse myself when I realize he can hear it.

"Jesus, baby. Don't make that sound. I'm going to come in my pants," he groans. I hold in a breath and clench my hands around my towel with my left hand to keep it from falling.

"Cole," I warn hastily.

"Undo your towel," he orders hoarsely. I don't know why I am even considering this, but I play along and do as I'm told.

"Cole, where are you?" I ask breathily.

"I just got home. I'm about to run up stairs to my room. Hold on," he says nearly panting.

As I wait for him to go upstairs, I close my eyes and take a deep breath. *I can't believe I'm actually considering this after all this time.* Then I remember him picking up the phone the other night, and suddenly I feel like a bucket of ice has been thrown on my libido.

"Does Erin live with you?" I ask with my eyes screwed shut, as if it'll make a difference once I hear the answer.

He exhales harshly. "No. Can we please not talk about her?"

I stay silent unsure of what to say. I know if we continue what we're doing, everything between us will change, and the more I think about it, the more I want it to. I don't want Erin in his life anymore.

"Baby," he says hoarsely. "When I stroke myself, like I'm doing now, you're the one I think about. I see your stormy gray eyes looking into mine, wanting me. I feel your small delicate hands wrap around my dick. I feel your plush pink lips wrap around me and your sweet tongue circle around it."

His silky voice makes my eyes flutter closed and my lips part slightly. I'm lying in bed, chest heaving, heart stammering against my chest, thinking about all the reasons I shouldn't do this.

"Cole," I moan. "We shouldn't do this. This is wrong."

"It's not wrong. It's you and me, baby," he whispers. "Touch yourself. Please. Close your eyes and picture me looking down at you." And I do. I picture his hooded green eyes looking at me as he positions his body over mine. "I'm cupping your breasts with my hands and flicking your nipples with my thumbs as I lick the shell of your ear. I'm nibbling on your earlobe the way you like." His words make me throw my head back and let out a low moan. "I'm running my tongue down your neck to your nipples. I pull one into my mouth and nip it the way you like—"

"Cole, Oh God," I pant as I follow my body with his words, replicating the beautiful torture he's describing.

"That's right, baby," he husks.

Suddenly there's loud pounding on my door.

I let out a frustrated groan. "I'm on Aubry's phone. He's knocking on my door. He might need it."

"Fucking fuck," he shouts. "Fucking Aubry and his ability to cock block even when I'm miles away from you," he says, his breathing heavy.

I let out a strangled laugh as I get up and wrap the towel around myself again.

"What'd you need to talk to me about?" I ask, remembering that he called to ask me something.

"Aubry says you're not staying in my house when you come this weekend. I can assure you, especially after this conversation, that you're not staying anywhere else."

"Cole," I start as I open the door and find Aubry with an eyebrow raised. I'm sure my flushed face has "guilty" written all over it. "I'd rather stay at a hotel. I really don't want to see Erin after what happened the other day." I really don't want to see her at all, but I'll keep that to myself.

"We'll see about that," Cole says and I hand the phone over to Aubry.

Aubry gets it and greets Cole again. As he walks away, I hear him say, "Don't worry, Cole. I'll pick up where you left off."

I laugh and close my door. That night, I fall asleep smiling and dream about Cole's body over mine.

CHAPTER EIGHT

Present

"It feels so good to be getting out of here," Aubry says as we wait in the security line at O'Hare International Airport.

I was able to get out of staying in Cole's house. Luckily, he didn't argue when I told him I would prefer to stay in the city. His house is a thirty-five minute drive to the city, so I told him I'd rather stay with Becky and shop while he's at work.

"Sure does," I say, smiling.

I still haven't checked out the safety deposit box at the bank. I've gone and chickened out three times. I haven't even been able to step inside the iron doors. I contemplated telling Mark about it, but I still don't know how much I can trust him. Shelley did tell me to question everything, and even though she said he has my best intentions, she doesn't know what happened that night. Since I can't rely on the memory of my four-year-old self, I'll just have to question his motives.

We arrive in New York at noon and take a cab to the Waldorf Astoria, which is where Greg's team is staying. He was assigned to room with a teammate so that he would be less distracted, so Becky, Aubry, and I will be sharing a two-bedroom suite. I'm sure Greg will find a way to sneak in there as well, though. When we pull up in front of the stunning hotel, Aubry gets our suitcases out and tips the cabbie, who did not say one welcoming word to us during the ride. He did, however, make sure to tell us three times that the credit card machine was broken. Somehow, I doubt the machine was broken, but thankfully we had cash.

As soon as we step into the luxurious lobby, we are greeted by a shrieking fiery redhead. We hug, kiss, and examine each other's outfits and faces a hundred times. The last time I saw Becky was during Christmas, so I'm glad for this weekend with her. She informs us that Greg's coach is still being lenient and not enforcing rules yet since the real season hasn't started. The Chargers are playing the Jets in a scrimmage game tomorrow night. So while Greg is in a team meeting, Becky is ready to shop.

After checking out our glamorous suite, we leave to the stores. Becky and Aubry talk about work for the better part of the afternoon. When they're not talking, Becky and I are trying on outfits while Aubry text messages furiously. Cole calls us around six o'clock, when he gets out of work, and lets us know that he's meeting us for dinner.

When we get back to the hotel, we spot Greg and a few teammates in the lobby bar. When he sees us, he stops talking and stands up to greet us.

"Cowboy!" he booms as he sprints toward us, smiling with his arms open wide.

I skip over to him and throw my arms around him while his teammates make dumb remarks to Becky. Becky laughs it off and introduces us all. Aubry and I meet Trevor and

Donovan, two very big guys, and small talk for a little while before we head upstairs to get ready for dinner.

"Blake, you must wear this dress," Becky says as she hands me a ridiculously short black sequenced dress.

"Becks, aren't we going to eat dinner downstairs? Why do you want to dress up so much?" I ask.

"Umm ... hello? Where have you been? We're at the Waldorf, not Motel 6. You have to dress up here," she says with a puzzled look.

"True," I laugh. "I just don't think I'll be able to sit in this dress, let alone bend down for anything."

"Eh, whatever, you have Aubry and Greg to bend down for you if you need anything. When you sit, cross your legs—problem solved," she shrugs.

I know better than to argue with Becky about clothing, so I grab the dress and put it on.

"Becky," I shout from the bathroom. "I can't even wear a bra with this!"

"It's fine. It's too tight anyway. Your boobs won't have anywhere to move," she shouts back.

Aubry laughs loudly and says something about girls being weird.

"Yeah, or breathe," I mutter under my breath as I struggle to pull up the tank top. I really hope my boobs don't pop out of this dress tonight.

I put on a pair of tall black Louboutin peep-toe shoes that Becky lent me and pray that my feet survive the night. I towel dry my hair and apply anti-frizz serum. After I put on some light makeup, I make my way out to the living room area where Aubry is sitting.

"Becky's still getting dressed?" I ask.

"That girl takes for-fucking-ever to get dressed. Every single time," Aubry replies, looking up from his newspaper and whistles. "Damn, you look hot!"

"Thanks, Aub, you don't look so bad yourself." I wink.

He's wearing black dress pants, a blue long sleeve button down, and suspenders. Only Aubry could pull off suspenders. Instead of making him look dorky, they add a sexy appeal to his boy-next-door look.

Becky comes out of her room wearing a short gold dress and killer heels.

"I don't know how you walk in these heels, Becks. I already feel like I need a foot massage," I groan as I practice my walking. I really don't want to eat pavement in these. Or in this case, marble floor.

"Blakey," Becky says rolling her eyes. "Stop whining. Let's go."

When we get downstairs, Greg is waiting for us with Trevor and a different big guy. *Where do they breed these guys? They're so freaking big.* Greg's brown eyes light up at the sight of Becky, and my heart swells for them. *Maybe someday.* My thoughts are interrupted by a whistle.

"Blake, you look stunning," Trevor says, eyeing me from head to toe. "You can be my date tonight."

I laugh. "That depends. Do you have a wife, fiancee, girlfriend, or anybody you're casually dating?"

He raises his eyebrows. "Damn, that's a hell of a list. No, no, no, and sort of," he replies with a smirk.

"Sort of casually dating someone?" I ask, pursing my lips.

"Well, I went on two dates with the same girl, so I guess that counts," he chuckles.

"You get an A for honesty. I'll be your date tonight," I reply, sticking my arm through his.

Aubry laughs behind us and coughs out, "Russell."

I turn on my heels and playfully slap his arm. Russell and I are on a break. Really, we're broken up, even if he refuses to accept it. Either way, I'm not planning on doing anything with Trevor; he's just my pretend date for the night, no big deal.

We're all sitting down, laughing over drinks, when I feel the hairs on the back of my neck spike up. I instantly know he's here and can feel his eyes on me before I look up to meet them. I'm surprised to see him here by himself. I smile warmly at him, but instead of returning my smile, he glares at me. He fixes his eyes on the arm that Trevor has draped over my shoulder. I roll my eyes dramatically and shake my head in disbelief. Cole greets everyone and extends his arm out to Trevor, successfully getting him to remove his arm away from me.

"Mind if I scoot in between you two?" Cole asks. "I haven't seen my *friend* in a while, and we need to catch up."

"No, that's fine," Trevor replies, shooting me an apologetic look. I give him a small smile as he gets up and moves over a seat.

"You look beautiful, baby," Cole says in a low whisper, stirring the butterflies in my stomach. My breath falters when he leans into me and kisses the spot just below my ear.

I let out a low gasp. "Cole, we're in a public restaurant. People will most likely recognize you. You need to think," I reprimand through gritted teeth, but he just shoots me a devilish smile, showing me his dimple.

The rest of our meal flows smoothly. Greg, Aubry, and Cole tell stories about their teenage years as Greg's teammates egg them on. From the corner of my eye, I see Trevor lean forward to look at me when Cole is recalling a prank he pulled on Aubry once. I lean forward as well, careful to not let my boobs spill out of my dress and all over the table.

"So, Blake, what room are you guys in?" Trevor asks in a hushed provocative tone.

Cole, who is talking to Greg, grabs the hand I had resting on my lap and squeezes it tightly.

"One of the suites," I respond coyly.

"Oh, it's like that?" Trevor jokes. "I'm staying here too. I could just follow you up, you know?"

"You need a key to stalk," I flirt with a wink.

Cole lets go of my hand and squeezes my thigh. Trevor's eyes travel down and notices.

"So, Cole, are you still dating Erin?" Trevor asks, cocking his head to one side.

I feel the blood draining from my face at the mention of her name, and I turn away quickly, focusing my attention on Becky. Becky is talking about her and Greg's new place by the water, but I'm only half listening since my ears are tuned into Cole's answer.

"We broke up recently," Cole says, and I unintentionally tilt my head to look at him. He gives me a crooked grin, showcasing his dimple and the mischief in his twinkling green eyes. He draws circles on my thigh where his hand still rests, and I feel like my heart is going to burst out of my chest. I look back toward Becky in an effort to keep the composure that is slowly fading away from me with every touch and look he gives me.

"Oh, sorry to hear that. She's a great girl. We've met a few times," Trevor responds.

"Yeah, she is a great girl. She's just not *my* girl," Cole responds, and I could feel his gaze heating the side of my face. I bite the inside of my cheek as I feel a blush creep up my body, and I silently thank baby Jesus and Becky for the deep bronzer I have on.

We finish dinner and walk toward the lobby to continue our conversations. Cole excuses himself and goes to the bathroom. Aubry trails behind him since they're still discussing last night's Cubs game. I stand with Trevor, Becky, Greg, and their other teammate, Jimmy.

"Are you guys dating?" Trevor asks, nodding his head in the direction Cole disappeared to.

I scrunch my eyebrows and look up at him. "No."

"Doesn't seem that way," he says, pursing his lips.

"Yeah, he can be a bit overprotective of me," I explain.

"That's more than a bit overprotective, Blake. That's ... something else," he mumbles.

I laugh and playfully slap his chest. "Something else?"

He holds the hand I used to slap him and he watches me intensely. The desire swimming in his deep brown eyes cuts my laughter short.

"You do look beautiful, by the way," Trevor says before he kisses the top of my hand and lets it go. "I'm in room 824, if you want to hang out ... or whatever."

I smile at his invitation, but don't reply. I'm not sure what I'm supposed to say to that. Thank you for inviting me to have sex with you, but I'll pass?

I feel an arm snake its way around my waist. When I look up, I'm met with Cole's icy green eyes. Trevor says good night with a salute before walking to the elevators.

I wave my hand, but my eyes are still on Cole's. I smile at him, remembering the last time he did this to me, and I see his eyes soften. He turns my body in his embrace so that I'm facing our friends and nips my earlobe lightly.

"I love you too, baby," he says in a low voice that makes me shiver. Cole has been saying those words to me for the past nine years. I've never said them back. He stopped asking me to years ago. He accepted that I couldn't and that I was scared to for what I think are good reasons. Every time I've said those words to somebody, I lost them. He always assures me that I wouldn't lose him, Becky, Greg, Aubry, or Maggie, but I can't take that risk. I love them too much. They are my world.

We crowd the elevator on our journey upstairs. Cole presses me against his solid chest and puts both arms around me, knotting them together in front of me. When we reach our floor, I stop him and hold on to his arm as I step out of my heels. I cannot take one more second of having them on.

"Blake!" Becky squeals. "You're kidding, right?"

"Ugh. Shut up. My feet are about to commit suicide," I groan painfully.

The guys laugh and Becky rolls her eyes. "You're such a baby."

"Yeah, whatever, diva," I grumble before I let out a loud screech when Cole lifts me off the floor. "Cole, are you crazy?"

"Only about you, baby," he murmurs into my hair. I bite down on my lip as my heart hammers relentlessly against my chest. I feel like butterflies are having a sock hop in my stomach. When my eyes meet his, I'm expecting them to look amused, but they're completely serious and a little sad even.

"You can put me down. I can walk just fine," I say pointlessly because we're already in front of our door. "I probably flashed everybody."

He puts me down slowly, never taking his eyes off mine. I want to look away from the intensity in them because they are making me feel like I have a gaping hole in my stomach.

"Uh ... guys? Are you coming in or are you going to stand in the hallway, eye fucking each other all night?" Becky asks with a laugh. I snap out of my trance and push off of Cole. As I make my way past Becky, she nudges me playfully. She is so obvious that I can't help but laugh as I walk to my room.

I change into a pair of blue shorts and a red T-shirt that reads "Murphy" in the back. It's Cole's football shirt from high school and my most comfortable sleeping shirt. After I scrub my makeup off and tie my hair back, I go back to the living room. Becky and Greg are already tucked away in her room, but I find Cole and Aubry flipping through channels in the living room area.

A large brown duffel bag that I don't recognize catches my eye. "Is that Greg's?" I ask to no one in particular, but look at Aubry.

Aubry's eyes widen as he bites down on his lip to keep from laughing, but doesn't reply.

"It's mine," Cole says nonchalantly.

"You're staying here?" I ask confused. "What's wrong with your place?"

"You thought that you were going to get rid of me just because you decided you were too good to stay at my place?" he asks with a raised eyebrow.

"Um, no, I never said I was too good for you," I reply quietly as I wring my hands together.

"You're right. You told Aubry that you were going to hook up with somebody," he says looking amused, while I glare at Aubry. "You told me, that you were staying here for Becky and shopping. I don't care either way. I don't like being far from the action, and since we're both here and you need a hook up partner, hey," he shrugs.

My mouth pops open. I close it. I process his words and start laughing.

"You ..." I say, smiling and shaking my head, "are easily the most controlling person I know, and that's coming from me," I joke. He really is controlling. I know why he needs to be in control. Problem is I need to be in as much control as he does. Our past taints us. As much as we try to paint our own canvas, our past is always there, hovering over our lighting.

"I prefer the term planner, but you can use controlling if it makes you feel better," he says, winking at me before I head back to my room.

Cole steps in as I'm getting into bed and goes straight to the bathroom. I stop leafing through my gardening magazine and look up when he comes back out; he's dressed only in his boxers. I don't know how he keeps his body in such great shape, even after he stopped playing football. I bite down on my lip to keep my mouth from opening as he strides over to the bed. His movements flex the perfectly defined muscles on his stomach. He crosses his arms, displaying his bulging biceps and strong forearms.

"I think you may have drooled on yourself," he says before he darts out his tongue and licks his lips slowly. A shiver runs down my spine at the sight of it.

"Says the guy that ran Trevor off when he saw him talking to me?" I ask, arching an eyebrow.

"Talking to you?" he growls. "He was practically eating you with his eyes. What was he telling you when I was in the bathroom? When I came out, he was holding your hand, and you were looking at him all dazed and shit," he says. His jaw is clenched and his fisted hands are resting on his waist.

I laugh. "Some things never change. I have a boyfriend, remember?" I don't, but he doesn't know that—I don't think. Aubry might have opened his big mouth.

"Do you?" he asks with narrowed eyes, making me squirm.

"Uh ..." I start as I make a mental note to kill Aubry tomorrow morning.

His eyebrows furrow. "Blake?"

"No," I reply quietly as I draw circles on the comforter with my finger.

"What happened?" he asks, tilting his head.

I shrug one shoulder. "The usual." *He's not you.*

I've dated four guys in the past seven years. They've all been extended one-night stands. That's how I define my relationships. I'm still friends with all my ex-boyfriends. I've attended two of their weddings, so that should tell you something. I never let them get attached to me, and I don't attach myself to anyone. I know the underlying problem to all my bullshit excuses is that they're not Cole. I've hoped that if I found someone that I shared a deep connection with, I wouldn't let them go so easily. Unfortunately, so far, I've only shared that deep connection with one person, and that one person is standing in front of me half naked, again. Usually I don't have a difficult time not getting caught up in Cole's presence. I just think about our past or the fact that we're both taken. Tonight, something feels different. I feel different. He feels different. As much as my body yearns for him, though, I refuse to make the first move.

"And he let you go? Just like that?" Cole asks as he sits on the opposite side of the bed.

I throw my head back to look at the ceiling and let out a breath. "He's in denial."

My head snaps back to Cole when his laughter echoes the room.

"What?" I ask annoyed.

"Nothing. Russell's a smart man; I'll give him that."

I frown. "You think he's not going to give up?"

"Pfff. I know he's not going to give up. I knew he was going to be difficult to get rid of with his annoying accent and everlasting patience."

"His accent is sexy," I muse quietly. He narrows his green eyes at me and gets up from his side of the bed.

He strolls over and stands in front of me, making me crane my neck to look at his face.

"What are you doing?" I ask cautiously.

His eyes bore into mine as he grabs my hand and runs it from his still damp stomach to his chest. My fingertips graze every line on his defined body before he brings it up to his mouth, forcing me to sit up on my knees. My hooded eyes mirror his, and my heart begins to quicken. My lips part slightly when his teeth nip each of my fingertips.

"Is this sexy?" he asks, lowering his voice as he stares at my lips.

I can't answer because my heart is stuck in my throat. I lick my lips and swallow, hoping it helps my dry mouth.

His eyes are blazing with desire when he lets go of my hand and frees my hair from my ponytail. He massages my scalp before running his hands down the sides of my body, making me shiver.

"I love it when you wear my old shirts," he whispers as he leans his head down and kisses my neck softly on each side. He runs his soft lips along my jaw—achingly slowly. If I were with anybody else, I would have been embarrassed by my now very loud panting.

He runs his tongue along the shell of my ear. "Is this sexy?" he breathes into my ear. I bite down on my lip to keep from whimpering loudly and shake my head vigorously.

"No," I say trying to sound resistant, but I can hear the breathlessness in my voice. He chuckles near my ear, making my stomach flip at the sound.

"No?" he asks, dropping his mouth back to my ear and nipping it lightly before backing up to look at my face. The amusement in his piercing green eyes contradicts his serious face, and I know he's expecting an answer from me. I roll my eyes at him, and he shakes his head in response before continuing his torturous tease as he cups my breasts over my shirt. He grabs the edge of my shirt and searches my face for a minute before he slips it off. He continues to take my clothes off slowly, leaving me exposed.

He lays me down and examines every inch of me, and I'm glad that I'm already lying down because the look he's giving me is making my knees quiver. I lick my lips slowly as my eyes roam his body and land on his tented boxers. He notices my traveling eyes and takes a deep breath as he runs his tongue slowly over his top teeth. My chest is heaving. I start to sit up to ask him what the hell he's waiting for, when he moves over to me and swiftly grabs my wrists together in one of his hands and pins me down to the bed.

"Cole—" My thoughts vanish with the searing kiss he gives me. When his tongue enters my mouth and begins to slowly stroke mine, I allow myself to lean into him. When he tries to slow down the kiss, I lift my head from the bed and kiss him carelessly, ravishing his mouth. He groans against my lips before grabbing my chin with his free hand, tearing my mouth from his.

My protest gets lost in my throat when I see the hurt look in his eyes. He doesn't give me time to wonder if I should bring up the past or just let it be. He plants wet kisses along my extended arms before reaching my neck and making his way down to my breasts. He lets go of my wrists, and my hands automatically move to his head as he continues kissing down my stomach and finally hovers between my legs. He licks my thighs, blows on my skin, and slowly drags his tongue from one side to the other, taunting me with a promise. When he swipes his tongue from the bottom up landing on my sensitive bud, I throw my head back with a moan and grab handfuls of the plush white hotel comforter under me.

"Cole," I plead, breaking my silence.

I feel him smile against me, empowering him with the sound of his name. He continues to suck and lick tantalizingly slowly until I'm breathing heavily and moaning his name loudly. When my body is shivering, on the brink of ecstasy, he stops. A disgruntled sound escapes my throat, and I prop up on my elbows and open my eyes.

His chest is heaving when I look at him. "Was that sexy enough for you?" he asks as his narrowing eyes burn into mine.

I groan and fall back on the bed, covering my face. "Cole, you're the sexiest man I've ever known. Plenty of women tell you you're sexy. You don't need me to feed your fucking ego."

I feel him shift and uncover my eyes, but I keep them closed. "Look at me," he orders in a low tone. I open my eyes. "I don't give a *fuck* what other girls say. You're the only one that matters."

I forget about my impending orgasm. I forget about not being in control. I forget about the ways we've hurt each other in the past. In this moment, I only want Cole. *My Cole*. I grab him by the back of the neck, pull his face to mine, and kiss him deeply. I kiss him to make up for all the years that I've missed out on not kissing him. I kiss him like it's the last time I will ever have his mouth on mine—because maybe it is—and I force the thought out of my head quickly. He moans when I slip my tongue into his mouth and reach to pull his down his boxers. I grasp his length and squeeze, making him hiss through his teeth.

"Do you have a condom?" I ask, looking at him through my lashes. Before he answers, I push him off of me and position myself to take him in my mouth. I circle my tongue around his tip a couple of times before I put my lips around him, taking him in deep.

"Shit, baby," he groans. "I have one ... oh God … I have one ... but ... but … I'm clean," he says desperately.

I stop and lean back on my heels to look at him.

"Cole," I warn. I'm on the pill. I know he knows this. He knows I'm clean, too, because I'm as much of a control freak as he is. I'm still hesitant about not using one though.

"Relax, baby, we're not seventeen anymore," he says, caressing my cheek softly.

I close my eyes and nod once. "It doesn't matter that we're not seventeen. We still need to be careful," I say.

He picks me up and positions me higher on the pillow before blanketing me with his warm body. He ducks down to nip my bottom lip and kiss me tenderly, before slowly pushing himself inside me.

"Fuck, baby," he moans as he thrusts all the way in. "You feel so good."

I whimper and lift my hips to meet him, forgetting my apprehension. It had always felt different with Cole. Always better.

"So fucking good," he repeats hoarsely. He buries his face in my neck and breathes me in as he pounds into me. "It's been too fucking long. I feel starved without you."

His words have me on a high I hadn't experienced in a long time—if ever. I'm consumed by Cole's raspy voice, his movements, his touch, his warmth.

"You're the only one that matters," he says as he drives into me faster. "You're the only one that fucking matters ... only you ... always."

I feel tears in the back of my eyes, and I grab on to his face and kiss him, pouring my soul into his.

Our bodies are slick—covered in our sweat and my arousal. We're both screaming profanities and each other's names in between passionate kisses. We never take our eyes off each other. My eyes are telling him what my voice can't say. His eyes are singing back the same words as we both find ecstasy and fall together.

"I love you, baby," he whispers into my hair as he cradles my body into his.

I find sleep easily that night. Dreamless sleep.

The next morning, I feel sunlight hitting my face and open my eyes slowly. I try to move, but I'm being held hostage by a strong warm arm. I look over at Cole and find him awake, his eyes smiling at me.

"How long have you been up?" I croak out.

"About thirty minutes," he says, looking at me in wonder.

"Why didn't you wake me up?" I ask, trying and failing to shimmy out of his hold.

"I was watching you sleep. I love watching you sleep," he says dreamily.

I smile. I love watching him sleep, too.

"I have to pee," I say, squirming again.

He chuckles and kisses my lips roughly before letting me go. A couple of minutes later—as I brush my teeth—Cole comes in and stands behind me.

"Whatever you're thinking—stop," he warns, wrapping his arms around me and looking at our reflection in the mirror.

I half smile with the toothbrush in my mouth. *We look good together. Always did.*

"I'm not thinking anything," I mumble in protest before I spit out toothpaste and rinse my mouth.

He turns my body to face his and lifts me to sit on the counter. He takes a deep breath and puts his forehead against mine.

"You're not getting away from me this time, Blake," he says seriously.

I back away a little so I can look into his eyes. He's dead serious. I inwardly curse myself for having sex with him last night. As much as I love the idea of being with Cole, it also scares me out of my mind, which is why I hadn't entertained the idea in such a long time.

"I never got away last time, Cole," I say, tearing my eyes away from his and concentrating on the nice bathroom tile.

He stares at me for a long moment before taking a deep breath and walking over to the shower to switch it on. As he walks back, he strips off his boxers, stands in front of me, pulls my shirt off, and takes my mouth in his.

"It doesn't matter, baby," he says against my lips. "That's in the past."

He lifts me up and walks us over to the shower, holding me tightly against his body. I lean my head on his shoulder and smile contently. As scared as I am to get involved with him again, I know I can't continue to live my life with him as just a friend. I can't keep letting him date other women and act like I'm okay with it, because I'm not. As he slides me down his body, I smile at him and let myself feel happy. I just need to figure out how to keep him in my life. Safely.

CHAPTER NINE

Past

I was waiting for Cole to pick me up for our anniversary date. I knew he had planned something special because Becky made sure I pampered more than usual. She asked me about a hundred times if I remembered to shave my legs. She even checked my underarms. That girl was something else. She gave me the "birds and the bees" talk—in her own strange way—which was hilarious.

"You're still on the pill, right?" Becky asked anxiously.

"Jesus, Becky, yes!" I replied, rolling my eyes.

She let out a breath. "Chill out, Blake. I just want this to be perfect for you. I don't want you to worry about anything later."

Cole and I hadn't gone past second base—mainly because we were interrupted every single time we were about to do more. I had no idea how Becky and Greg found a way to have sex in our house when they stayed here on weekends.

When I heard the doorbell ring, I smiled and sprinted to the door. The butterflies in my stomach fluttered when I saw

Cole leaning against the doorframe. The backward baseball cap he was wearing hid his messy brown hair and made his green eyes look bigger and brighter. He was wearing his dark-wash jeans, black boots, and a black cable sweater that hugged his defined body. He licked his lips slowly as his eyes wandered over my body. He took every inch of me in, making me feel exposed in a way that only he could. I smiled and threw my arms around his neck, as he chuckled and pulled me close to him, lifting me and snuggling his face in the crook of my neck.

"I love how you smell," he whispered. "You look beautiful as always."

"So do you ... as always," I replied with a smile.

I inhaled his scent, a mix of his favorite Jean Paul Gaultier cologne and the pine-and-clove body wash he used. He smelled like a masculine Christmas tree. My favorite smell in the world was *Cole*. He closed the door behind us and walked me to his car. I still had no idea where he was taking me, but that was what usually happened when Cole took me out. He insisted that everything be a surprise, and even though I hated surprises, I always loved his. When we got into the car, he took out a blindfold and showed it to me.

My eyes widened. "No. Hell. No!"

He bit down on his lip to keep from laughing at the expression on my face. "Please? It's only until we get there. I want this to be a surprise," he pouted. Damn it. I hated when he pouted, he looked so cute.

My shoulders slumped. "Fine, but if I start freaking out, you'll take it off, right?"

His smile was replaced by a frown. "Of course, baby. Why would you freak out?"

The truth was I didn't know, but as soon as I saw the blindfold, my heart went into overdrive. I took a deep breath and let him blindfold me. I was with Cole. I was safe.

We drove for what seemed like hours, even though Cole assured me it had only been ten minutes. When the car stopped, I heard him take a deep breath and shift in his seat.

"I'm going to take it off now, okay?" I faced the window so that he could untie it.

I blinked a couple of times before my face broke into a smile. I stared at the Bed and Breakfast in awe; I couldn't believe he remembered. We'd gotten a flat tire in front of that place before we started dating. I remembered telling Cole something about it looking romantic and hoping my future boyfriend would take me there someday. I remembered him choking on the water he was drinking at the mention of a future boyfriend taking me to a bed-and-breakfast but never thought anything of it.

"I hope you didn't make plans for tomorrow morning," he said, snapping me out of the memory. I looked over to him and smiled so wide my face hurt.

"I can't believe you remembered," I said, shaking my head.

"How could I not remember? I would never forget anything my favorite girl tells me," he replied before giving me a soft peck on the lips.

After checking us in, Cole led me to our room. The rooms were close together, and I wondered if Cole was out of his mind booking this place for our first time—because this *had* to be our first time. The rooms were closer together here than they were at Maggie's. When he opened the door to our room, we stepped into a spacious Victorian-style mini palace. It had a large white four-post king-size bed, an adorable vanity, and a bathroom bigger than the one we had at Maggie's.

"This place is beautiful," I said in awe as I looked around. I heard voices in the hallway and gave him a panicked look. "Oh my God, the walls are so thin," I whispered as I buried my face in my hands.

Cole chuckled and made his way to me, wrapping me in his arms and kissing the top of my head. "I know, baby, but we can never be alone at Maggie's. We have the worst luck in the world," he pouted. "Besides, you said you wanted your boyfriend to bring you here, and since you're never going to have another boyfriend, it was bestowed upon me," he said as he winked.

I tilted my head and pressed my chin on his chest to look at him. "You're right." I smiled.

"I brought you clothes. I had Becky pack your stuff, so if there's anything you don't approve of, blame her."

I laughed. "No wonder she was prepping me so much."

"What do you mean prepping you?" he smirked, showing me his dimple.

I rolled my eyes. "Girl talk."

We took turns showering, got dressed, and headed downstairs. The couple that owned the bed-and-breakfast invited us to a dinner they hosted for their guests, and we agreed to go. It turned out that we were one of three couples staying there that night. The other two couples were on the opposite side of the house. Cole gave me a knowing smile when he heard that. As we spoke to the other guests, we learned they were all much older and happily married. They told us what a cute couple we made and asked us how long we'd been together.

"She's a real catch this one. Don't you let her get away." Betty, one of the guests, told Cole as we ate dessert.

Cole lifted my free hand and put it against his lips. "I wouldn't dream of it, ma'am," he replied while gazing intently at me. The look in his eyes made my heart skip a beat, and my hands started to shake.

The older couples went back to laughing and talking about how they met, their weddings, and their grandchildren. It was bittersweet to see them together, whispering declarations of love and holding hands. I wanted that in my future—but whenever somebody asked me to imagine where I would be in five, ten, or twenty years, I drew a blank. I couldn't answer because I always thought *I don't know if I'll be alive in one, two, or three years; people die every day.*

As we walked up the stairs, Cole hugged me from behind and began to kiss my neck softly. By the time we made it into our room, I was panting. He pulled me towards him and murmured "I love you" against my lips, before taking them in his and exploring my mouth with his tongue. The taste the chocolate cake we had for dessert and Cole had me in going into a sweetness frenzy. I grabbed on to his long brown hair and gripped him as he continued to kiss me down my neck. My low-cut dress gave him access to the swells of my breasts. While he gave me wet kisses, he unzipped the back of it. I let go of his hair and let the dress pool at my feet. He took a step back and crossed his arms over his chest. Desire curled my gut as he watched me through hooded eyes with his tongue coaxing his bottom lip slowly. He looked like he was taking a mental picture of every inch of my body as his eyes traveled from my feet, up to my eyes, and slowly back down.

The hungry look in his eyes reminded me of a man on death row looking at his final meal, and it made me shiver in anticipation. He stepped forward and ran his fingers over my shoulders before unhooking my bra strap and tugging it down. When my bra fell to the ground, he let out a shaky breath and pressed his body against mine. I reached up and started unbuttoning his shirt as we kissed deeply. He broke the kiss and finished taking off his shirt, never taking his eyes off mine. I started to feel breathless when his eyes roamed my body and he bit down on his lip.

I was glad to be experiencing something so intimate with Cole because I didn't feel nervous to be almost naked in front of him. What made me nervous—and the reason I was scared to go all the way with him—was that he had been with so many other girls. I was scared that I wouldn't live up to his standards or be the worst lay he'd ever had. What if I did something wrong with him—or worse *to him?* I knew Cole would never laugh at me or make fun of me about anything, but the thought had been eating away at me since we got together.

He finished getting undressed—only leaving on his black boxer briefs—before he slipped off my panties and walked me backward to the bed. I sat when the backs of my legs hit the frame, and then shifted myself to lie down. Cole was standing, his deep green eyes boring into mine as I lay naked before him. His eyes traveled down my body again before he closed them and muttered a curse. He leaned over me and kissed me softly, nibbling and teasing my bottom lip before sucking it into his mouth. When he slipped his tongue into my mouth, I sucked on it and he let out a low growl.

He held himself up, caging me in his arms as we kissed. I held his gaze as I sat up and touched his cheek with the back of one hand as I ran the other down his body until it landed above the edge of his boxers. I inched them down until I could see just the tip of his manhood, waiting to be let free. I wiggled my body down until I got closer and pulled his briefs down with both hands. When he stepped out of them, I wrapped my hand around him and squeezed. He let out a deep moan and tilted his head back as I continued to stroke him softly, reveling in the smooth yet hard feel of him in my hand.

"Baby, you're going to have to stop," he said in a husky whisper as he took my hand away from him. He leaned me back on the bed and went down with me, careful not to put all his weight on me. We kissed longingly, holding each other tightly as our bodies melded together. When our lips parted, he began placing kisses on my cheeks, my nose, my eyelids, my mouth, my chin, and my jaw. He moved down my neck to my chest until he landed on my breasts. He licked around my breast until he got to the sensitive middle. He took my nipple in his mouth and swiped it with his tongue slowly. I arched my back, offering for him to take it all and felt him smile against me when I moaned out his name. He turned his attention to my other breast, repeating the same sweet torture.

"Cole," I said, breathing raggedly as I grabbed his hand and placed it between my legs.

"What, baby?" he murmured against me and then grazed me with his teeth, making me yelp.

"Touch me, please," I begged as I screwed my eyes shut. I couldn't believe I had just said that.

He circled his thumb on my lower stomach before trailing it lower. I bowed my back from the bed.

"Relax, baby," he chuckled.

"I am relaxed. I just want you to—" I squeaked when he inserted his finger inside me.

"You want me to what?" he asked, breathing hotly against my breast while continuing to circle his thumb over my outer layers and hook his pointer against my inner walls.

"Oh, God ... Cole ... oh ... God," was all I could say in between pants before a wave of relief swept over me followed by a tingling sensation.

He continued to touch me softly, wetting me with my arousal before he started to kiss me—everywhere. When I felt his lips on my thighs, I stilled. My hands flew to his hair, and I pulled his face up. He gave me a bewildered look.

"Cole, you're not going to do that, are you?" I squeaked.

He smiled. "Yep, can you let go of my hair, please?"

I bit my lip as I thought about how to talk him out of it. "Cole, I really don't want you to do that."

He shook his head once, making me loosen my grip and release his hair. He placed his chin on my lower abdomen and looked up at me for a while, searching my face before speaking.

"Baby, it's me. There's nothing to be embarrassed about. There's nothing to be weirded out about. I haven't done this before. You think I'm not nervous?" he asked softly.

I gasped. "Cole, you have done this before—a gazillion times," I exclaimed, slightly turning myself away from him.

He held my hips in place. "No, Blake, I haven't. I've had sex before—yes. Casual, meaningless, stupid sex. I might as well not have done it to be honest. This," he said motioning between us, "is not casual, it's not stupid, and it sure as fuck is not meaningless." He tilted my chin to make sure I looked him in the eye. "I'm in love with you, Blake. I've been in love with you from the moment I saw you. I've been in love with you from the day I was born and possibly even before then. I belong to you. My body belongs to you. My heart belongs to you. Please let me make love to you."

My hands were shaking, my heart may have stopped for a beat or two, and I felt tears form in my eyes, but I was able to nod my reply.

"Besides," he said, smirking as he parted my legs again. "This is my first time, too. I've never kissed anybody … down here."

My eyes widened and my mouth dropped open. I would have said something, but when I felt his tongue flicker against me, I was a goner.

He dragged his body against mine as I shook in the aftershocks when he started placing soft kisses on my neck and began to touch me again.

“I have to make sure you’re ready for me, baby,” he said gruffly. “But you’re so fucking wet already. I don’t think I need to do anything else.” He ravished my mouth again before opening my legs wider and teasing me with his tip.

“Cole, please,” I moaned as I pushed my body toward him.

“Hold on, baby,” he groaned as he slowly pressed himself inside me.

I squeezed my eyes shut and bit down on my lip when discomfort rippled through me. I felt like I was being torn apart from the inside. I squeezed his shoulder tightly to keep from crying out.

“Are you okay, baby?” he asked as he stilled.

I noddcd furiously. “Ycs, ycs, just kccp going, plcasc.”

He pushed inside a bit more and paused again, letting me get used to the feeling. After he had pushed himself in and out a couple of times, he picked up his rhythm.

“Fuck, baby,” he said in a low voice. “Fuck. Fuck. *Fuck.* You feel so fucking good.”

All I saw were Cole’s green eyes boring into mine, not letting me look away. My heart felt full as he kissed me affectionately, told me how much he loved me, and how good it felt to be inside me. I felt him throb inside me a couple of times and his body tensed.

“God, Blake, I love you so much, baby,” he grunted as he pushed inside me one last time.

He placed his head on my shoulder and kissed me softly. “I’ve never felt that before either,” he let out a breath. “That—I can only feel that with you, baby. Only you.”

I saw the sincerity in his eyes, and I knew he was right. If I hadn’t fallen in love with Cole before, I definitely knew I had then. With a tightening pang in my chest, I had the sudden urge to cry.

Between his loving words and the intimacy we'd just shared, I knew I'd never be the same again. It wasn't a bad thing necessarily, but I knew I could never love anybody the way I loved Cole. I hugged him tightly, wishing I could tell him how I felt. Wishing I wasn't so scared of everything. Of loving him. Of losing him. Beyond that, I was thankful that he loved me the way I was—scars and all.

CHAPTER TEN

Present

"So what now?" I ask Cole as he walks Aubry and I through La Guardia Airport to the security area.

Cameras flash here and there as photographers recognize his face. Guys come up to him, say hello, take photos, and tell him how great he is. A couple of girls smile and take a picture; they say their boyfriends are going to be so jealous. The fact that Cole has this whole "bro" following makes me laugh. After all those years of guys not liking him because their girlfriends did, the opposite is happening, and it's pretty funny. Now girls don't like him because all their boyfriends do is watch him on the tube. Aubry and I share this joke as we step aside and let him talk to some more people.

"What do you mean?" Cole asks when we get away from his adoring fans. Aubry has his back to us and is acting like a bodyguard, shielding us from everybody's view, and effectively eavesdropping on our conversation.

"I mean what now? Are you going to get back together with Erin?" I ask, avoiding the real question on my mind.

He gives me an incredulous glare before his green eyes start twinkling and his mouth slowly turns up on one side. "Hmm ... How about hell no?"

"Why not?" I ask, biting my lip and fluttering my lashes.

"Let's see," he starts as he tucks a strand of hair behind my ear, making me let out a quaking breath. "You and I had amazing sex this weekend." He slaps Aubry upside the head when he starts laughing loudly. "And quite frankly, I think it would be *very* stupid to let the love of my life walk out on me—again." He raises his eyebrow and looks at me intently.

I nod my head and smile. "I'm going to agree with you on that," I whisper.

He tilts my chin so I can look directly into his eyes. "I'm not kidding, Blake. I'm not letting you walk out of my life again—ever."

He places a soft kiss on my lips, and my apprehension disappears briefly. The only thoughts of running I have include me on a treadmill tomorrow because I ate too damn much in New York City this weekend.

We stand there for a while, staring into each other's eyes, not wanting time to tear us apart, even though we both know I have a plane to catch.

"I'll be in Chicago next weekend, okay, baby?" he says softly as he pulls my body against his to hug me.

"Okay," I whisper. I feel unshed tears in my eyes, and I silently pray that I don't cry because I'll feel so stupid if I start crying over this.

"I'll be there every single weekend. And if I can't go, I'll fly you to me, okay? If that's what it's going to take to keep you from freaking out on me, I'll sell everything I own and buy a damn jet." He backs out of our embrace and looks at me with a serious expression to make sure I'm still with him. I nod sadly. "Not letting you go, baby."

I laugh lightly. "I'm fine. I'm fine. I'm not a teenager anymore, Cole."

He grins widely and leans in to take my lips in his one more time. He moans when I slip my tongue into his mouth and suck on his.

"Fuck ... I hate that you have to go," he pouts.

"Are you fucking done, Romeo?" Aubry asks, turning around. "This flight isn't going to leave my ass. I'm not about to pay a hundred dollars to get on the next plane, and I kinda wanna get laid tonight."

I roll my eyes at him as Cole laughs and bumps fists with him. We kiss one last time and sadly say our goodbyes before I get on the airplane to head back to Chicago.

When Aubry and I get back to our apartment, I check the stack of mail and find a white envelope with my name on it. I notice it's missing a return address and grab it along with my bills before heading to my room. I place my suitcase on the bed and stare at it for a while. I hate unpacking and doing laundry. If I could pay somebody to do it for me, I would. I know staring at it won't get the job done, though.

"Aubry," I call out loudly. I haven't locked my bedroom door, so he comes in and stands in the threshold with one hand on his hip and the other holding his phone.

"Hold on, Aimee," he says to the phone. "What?" he asks annoyed.

I laugh. "What?" I ask with faux attitude and snap my fingers in front of me as I sashay my body. "Let me just tell you. You have me to thank for hooking you up with princess over there. Anyway, do you wanna do my laundry? I'll pay you."

Aubry laughs and shakes his head as he tells Aimee what I asked him to do. She laughs loud enough that I can hear her when Aubry extends his arm to move the phone away from his ear.

"Sure, I'll wash your shit. Do you have underwear for me to wash? Or did Cole rip them all?" he asks, laughing. Bubbled laughter escapes me as he walks away, because I'm pretty sure Cole did rip them all.

I hadn't considered that Cole was going to meet Aimee soon. I'm sure Aubry is already trying to set up a double date for next weekend. The thought of a double date makes my heart speed up. I'm really going to do this. No fear this time. *No fear.* I'm not going to lose him. I love him, and I'm not going to lose him. I open the white envelope with no return address. The letter doesn't even have a header. *That's odd.*

August 14, 2011

Ms. Blake Brennan,

We are interested in buying a plot of land that is under your name. The address of the land is 600 Rockwell Street. We would like to offer you $400,000 for it. Please contact us when you are ready to sell.

Best,

O'Brian Investment Group

I dismiss the letter and put it away. *How'd they get my address?* I guess it's a public listing and they found my name. That's the problem with living in a world of technology. Google can make anybody a stalker in two clicks. I sort through the rest of my mail and pay a few bills online. My phone rings as I'm looking for my PJs, and I smile when I see Cole's face on the screen.

"Hey," I say, grinning like an idiot.

"Hey, baby," he replies, and I can hear his idiotic smile, too.

"Miss me, already?"

"I always miss you," he pouts.

"Aww, I always miss you, too," I coo as if I were talking to a puppy.

"Is it too soon to come see you?"

I laugh. "Cole Murphy, you have lived without constantly seeing me for the past seven years. I'm sure you can survive five days."

He sighs noisily into the phone. "No, I can't. I didn't want to not live with you for seven years. I was dying a slow, agonizing death without you. You just didn't know it."

I roll my eyes even though he can't see me. "I'm so sure you were dying when you were with Erin … and Kim … and Taryn … and Rita … and Sandra … and Jessica … and Sasha … and Ana … and Meredith."

He laughs loudly. "I was dying the entire time I was with all of them. In fact, you remember more names than I do. I was just killing time with them waiting for you to save me."

"You're an idiot—" I'm interrupted by a knock on the door, and I groan. "I have to go, baby. I'll call you later," I pout with slumped shoulders, totally acting like a toddler.

"Fine," he whispers. "Miss me a lot."

I blow him a kiss through the line and hang up. When I open the door, I'm met with his emerald green eyes and his wide grin. I scream loudly and jump on him, hooking my legs around his waist as he grabs my butt to keep me from falling. I kiss his laughing face over and over.

"I thought five days was nothing?" he asks playfully.

"I lied. It's too long," I say, smiling as bright as my heart feels before giving him a tight hug again.

"Good because I wasn't sure how you were going to react. I kept thinking that maybe I shouldn't have taken the next flight out here."

I throw my head back, laughing. "Why didn't you just fly with us, you dweeb?"

"I didn't know how much I missed you until I saw you walk away from me. Maybe it's stupid, and I know I sound like one of those corny-ass guys I make fun of, but it's the truth. I couldn't bear the thought of not waking up with you in my arms tomorrow morning."

If there was ever a time that I wanted to scream that I loved this man, this was it. *I. Love. This. Man.*

I throw my arms around him again and kiss him, pouring all my love into his mouth. He groans as I slip down his hard body.

"We should have been doing this for the past seven years," he says, lifting me up and kicking the door shut behind him as he walks me further inside my room. He throws me on the bed and unbuttons his dress shirt as he kicks off his shoes. His eyes are boring into mine, and my heart is pounding wildly in anticipation. My skin is flushing, and my breath is coming out in short pants as I watch him. When he finishes stripping, he stalks toward me, his hooded eyes never leaving mine. He pulls me by my ankles and undresses me quickly. I notice his breathing hitch when he sees my black lace bra and panties.

"You were wearing this under your clothes this morning?" he asks huskily.

"Yes," I reply, slightly confused. I always wear nice underwear. Then I realize—holy shit—he wouldn't know. He hasn't seen me naked in seven years before this weekend. I smile widely because now I know he likes what he sees, and I know that he'll always like what he sees.

He trails wet kisses up my calf, past my thighs, and works his way up to my mouth slowly, stopping only to nibble on the sensitive parts of my body that he knows so well. I struggle to keep my breath even, but when he pulls the cup of my bra down and I feel his mouth close on my nipple, I am a goner. I put my hands on his head, wishing he had more hair for me to grab.

"Why'd you cut your hair?" I groan.

He clamps my nipple with his teeth, making me yelp before he looks at my face with his lips upturned, showing off his dimple. "I didn't want anybody else to touch it."

He lowers the other side of my bra and caresses my nipple with his tongue while he massages the other one with his fingers, not leaving any part of me ignored. I moan his name as he continues his sweet torture. He brings his lips to mine and kisses me softly as he shimmies my panties down my legs. He centers his hard, muscular body between my legs and enters me slowly, relishing the feel of me. His face watches mine in wonder, in awe, in love—and my expression returns the sentiment. We move in sync, pumping with emotion and sensual pain, and we fall together.

"What did you mean you didn't want anybody else to touch it?" I ask as I look up at him with my head on his chest and thread my fingers through his short brown hair.

He smiles sadly. "When you broke up with me and I went to North Carolina, I just wanted to start over. I was forced to start over. I didn't want to," he gives me a knowing look. "My second week there, I met some random girl at a party," he caresses my face when I cringe at the thought. "She was flirting with me, asking me about my classes and football practice, and she leaned up and ran her hand through my hair. It made me think of you, and I decided to cut it off the next day. I didn't want to ever be with a girl and have her pull on my hair like you did. It was bad enough that when I was with girls I wished they were you. I could only picture being with you," he shrugs. "My hair was for you. Only for you."

I give him a small smile. "You know those three words that you say to me, and you know how I feel?" He smiles and nods. "If I weren't so scared, I'd say them right now."

He kisses my head softly. "You know that nothing is going to happen if you say them, right? They're just words, baby."

I shake my head, my eyes tearing up. "No, Cole. When I say them, it's like I'm asking the universe to make something bad happen. I hope I get over it someday. I hope I can say them and not feel guilty for it. I just—unless I think I'm going to die tomorrow—I won't say them."

He chuckles. "Oh, Blake, I love you. To the moon and back," he says with a wink.

The following afternoon, we're sitting on the living room floor watching TV when my doorbell rings. I look at Cole, confused. He tilts his head as if to remind me that he doesn't live here. I get up, look through the peephole, and see blond curly hair and hazel eyes staring back at me. *Shit.* Russell. I completely forgot about him. I run back to the living room quietly where Cole is looking at me expectantly.

"Russell's here," I whisper loudly.

"So?" he asks nonchalantly as he mutes the television.

"So? Get dressed!" I say.

"No. No. No," he shakes his head. "We're not playing this game anymore. I didn't want to play it while you were with the douchebag, and I sure as hell am not going to play it while you're my girlfriend," he emphasizes. "*My* girlfriend, Blake," he repeats loudly.

I throw my head back and let out a frustrated groan. "I know, I know. I'm not saying to pretend you're not my boyfriend—just put on a damn shirt."

He's wearing basketball shorts and nothing else. He looks at me with a raised eyebrow, and I look down at myself and shrug. *I look fine.*

"Hell no. You're not opening the door wearing that," he says as he turns to my room.

"Cole, I'm wearing shorts and a tank top," I say annoyed.

"You're wearing *tiny* shorts and a *tiny* tank top that doesn't even cover your stomach."

I laugh because—well, what else can I do? Should I explain to Cole that Russell has seen me wearing a lot less clothing? I'm sure he doesn't want to hear that. He hears it anyway, though, in my laugh.

"Blake," he hisses through his teeth. "I don't even want to *think* about that, so don't make me. Put on bigger clothes, and I'll open the door for the loser."

"No," I shriek. "Just let me handle this. You stay here. I'll change, and you can stay in here."

"Hell no. That's not how this is going to go. I'm not hiding anymore."

"Fine," I agree as I change.

"That's what you're going to wear?" he asks amused.

I look down at the white summer dress I'm wearing. Not tight and not too short.

"What now?" I ask confused.

"You're going to break up with the poor bastard—or let him know that you're not going to get back together with him—wearing that?" he asks again.

"Cole, shut up," I groan and walk past him.

He laughs and walks up behind me. "You look sexy in that," he purrs in my ear before biting my earlobe and heading back to the living room with me.

I take a deep breath and open the door to find Russell leaning on the frame.

"Hey, Blake," he says. *Damn his accent. Damn. Damn. Damn.* I feel so bad.

"Hey," I reply. "Want to come in?"

"Sure," he answers as he steps around me. "Are you busy?"

"Not really. Cole and I were just watching TV." I hope that by mentioning Cole's name I can break the fall a little for him. Actually, I hope Cole keeps his mouth shut and doesn't say that we're together.

"Hey, Cole," Russell calls out from the kitchen.

"Russell," Cole greets with a nod and a wave of his hand.

We sit down in the kitchen. I offer him something to drink and he takes a glass of water. I sit with my hands on the table in front of me, unsure if I should start the conversation or let him.

"So," he starts. "Have you had a good week?"

"Sure," I shrug. "You?"

"I've had better," he says as his hazel eyes search my face.

"Russell," I say quietly. "I think we're better off staying friends."

"I know. I figured you would still feel that way this week."

I blink at him. He doesn't look angry. He looks a little tired, but beyond that, he looks fine. We'd only been together for six months—maybe he didn't get too attached. I can only hope.

I smile. "Good. So we can still be friends and study together and all that fun stuff?"

He chuckles. "Who am I to turn down a darling girl?" *Goodness, that accent.*

I bite down on my lip. "Thanks, Russ. Would you like to stay for dinner?"

"No, thanks. I better get going. I'll catch you later, Cole," he calls out as we get up to walk to the front door. He stops with his hand on the knob and turns to me. He lowers his head and gives me a soft peck on the lips before letting himself out.

"Did he just kiss you?" Cole booms as he walks toward me. My eyes widen and I lock the door quickly and stand in front of it.

"Cole, it was barely a kiss. It was a closure thing," I reply while I encircle my arms around his waist.

"That little shit better be thinking closure. Make sure he doesn't kiss you again," he replies, pulling back to look me in the eye.

I smile. "Yes, sir. These lips are all yours."

He smirks and scoops me up to take me back to the living room.

"I know, but I can't believe he fucking kissed you," he groans into my hair.

CHAPTER ELEVEN

Past

The summer had finally arrived, and Cole and I were going to the lake with Becky and Greg for the day. Aubry was working all day, so he couldn't join us. We crammed our things into Cole's small black Accord and blasted the music loudly on the way there. Cole was stroking my thumb softly as he cradled my hand in his. We'd been arguing a lot—about everything—and I knew that even though he wouldn't admit it, college was the source of the problem. Cole was upset that we were going to be in different states. I was upset because I knew I had to let him go. He hadn't mentioned breaking up, but it would be impossible not to. Cole was every woman's dream, and since I had him, I was every woman's envy. I knew that high school was filled with drama, no matter which one you go to or who you are. Still, my four years of high school had been hell, and I was relieved to be out of there. I was ecstatic to be getting out of this small town, so I didn't have to deal with seeing anybody from school again.

Cole and I were together most of junior year and all of our senior year. The first day when we walked into school holding hands, most people cheered and said, "Finally." I think it was the beginning of senior year when the girls started getting catty with me. Some guys, Steve in particular, started getting on Cole's nerves. I guess even though we were together, they figured with Cole's track record with girls we would break up eventually. When we didn't let them get to us, they upped their game. Girls started purposely putting underwear in his car, which he never locked. *Freaking underwear! Who does that?* Steve made an effort to blatantly flirt with me in front of everybody. When Cole found him cornering me one day after math class, he grabbed Steve by the back of the shirt and swung him across the hall. It was like a scene out of an eighties movie where the bully beats up the nerd. Except Steve was no nerd, and he'd overplayed his innocent card.

For the most part, I didn't let the girls' foolishness upset me. I knew Sasha, the head cheerleader, was behind most of it. She and Cole had a heated relationship in the past. She had a heated relationship with most of the athletes in the school, though. Apparently, Cole was her favorite. The thought made me sick, but I shrugged it off. If this was high school, I could only imagine what things would be like for him in college. Cole got a scholarship to play football at Duke University. Scouts flocked to most of the games during his last two years. He was the protégé everyone was after. He was the hot quarterback with the striking green eyes, killer smile, and effortless charm, who also happened to be book smart.

I realized the opportunities would be endless for him once he got to Duke. Girls would be throwing themselves at him left and right, and there, nobody would know or care about me. Hell, if they knew me here and didn't care about me, what would it be like there? As much as I trusted him, I couldn't live with the doubt. I knew it would only take a couple of days of his not calling me back to drive me insane with jealousy. I'd rather get a clean break and nurse a broken heart now than deal with it later.

Becky and Greg were both going to the University of Southern California. Greg got a football scholarship there. Becky had some money saved up, but she planned on paying for most of it with student loans. She was just glad to be getting out of Illinois and following Greg wherever he went. Aubry and I were going to attend the University of Chicago. I knew Aubry was secretly jealous of Becky because California was a good place for advertising, which they were both studying. He refused to let me go to Chicago alone though. Cole begged me to apply to Duke and go with him, but I couldn't do that to myself. Besides, I loved Chicago and was glad that I was finally moving to the city, and I couldn't ask Cole to give up his scholarship for me, either.

When we got to the lake, we batted off the usual batches of pesky flies—also known as cheerleaders. Or rather, ex-cheerleaders, since we were out of high school, and they were out of a hobby. I was sure some of them would go on to become great housewives and cheerleading coaches. Not to knock them all—less than a handful of them were nice to me and hadn't tried to steal my boyfriend. I waved hello to those three and continued my walk to the water. We put out lawn chairs and a cooler. I started to strip off my shorts and shirt when I noticed that Cole had run off somewhere. When I looked up, I saw him talking to Sasha. I felt the blood drain from my body as I watched her run her hand down his chest, and even though he stopped it from reaching the band of his shorts, I was already seeing red.

"Becky, can you please turn around?" I huffed through clenched teeth.

Both Becky and Greg turned their heads to watch Cole and Sasha's exchange.

"Cowboy, you know he doesn't like her," Greg said, trying to pacify my emotions.

"It doesn't matter, Gregory," I responded angrily. "Why is he even talking to her? Why is he standing so damn close to her? And why haven't I ever seen you doing anything like that?"

He took a deep breath, but said nothing. *Exactly.* Silence. Greg never had that issue because Greg knew when to keep his dick in his pants. I cursed myself a million times for letting myself love Cole. I cursed myself again for cursing myself for letting myself love Cole. He was one of my best friends—despite his past actions—and I knew he would never cheat on me. But still, that hurt.

The longer I watched their exchange, the more furious I got. I decided to walk over to where Steve and his friends were sitting. I knew it wasn't a good idea, but I was so livid that I couldn't stop myself. I was wearing the tiniest red and white polka dot bikini that I could possibly fit into, which got Steve's attention immediately. Cole hadn't seen it yet; I'd been saving it for that day since it was our last trip to the lake together. Steve's friends left us alone and we started small talking about college. Steve was going to Northeastern University in Boston. He had plans to become a doctor like his father. At one point, he leaned into me, tucked some loose hair behind my ear, and caressed my earlobe. I shook his hand off, and looked at him, my wide eyes asking him what he was doing.

"We could have been good together, Blake," he said quietly. "Still could be, you know."

I took a step back and laughed lightly. "Nah, you'll be off in medical school before you know it, and you won't have time for me anyway," I joked, trying to make the situation less awkward.

He pushed himself off of the tree he was leaning on and stepped closer to me as I took a step back. He stepped forward again, I stepped back. I felt like we were playing a game of cat and mouse. Maybe trying to get back at Cole this way wasn't such a good idea after all.

"I'll tell you what," he said, stopping close enough for me to hear him, but far enough that we didn't look like we were having an intimate conversation. "I would never fuck around behind your back like he would."

I gritted my teeth and tried to reign in my temper—to no avail. "He …" I emphasized by pointing my thumb behind me in the direction to where I thought Cole might have still been standing. "Wouldn't do anything to hurt me. You don't know him, so stop making assumptions. And you," I said, taking a step closer and jabbing his chest with my pointer, "are just mad because you couldn't have me. The only reason you were trying to get with me in the first place was to show him that you could do it."

A sly smile spread across Steve's face. "You're very smart, Blake. I'll give you that. I wish you well, and I hope you're right about Cole."

He saluted me before he turned around and left me fuming. I clenched my hands in a fist and turned around to stomp toward Cole. *God, help me if he was still talking to that little skank.* I looked around and finally found him. He was no longer speaking to Sasha. He was standing next to Greg with his arms crossed at his chest and a pissed off look on his face—which I returned with a raised eyebrow. I sat down next to Becky and lathered myself up with oil and didn't look up when I saw him plant his feet next to me. After a couple of seconds of burning holes into the top of my head, he sat down.

"What were you talking to Steve about?" he asked in an even tone.

"What were you talking to Sasha about?" I retorted.

I pictured his jaw muscles working, though I didn't want to look. I focused my eyes on the blue and green lines on the towel below me until he lifted my chin so that I was forced to look at him. "College." His eyes were flashing with anger.

I snapped my face out of his hold but held his glare. "Was she teaching you how to shower in college?" I spat irritably. "Maybe I should go ask Steve to give me a demonstration. Hold on, I'll be right back."

I stood up with no intention of finding Steve. I just needed a breather because I felt like at any moment I might slap the shit out of Cole. He grabbed my arm firmly and pulled me back down.

"If you do that ..." he said through gritted teeth before he let out a shaky breath.

I narrowed my eyes at him. "If I do that, what?" I asked a little loudly. "You're going to break up with me?"

His anger was replaced with distress, and he pulled me into a hug. I tried to squirm away, but his arms held me tighter. Suddenly, I felt like crying—and I did. I buried my face in his chest and cried quietly. Nobody could see or hear me, only Cole. When he loosened his hold, I wiped the tears from my face and took a deep breath.

"I would never break up with you, baby," he said into my hair. "Never."

I didn't respond. I was the one that was going to break up with him, and I had a feeling he knew this. The rest of the afternoon we splashed around, ate pizza, and went for ice cream. We acted like teenagers in love, and that's what we were. That was the last time we were together as kids. In love, without a care in the world. I was happy that day. I was happy that summer. I was with the people I loved, and they were all happy. They were all safe.

A week before we were all leaving for college, Cole took me on a date. He left me a note on my bed, telling me to dress comfortably and to be ready by six. I threw on a green halter maxi dress and a pair of flip flops. Becky fixed my hair so that it curled widely at the bottom and smoothed out the frizz at the top. She gave my eyes a smoky look, making my gray eyes stand out. My eyes had come alive since I'd been in this house; they were no longer stormy and depressing. I put on lip gloss and went downstairs to wait for Cole. He came up with this idea when we started dating. He said that since we lived together I was missing out on the "fun" part of dates, which was him picking me up and knocking on the door to wait for me. He always asked me to be ready at a certain time so that he had enough time to get ready and leave the house, just to come back to pick me up.

The doorbell rang at 6:00, and I squealed in excitement as I got up and ran to it. I beamed at him when I saw the bouquet of sunflowers in his hand. His eyes greedily ran down my body as he handed me the flowers. He wrapped an arm around my waist and pulled me into him, taking my mouth in his and kissing me arduously. The flowers slipped from my hands when I clutched on to his messy hair and pushed myself closer to him. His hands traveled down the thin fabric of my dress, down backside squeezing my butt. He let out a deep moan into my mouth that echoed through my body and made me quiver. When his mouth suddenly left mine, I whimpered in protest. Resting his forehead against mine, we caught our breath before he leaned down, scooping up the flowers and handing them to me again.

"Sorry about that, baby," he said gruffly. "You look ... You just ... You make me lose my mind."

I laughed and kissed his lips softly. “Thank you for the flowers. They’re beautiful.”

Once I placed the flowers in a vase, Cole grabbed my hand and led me to his car. We drove for a little while; I wasn’t sure where he was taking me. We drove by restaurants, the movie theater, everything we normally frequented before he pulled into a narrow road and started driving on gravel.

“Where are we going?” I asked hesitantly. “This place seems like the perfect place to become victims of *The Texas Chainsaw Massacre*.”

Cole laughed and squeezed me hand. “Good thing we’re not in Texas,” he said with a wink. He laughed louder at my “I’m not so sure about that” expression.

We pulled up next to a large abandoned house, and I was really starting to freak out. *Where in the world are we? Holy crap, we’re going to die here.*

“Cole,” I asked in an uneasy voice. “Did you let anyone know where we were going?”

He laughed. “Baby, it’ll be fine. You’re with me.”

“Yeah, but you don’t have a gun or a machete or a chainsaw,” I squeaked.

He chuckled and shook his head before grabbing both sides of my face and giving me a long, lingering kiss that made my head swim.

“I love you, Blake. You’re so damn cute.”

There were so many truths in his green eyes and so much more that scared me. I dubiously let him lead me toward the back of a large abandoned house—and that was when I saw why he brought me.

Behind the house, there was a meadow. There were little purple flowers on both sides of us and acres of unused land. I wondered how he found this place. He didn’t let go of my hand as he walked me to a recently mowed spot surrounded by tall grass. In the middle of the freshly cut grass were four unlit lanterns, one on each corner of a checkered blanket that had a large basket in the middle.

I turned my smiling face to him. "A picnic?"

"Yes, ma'am," he said, leaning down to kiss the tip of my nose.

We sat down in the middle of the blanket, and he took out two plates and two cans of pop.

"How'd you hear about this place?" I asked.

His green eyes roamed my face before he let out a breath and answered. "Maggie gave me a letter a week ago. I've been wanting to talk to you about it, but I wanted to bring you here first. The letter had information for the bank account that my dad had set up for me. It also had this address on it. It said that I own this land—ten acres to be exact."

I gaped at him. "What? Did it say why? Is it from your dad?"

He shrugged. "It didn't give any specifics. The land was put under my name when I was born. Maybe my dad was dying and that's why he dropped me off? I mean this is a lot of land, and everything looks pretty abandoned. I walked the property yesterday, and there's an abandoned farmhouse if you keep walking that way. It's full of mold, and it's practically falling apart, but I could tell it used to be well kept. I'm guessing this was the main house. Either way, if my dad used to live here, he hasn't for a very long time."

"What are you going to do with it?"

"I'm not sure," he said before taking a bite of one of the sandwiches he put out for us.

"So the bank account? He's been putting money in it since you were born or since you were dropped off?"

He raised an eyebrow. "Good question. I have to find out. There's enough money in there for me to live on for years without working, so I guess that's a good thing. Maggie's been giving me an allowance for years; she said it was from the money my dad left with her. I just always assumed it would have run out by now."

I pursed my lips deep in thought. I knew that my bank account was set up by my aunt and that she had nobody else to leave her money to. Cole's situation was just plain weird though.

"I don't get it, though. How is money still going into the account? If your dad is dead—and obviously he hasn't been living here for a long time—who's been depositing the money?" I asked confused.

"I don't know, Blake, but I'm going to find out," he said, determined.

We finished eating and lay down close to each other. Cole was supposed to leave for North Carolina soon, and I was leaving for Chicago. We hadn't spoken about the elephant in the room in a long time, and I felt like we needed to address it soon.

"Cole," I whispered. "You know that I ... really, really care about you. More than I care about anybody else in the world, right?"

"I know, baby. I love you, too," he said sleepily while he stroked my hair.

"Well, because of that, I think maybe we should take a break," I whispered in a rushed voice before I had the chance to back down like the coward that I was when I was around him.

"Baby, not this again," he groaned as he sat up.

"Yes, this again. I'm not kidding, Cole. I'm already sick with jealousy, and you know I don't do jealous!"

"Blake, I'm sorry about the Sasha thing. She was being stupid, and I acted like an idiot. I shouldn't have let her stand so close to me. I shouldn't have spoken to her at all. She was telling me about a couple of friends of hers that are going to my school, that's all."

I felt my jaw clench. "See? That's exactly what I'm talking about. Sasha's friends are going to college with you. She'll probably go over there at least once to try to screw you, and I have to be in Chicago—hundreds of miles away—thinking about whether or not that's going to happen."

He closed his eyes and took a deep breath. "Blake, I wouldn't cheat on you."

"Cole, it doesn't matter what you say. Don't you get it? I'm scared. I'm freaking scared to lose you, and I don't want to lose you like that," I said, blinking back tears. "I can't stand the thought of you with another girl. I hate that you're so good looking. If you were ugly, we might not be in this situation."

He barked out a laugh. "Blake, you're the most beautiful girl in the world. You're sexy as hell, you're smart, and you're funny. Life has handed you shit cards, and you've still managed to make the best of it. *You* are all I want. *You* are all I need. When will you accept that?"

I shook my head slowly. "That's not enough right now. Just go to college and have fun. I don't want to hold you back from a college experience. I ... care about you too much. If we're meant to be together, we will be—later on in the future."

He got up and knocked over our empty cans. I watched as he angrily put our things in the basket. He was pissed—really pissed, so I stayed quiet and got up slowly to help. He didn't say a word to me as he lit two lanterns and handed one over to me, so that we could walk back to the car. We drove back home in heavy silence. The kind of silence that you didn't want to break—because you knew that if you did, it would turn into a screaming match. Cole went to the kitchen to put things away as I hovered around silently watching.

Finally, I headed upstairs. I heard his loud footsteps behind me, and turned to enter my room when he grabbed my arm to stop me.

"My room," he ordered in a low voice, and I could only nod and follow.

He closed the door behind us, and he held me from behind, crushing my back to his chest as he squeezed his arms tightly around me.

"Why are you so adamant about getting rid of me?" he whispered into my hair. "I fucking love you. I care about you. I want to take care of you. Let me."

I shook my head as new tears formed in my eyes. *I'm scared. I love you. I'm scared of losing you for real. I can't be with you if I can't see you. I'm stupid. I don't deserve you.* I didn't say any of this.

"I can't," I said brokenly. "I want to, but I can't. I want you to live."

He turned my body to face him and scooped my face in his hands, wiping the tears with his thumbs.

"I'll live happier with you, baby," he said softly.

"And I'll live happier knowing you're living—even if it's without me," I replied quietly, dropping my gaze from his before looking back.

He nodded.

It was over.

The pain in his eyes was so potent that I could feel it reaching into my heart and shredding it with its long vicious claws. That night he made sure to show me that I belonged to him—repeatedly. His kisses and caresses would be forever embedded in my brain. He made sure that no man would ever live up to him. In the end, he hurt me more than I hurt him. I broke his heart, but he tore mine into a million pieces. Even if I wanted to piece it back together, I would never find them all because he would always be holding some.

CHAPTER TWELVE

Present

I arrive at Amalgamated Bank and stand stock still by the front door for a couple of minutes. The bank has an old eerie feel to it, and most of the people in here are older men dressed in suits. I am hesitant to continue in, but the security guard at the front glares at me, and I know I have to move. I stand in line, shifting from one foot to the other as I wait to write my name down on the list. The tellers are to my right behind a tall desk. *This place is giving me the creeps.* I'm half expecting for someone to pull out a machine gun and yell, "Manolo, shoot that piece of shit." Scarface style. I continue to look around while fidgeting my hands until I finally wrangle them together tightly, creating my own bondage. I take a deep breath to calm my nerves, but it doesn't help. I'm so scared to take my eyes away from my surroundings that I don't even want to dig in my purse to take out my phone and text somebody to keep me false company. When I finally make it to the sign-in sheet, I jot down my name and make my way over to the waiting area.

I sit down and look at the old men—or older men, I should say. They all look like somebody pissed in their coffee this morning. I spot a group of them circling around an older gentleman with white hair, who is making his way toward the exit that is located behind me. He's wearing a sharp navy suit, a white shirt, and a blue tie. He has charcoal eyes that compliment his salt and pepper hair. I smile at the sight of him even though he's not looking at me. He seems like a kind man, but I can tell he's influential. I purse my lips and wonder what he does for a living. He catches me staring and scrunches his eyebrows together as if he's trying to figure out where he knows me from. I'm kind of doing the same to him even though I couldn't possibly know him. Our eyes stay focused on each other until a woman touches my shoulder and asks me if I'm Blake. I break eye contact with the old man, who's still frozen in place, to nod at the banker before getting up to follow her.

"Miss Brennan, did you bring your key and identification?" she asks.

"Yes," I reply.

"Good. My name is Alicia. I'll help you access your box, and then I'll step outside and give you some privacy. You just have to press this red button, and I'll come right in if you need any help."

I thank her and step aside so she can show me to the box. The room is filled with big and little boxes. If it weren't for the adorned circular gold door, I would have confused this for a nicer-looking post office.

I take a deep breath as she pulls the drawer out of the wall and places it on the large marble table in the center of the room. She excuses herself and exits, leaving me alone in my nightmare. I take a couple of deep breaths to ease the tensing in my stomach as I step closer to the table. My heart is pounding so loudly that it's the only noise filling my ears. I circle the table once and stop directly in front of the drawer.

"Here goes nothing," I mumble to myself.

Sitting in the drawer are three large yellow manila envelopes. I take the first one out; it's heavy and fat. I open it slowly—scared of what I might find. I thought I was prepared. I thought I could do this, but when I find myself looking at a picture of myself as a baby, my hands start to shake uncontrollably. As I gather the manila envelopes in my hands, I notice a standard-size envelope with my name on it is taped to one of them. I tear it open and sigh in relief when I recognize Shelley's handwriting.

Blake,

In these envelopes you will find photos of your childhood. There are some from when you were still with your parents before you lived with me, and there are some with me. I'm sure you're questioning whether or not you want these. I'm sure it will hurt to look at them, but please take them home with you. Try to keep them even if you lock them away in a box. You don't have to look at them. Maybe someday you will have children of your own, and you might want to show these to them. Someday you will know the truth, and your heart might hurt less. At least, I hope it will.

I love you, Doll.

Love,

Shelley

I smile weakly at the nickname she used for me when I was little. I take another deep breath, inhaling the smell of

Pine-Sol that surrounds the room, and decide to take them home with me. I can't look through them now. Shelley's right—it hurts too much. It only brings back memories of *that* night. I press the red button, and Alicia comes sauntering back in, her heels clicking loudly against the marble floor.

"Are you all finished?" she asks sweetly.

"Yes, I'm just going to take the contents with me if that's alright," I reply.

"Of course. You will always have this box here. If you'd like to bring anything back, you may," she says.

I wrinkle my forehead in thought.

"Can you tell me whose name this box is under?" I ask curiously.

She blinks rapidly. "I ... I'm not allowed to say. Your name appears in the paperwork though."

I frown. "If I guess the name, will you tell me if I'm right?"

"I'm not really allowed," she says and then adds quietly, "but you can try."

I smile at her, and she smiles back gently. "Shelley?"

She shakes her head slowly and gives me an apologetic look. "Sorry. I'm here if you need me, Miss Brennan."

I shake her hand, thank her, and leave the bank with some pieces of my life in my hands.

On my way home, I send Cole a text message to tell him that I miss him—because I do. I desperately want him next to me when I open these envelopes, but I also want to keep him as far away as I possibly can. I'm not going to tell him about it yet. I think I'll give myself some time to stew over it. I know if I tell him or Aubry, they'll open these for me. I get home, throw my keys on the kitchen counter, and notice that Aubry's not home yet.

I go to my room, lock my door, and check the messages on the machine. The first message is from Veronica Stein at

Mark's office, asking me to call back. The second is from a rough-sounding man, saying he needs to speak to me about a plot of land. I'm both shocked and nervous when I hear this message. *They have my address and my home phone number? Who are these people?* I make a mental note to call Veronica on my way to work tomorrow. I need to figure out how to remove my personal information from these properties.

As I make myself a grilled cheese sandwich, I pick up a note that Aubry left me. It reads *Went to pick up Aimee. Be back later. Remember—movie night.* I remember his telling me that he was bringing her over to watch a movie. As I eat, I idly wonder which one they'll choose. When I'm done eating, I pour myself a glass of red wine, turn the alarm on, and go back to my room.

I'm lathering my hair, totally relaxed from the wine I just had, when I hear my alarm go off. I hold my breath, trying—and failing—not to panic. The alarm always beeps ten counts before it goes off. If you know the code, you should be able to turn it off by then. *Who the hell is in my house?* My hands are shaking as I turn off the water. My eyes dart to the bathroom door. *Locked, thank God.* I climb out of the shower, dry myself quickly, and put on my clothes as fast as I can. I grab my cell phone from the counter and hear my house phone ring. My heart is beating so damn loud that I'm surprised I can even make out the words that the person from the alarm company is saying. I jump when my cell phone vibrates in my hand. It's Henry, the door man.

"Hello?" I say in a hushed tone as I hold one shaky hand over my throat.

"Blake, is everything alright?" he asks concerned.

"I don't know. I'm locked in the bathroom."

Henry is an older gentleman, a grandfather type. He's always looking out for us. When we first moved in, we bonded over baseball. When we got our alarm system installed, Aubry made a joke about it to Henry. Instead of making fun of me, Henry said I was a smart girl.

"I'll send Sean right up," he says.

Sean is a doorman in training. He's much younger than Henry, but he seems nice and on point.

"Thanks," I whisper. "The alarm company is calling me on the other line."

I click over and tell the patient lady that I'm in the bathroom. She says she's going to send the police. I don't tell her it isn't necessary because, truthfully, I'm not sure and I would feel safer with them here.

Even after the alarm lady shuts the alarm off so that I won't have to, and lets me hang up with her, I continue to look at my phone every two seconds. I wonder if I should call Cole. *No. I can't do that. He'll flip out.* Maybe I should call Aubry and ask him to stay where he is just in case. *Oh my God, I'm freaking the fuck out.* I wonder if anybody is still in here. I wonder what they want. I wonder who it could be. I'm sitting on the toilet, and the only noise I hear is the lid rattling under me from my shaking leg. Twenty minutes go by, and I'm still locked in my bathroom, clutching on to my phone and biting on my finger nail. I'm sure Sean is outside, but he hasn't banged on my bedroom door. I finally call Aubry and tell him what's going on.

"What the fuck?! What do you mean somebody broke in?" he screams.

"I said I *think* somebody broke in, Aub. I don't know for sure," I say rapidly.

"Whatever, I'm on my way," he says quickly.

"No! Please don't. Let me just figure out what's going on. Sean is out there, and the cops are on their way. Aubry, please promise me you'll wait until I tell you that it's okay for you to come," I plead.

"What?" he yelps. "Are you fucking out of your mind?"

"Please, Aubry. What if this is something bad? Do you really want to put Aimee in danger? If you love me, please stay out of the building until I tell you."

I hear him breathe heavily into the phone. "Cowboy, I hate you for this, but fine. I'll wait around the goddamn corner."

My phone vibrates as soon as we hang up, and I think it's probably him again to tell me that he's coming over here anyway. When I look down I see *Cole*. I close my eyes and take a deep cleansing breath before answering.

"Hello?"

"Hey, baby," he says. I can hear the smile in his voice.

"Hey," I reply, my emotions resurfacing at the sound of his voice.

"What's wrong?"

"I think somebody broke into my apartment," I say quietly.

"What?" he screams. "Where are you?"

"Locked in my bathroom."

"Don't you dare move. Where's Aubry?" he asks, and I can picture him pacing nervously.

"I asked him to stay away," I say in a small voice.

"What do you mean you asked him ..." he trails off. "Fuck, Blake. I'm calling him from my house. Do not hang up."

"No," I shout and then lower my voice again. "Please don't."

"Why? Nothing is going to happen to him, baby. You can't be by yourself," he pleads.

"Henry sent Sean up. I'm sure he's here. I'm just too scared to leave the bathroom."

He lets out a breath. "Oh, baby, I'm sorry I'm not there with you." I can hear the mix of regret and concern in his voice.

"It's okay," I say, forcing a smile. "You're here now."

"No, I'm not. I'm too far from you," he sighs. "I applied for a job in Chicago."

I'm taken aback by this, but before I can reply, there's banging on the door of my room.

"I have to go; someone's knocking."

"Stay on the phone with me, please," he asks, so I do.

The police are on the other side, and when I open the door, I see Sean is there as well. I tell Cole I'll call him back after they leave, and he hesitantly lets me hang up. I speak to Officer David Martinez and Detective Larry Ginsburg, who happened to be in the building next door when the alarm company called. I tell them what happened, which isn't much. They ask me to look around the apartment to check if I see anything unusual. I stroll around with a confused look on my face because everything that should be missing is there.

The TV is there; microwave is there; our stereo system is there. I walk to the guest room, and everything looks untouched. I close my eyes and praise myself for always having my Jack-and-Jill bathroom connected to the guest room locked. The thought of what might have happened makes my skin crawl. I do a little shimmy dance, shooing the creepy crawlers off of myself. Detective Ginsburg, who's standing right next to me, asks if I'm okay. I blush and nod my head yes. He says it's okay to be freaked out. I check Aubry's room, and while I'm in there, he and Aimee barge in frantically. I run to them and hug both at once.

"Are you okay?" they both ask in unison.

"Yes, thank God. Nothing happened to me. They didn't even bang on my door. I'm trying to figure out if they took anything. Will you help me?" I say quickly, my sentences practically overlapping one another.

We look around a couple of times, but nothing looks different. I spot a paper on the kitchen counter under my keys and furrow my eyebrows together. I walk toward it and study it. I'm careful not to touch it. I've watched enough detective shows to know that you shouldn't put your fingerprints on evidence.

"That wasn't there when I got home," I say, pointing at the paper with my trembling pointer.

Both Detective Ginsburg and Officer Martinez walk over and look at the paper.

"Are you sure?" Detective Ginsburg asks with furrowed eyebrows, looking between me, Aubry, and Aimee.

"Positive," I say. "Those are my keys," I point. "I tossed them up there when I got here and that paper wasn't under them."

Detective Ginsburg puts on one latex glove and picks up the paper.

"It's addressed to Blake Brennan," he says as he reads.

"What does it say?" I ask quietly as I shiver for the millionth time.

"It says, 'Blake Brennan, call me (312) 555-2984. We need to speak about the land.' It's addressed O'Brian at the bottom."

"Oh my God," I gasp, covering my mouth with both hands as I feel my knees weakening. "I cannot believe this shit." Aubry and Aimee steady me to keep me from falling while Sean excuses himself and leaves.

"I got a call from some guy earlier today about this plot of land. He also mailed me a letter a couple of months ago. I've never even *been* to this plot," I say in a shrill tone. "I inherited the land from my dead aunt. I don't know how he got my information, but first the calling, then the letter, and now he breaks into my house!" I'm shouting and shaking vigorously by the time I finish my explanation.

Aubry holds me tighter while Aimee runs her fingers through my hair. Detective Ginsburg leaves me his information and asks me to call him if I hear from the guy again. He puts the paper in a Ziploc to test for fingerprints. He asks me a million questions, including what the name O'Brian means to me. I assure him that I've never heard it before. He looks like he's hesitant to believe me, but tells me that he will let me know if he hears anything back from the lab regarding the paper. He mentions something to Officer Martinez about being closer to cracking the O'Brian's, but I'm not sure what that means.

After replaying what happened again, Aubry and Aimee settle down to watch a movie. They ask me to join them, but I'm exhausted. They rented *The Notebook.* I warn Aimee, who has never seen it—*really?*—that she better be prepared to do the ugly cry in front of Aubry. They both laugh at me, but I'm dead serious. You can't watch that movie without doing the ugly cry.

I lock myself in my room and call Cole again. He picks up after four rings.

"Hello?" he answers, sounding like he just ran a marathon. My stomach drops at the memory of the last time this happened.

"Hey, bad time?" I ask, biting my lip to brace myself even though I know my Cole, and I trust him.

"No, no, I was downstairs," he says, catching his breath. "I heard my phone, and I ran up to get it. I didn't want to miss your call."

I smile. "Why is it that you have such a big house for yourself again?"

I remember he gave me a stupid answer the first time I went there, but I can't remember what it was.

"'Cause I thought it'd be a nice place to raise our babies," he replies.

I snort with laughter. "Oh, that's right," I say with an eye roll. "I forgot that was the excuse you used the last time I asked."

"I don't know why you thought it was so funny when I told you that," he protests.

"Umm ... maybe because you said it in front of your *girlfriend*?"

He chuckles. "That's right. Do you remember what you said after you were done laughing?"

I think about it for a second. "Not really."

"You said that you didn't want to have babies in a two-story house."

"Oh yeah, I did say that. Well, that was actually true."

"Yeah, I know. That's why I put it on the market the week after you left. Unfortunately for me, the market had dropped by then, so I had to un-list it and keep it."

"You put it on the market because I said I didn't want to have kids in a two-story house?" I shriek and then start laughing. He waits until I'm done giggling before he continues.

He exhales loudly. "Blake, when are you going to realize that everything I've done I've done for you?"

"Someday, Mr. Murphy," I smirk.

He groans. "It sounds so hot when you call me that."

"You say that about everything," I laugh.

"Yeah, because everything about you is so hot."

I try to stifle a yawn. "I'm going to try to go to sleep. Is it okay if we pick up the conversation of our beautiful future children and where we'll be living with them tomorrow?"

"Damn, babe, now you're really turning me on," he says in a low tone, making my body heat up. "Hearing you talk about our future children is hot. Go to sleep, baby. I love you. Call me if you can't sleep or if you have any nightmares."

"I will. Good night. Dream of me," I say and blow a loud kiss into the phone.

He groans and I smile, ending the call.

CHAPTER THIRTEEN

Present

"Daddy!" I shriek as I run toward him, out of breath from laughing so hard.

Nathan has been chasing me through the open plain. We're playing tag and Nathan's it. Daddy looks up and the crinkled lines on his forehead disappear when he sees me running to him. He smiles and opens his arms, so I can jump into them. In his embrace, he starts tickling me, making me laugh harder. He stops when I tell him I have to use the potty. Daddy gets up and tells Grandpa we'll be right back. Grandpa has black and gray hair, and his eyes are gray, like mine and Mommy's. I like that. Grandpa pats my head like a puppy when I pass him and tells Daddy that time is running out.

"Time is running out for what, Daddy?" I ask, turning to him.

"Nothing, Baby Girl. It's just grown-up talk," he replies with a smile. It's the smile he has when he's worried. I don't like Daddy worrying about anything. When he worries, him

and Mommy fight, and it makes me sad. They always tell me they love each other and that sometimes grown-ups fights. I don't want to grow up. I don't want to fight like Mommy and Daddy.

"Are we leaving soon?" I ask. I don't want to leave Nathan. We're having so much fun.

"Yes, baby, we have to. I have a lot of work to do when I get home."

I walk into the bathroom by myself and tell Daddy to stand by the door. He leaves it cracked open so I can see him while I do pee-pee. I don't need his help today because I'm a big girl. I'm going to be four soon. That's almost all of the fingers on my right hand. I smile. I wipe, get down, and flush the toilet.

"Daddy," I call out excitedly.

He steps in with a smile.

"I did it!" I shriek with a fist-pump jump. "Like a big girl."

Daddy smiles brightly and carries me to the sink so I can wash my hands.

"Yes, baby, like a big girl, but don't get too big on me now." He kisses my cheek and I laugh.

We go back outside, and I look for Nathan. I see his messy brown hair as he runs behind the bushes.

"Nathan," I shriek as I run to him. "I went potty like a big girl."

Nathan runs to me, his bright eyes happy. "Did you do it like I taught you?"

I shake my head. "No, Daddy says princesses sit to use the potty. Only boys potty standing."

"I thought you wanted to be a G.I. Joe?" he asks, making his forehead wrinkle like Daddy's. I can tell he's not happy.

"I do," I reply. I don't want to make him mad. "But I want to be a princess, too."

"You can't be both," he says.

"Is this a fight?" I ask, putting my fists on my waist.

He shrugs.

"We can't fight, Nathan. Only grown-ups fight."

He looks at me and messes up my sweaty hair. "I'm not fighting ... princess. Tag, you're it," he screams and runs away.

"Hey, that's no fair," I scream, laughing as I run after him.

Nathan is a lot faster than me. When we race, he always beats me. His legs are longer than mine. He always lets me catch him when we play tag though. I'm running after him, and I notice he's running way past the house toward the barn. When I get close to the barn, I see Michael writing on a piece of paper. Michael has pretty eyes the same color as the sky. Michael is my uncle. I've told him that he's my only uncle, but he says he's not. He asks me if I remember his brother. I only saw my other uncle a couple of times. He lives far away. I kind of sort of remember what he looks like ... I think. One day I'm going to have a brother, too.

"Uncle Michael," I scream.

"Hey, Baby Girl," he says, smiling. "Are you having fun playing with Nathan?"

I stop running. "Yes, but he's very fast. I have to make my legs go really fast to catch him."

He chuckles. "Wanna know a secret? One day he's going to be chasing you, and you're going to be the one that he can't catch."

I look at him confused. I like when Nathan catches me. "What are you drawing?" I ask, trying to peek at his paper.

"I'm not drawing. I'm doing homework."

"Oh, Mommy says they're going to give me homework when I start school this year."

"Your mommy is right. She's really smart, too. She used to help us do our homework when we were little."

I smile. Mommy is smart. I continue running to the barn, and I see Nathan standing under the shade.

"Slow poke!" he screams.

"Am not!" I shout back. "I was talking to Uncle Michael."

"Uh huh, sure," he teases.

I stand next to Nathan, but as I tag him, I hear Daddy's voice. "Blakey, let's go," he calls out loudly.

"I have to go," I say sadly to Nathan.

"It's okay. I have to go soon, too. Are you coming back next weekend?"

"Nope," I say, smiling. "Daddy and Mommy are taking me to Disney World for my birthday."

"Cool. Bye then."

I walk back to the big house and see Daddy talking to Grandpa and Uncle Michael. On our way home, I remember that I left my Rainbow Brite doll outside the house. I fall asleep before I remember to tell Daddy.

I wake up in a pool of sweat, breathing heavily. My heart is pumping so rapidly that I'm scared my blood flow will start streaming out of my ears. I lean over to my dresser and clumsily search for my phone, panting as I hit the dial button.

"Hello?" he says, his voice raspy.

"Sorry to wake you up."

"No, baby, I asked you to. Bad dream?"

"Yes ... no, I don't know," I spurt out.

He exhales. "3:32," he mutters, and I look at the time.

"I know. I'm sorry. I shouldn't have called."

"Stop apologizing. I'm glad you did. Do you want to talk about it?"

"Not really. I just wanted to hear your voice," I say weakly.

"Okay, baby. Just go to sleep with me on the phone. I love you."

"Thank you." *I love you. I love you more than you'll ever know, Cole Murphy.*

The next morning, I call Veronica and tell her that I urgently need to speak to her. She squeezes me in between two clients at 2:00. Classes start again next week, and this is my last week interning at Ross and Chevy Law. I'm going to take my lunch at 2:00 so that I won't have to ask for half the day off—again.

My day at the office flies by, and when I look at the time, it's 1:30. I call Cole on my way to Lewis'. Cole's on a show called *Around the Horn* today, but it airs at 5:00, so he should still be home.

"Hey, baby," he greets.

"Hey," I say, shuffling between a pack of angry lawyers in the lobby.

"What are you up to?" he asks with a smile in his voice.

"Just took lunch. I'm on my way to meet Veronica so I can discuss whatever she called me about and tell her about the break-in."

"Did you eat?"

"Nah, I'll eat a granola bar and drink a protein shake on my way back, though."

"Blake," he reprimands. "You need to eat."

"I know, I know. I just don't have time to stop today. What are you doing?"

"Waiting for a realtor," he replies nonchalantly.

That stops me in the middle of the crowded sidewalk. The afternoon rush bumps me from all sides.

"To put your house back on the market? I thought it was a bad time to sell."

"It is. I'm hoping someone will rent it for a while at least. If not, I'm willing to accept offers. We'll see."

I continue walking, speeding past some of the bumpers from a few seconds ago.

"Cole, shouldn't you just wait it out? Take your time. There's no rush for you to move. Have you heard back from the team?" He'd applied for a job with the football team here to be closer to me. I was thrilled, but uneasy about it since his job paid so well in New York.

"I'm not taking my time, there is a rush, and I did hear back from them," he says, and I can hear his grin again, which makes me smile.

I bite my lip. "And?"

"And … they have a job for me, dummy."

"That's great," I squeal. "Is it a good one? Did they make you a good offer? Are you still going to get paid the same amount? Oh my God, are you taking a pay cut? Maybe this isn't the right move for you."

"Blake," he shouts laughing. "Calm down. The offer is great. It doesn't matter, though; I was moving with or without a job. Trust me. I have enough money to survive without one. I just love what I do, and I'm glad I'll still be able to do it. I need to be near you—that's all that matters to me."

I let out a sigh of relief and agree to call him after my meeting. I'm still smiling at the idea of Cole moving to Chicago when I walk through the lobby. I take the elevator up and greet Barbie's kid sister. She asks me to sit as she calls Veronica. When the door opens, I look up expecting her, but see Mark instead. He signals me to follow him and I look at Skipper, who's smiling at Mark while fixing her bleach-blonde hair. I close my eyes, take a breath, and follow Mark as he ushers me into his office and closes the door behind us.

"Veronica told me you were taking your lunch hour to meet her," he says, fixing his blue gaze on me.

"Yes," I reply blinking rapidly.

"Did you eat?" he asks.

What's up with this question? I look down at myself and awkwardly shake my head. You would think I look like a rail. "I'll eat when I leave. I only have an hour."

He walks to the bar and signals me to follow. He pulls out a chair for me, and I sit. There are three Chinese take-out containers and two plastic plates.

"I hope you like Chinese food," he smirks.

"Sure," I say slowly. "I don't think there are many foods I don't like."

This is going very differently than last time. I serve my food. He serves his and takes a seat on the opposite side.

"Tell me, Blake. When did they start contacting you about the land?" he asks as he hands me my silverware.

I look at him in surprise. "How do you know about that?"

"They sent us a letter. The law firm is on the deed to your properties."

"Oh ... I got the first letter a couple of months ago. Then I got a phone call."

He closes his eyes and rubs the back of his neck. "What did they say when they called? What number did they call?"

"They called my house line. They repeated what they said in the letter."

"What did the man sound like? Did you save the message? Do you own the apartment you're living in?"

"I deleted it," I shrug. "I didn't think it was important. And I don't own it, we rent ... why?"

He exhales a deep breath. "Blake, save everything. Never delete anything before bringing it here, okay?"

"Ooookay ... Do you know who wants the land?"

"I have an idea, but I can't be sure," he answers, looking down at his plate.

"They broke into my house last night," I say as I watch his face.

His puts his silverware down as his eyes snap back to mine. I explain to him what happened in detail.

"Shit. You need to move. Hire security to be with you at all times. Tell your roommate to move out and get security for himself."

He gets up and starts to pace the room, running his hand through his combed blond hair. I gape at him as I stand up and put my hands on my hips.

"*What?*" I sputter as I shake my head. "I can't just tell my roommate to move. I can't just get security to follow me around all day. I have a life."

"Blake …" he pauses, his eyes softening. "That's why I'm telling you to do this. If you want to have a life—and you want your friends to live theirs freely—trust me on this."

I take a deep breath. "I had a dream last night," I start as I look into his eyes. "I was on a farm with my dad and grandfather. There was a boy ... The boy that was with me that night ... and you were there, too."

He closes his eyes and sighs as he clasps his hands behind his neck.

"I was playing tag with the boy," I continue, my eyes watering at the memory. "I went up to you and said something. I think I called you my uncle."

He opens his blue eyes, and I can see the sorrow swimming in them before he blinks it away and takes a deep breath.

"You have a vivid imagination, Blake. It sounds like a nice dream."

I purse my lips and narrow my eyes. "I liked being around you. I remember that."

He gives me a sad smile but gives away nothing else. For the next twenty minutes, we discuss how I can sell the land to those people without any trouble. He tells me he'll have Veronica write up a sale contract. I would get market value for it, which is low, but I don't care. I just want to rid myself of this.

"Mark, can you tell me if my father is dead?" I ask quietly before opening the door.

"Blake," he sighs. "Your father died a long time ago. Are you happy now?"

I tilt my head. "Yes … and no."

He gives me a baffled look.

"Yes, because you just admitted that you know. No, because I would have liked it better if he were alive."

A slow smile appears on his face. "You're going to make a great attorney, Blake."

I smile back. "Thanks for the food, Mark."

"Remember, security," he calls out.

Shit. How am I supposed to explain to Cole that my attorney thinks I need security to follow everyone I care about? I told him I'd call him when I left the meeting, but I decide to send him a text instead. I need time to think about this.

Me: I'll call you later. Back at work.

Cole: Okay, baby. I love you.

When I sit back in my cubicle, I check my email and see Veronica's name. The title of the email is *Security*. I open it and see a list of names. When your attorney—one that knows more about your life than you do—sends you a list of people to hire as your bodyguards, you know things are serious. I replay last night's dream in my head. I can't shake off the feeling that there's something in that dream.

I end up working on a case until 7:00, and I'm thankful that I ate at Mark's office. I say goodbye to Gina and the receptionist before heading out. The floor isn't completely empty; I see lights still on in various offices. In the elevator, I rummage through my purse for my keys and phone. I find them both as I reach the floor of the underground parking garage. Unlike the offices, the lot is drastically empty.

I walk over to my car, dropping my keys twice as I try to unlock my phone with my other hand. I hear shuffling behind me, but I reach for the handle before I look back, and lock the doors as soon as I get in.

As I drive away, I notice a figure of a man in the corner of the garage, and it startles me so much that I slam on the brakes, making my car jerk forward. I let go of the brake slowly and continue driving up the curve toward the exit, leaving the dark figure behind. I'm watching my rearview mirror—just in case the figure moves into the light. *Please walk into the light.* My heart is pounding rapidly with adrenaline as I bite down on the tip of my thumb. I don't care how late it is—when I get home, I'm hiring security.

I call Cole on my way home and tell him about my meeting with Mark and about what happened in the parking garage.

"Jesus, Blake, you're freaking me out over here," he says.

"I'm sorry. I had to tell you, though. I'm getting you security, too. You need it more than we do since you're in the public eye."

"Baby, I need it least because of that. Besides, don't you think it's a little awkward for someone my weight and height have someone shadow me?" he asks.

A bubbled laughter escapes me. "I hadn't thought of that. I guess it is weird, but they'll be trained and have a weapon, so I'm getting you one regardless."

He chuckles. "I'll get my own if it makes you feel better."

"It does, but we have a list of people, so I'd feel safer if we choose from these."

"Why are you trusting that Mark guy so much anyway?" he asks curiously.

This is a foreign concept—me trusting anybody outside of my circle.

I shrug, even though he can't see me. "A gut feeling, I guess."

"Hmmm, that's fine. Just call the guys, but I'm paying for them."

"Cole," I groan. "It's my fault we're in this mess. Let Shelley's money pay for them."

"Baby," he warns.

"Whatever, we'll figure that out later," I say quickly. I really don't need this to turn into an argument.

CHAPTER FOURTEEN

Present

After bath time, Mommy always reads me a story. I'm in my pajamas, sitting in bed, and waiting for her to pick one out. My mommy is the prettiest mommy ever. She has yellow hair and gray eyes that look like mine. She looks like a princess. Or a fairy. Everyone says I look just like Mommy. I hope so. I hope when I grow up I look pretty like my mommy.

"Tonight, we'll read Love You Forever," she says, smiling at me and showing me the book with the messy kid by a potty.

I giggle and crinkle my nose. "That boy is silly."

Mommy laughs and touches my nose. "Yes, boys are silly. Let's read the book, so you can go to sleep. Tomorrow is a very important day. Do you know what day it is?"

"My birthday," I squeal as I clap my hands together.

"Yes, your birthday," she says, giggling. "You'll be four. A big girl."

I see water in Mommy's gray eyes, and I kiss her cheek. I don't want Mommy to be sad. She smiles at me and reads me the story. I feel my eyes getting heavy.

The last thing I hear Mommy say before I go to sleep is "As long as I'm living, my baby you'll be."

"I love you, Mommy," I mumble as I drift into sleep.

I wake up with tears streaming down my face. I look at the clock. 3:15. *Of course it is.* I roll my eyes and get up and wash my face. When I step back in my room, I look at the envelopes on top of my desk and take a deep breath as I walk to them. I sit in my chair and spin around a few times before deciding to open the one I opened the other day. I take out a Ziploc with pictures. The first picture takes my breath away. It's her. My mom. I just saw her in my dream. She looks much more beautiful in the photo than in my dream, though. She has long dirty-blonde hair and soulful gray eyes. She's wearing a maxi dress with big flowers on it. Her face is beaming as she looks down at the smiling little girl. The little girl has dirty-blonde hair and big happy gray eyes. Her long eyelashes match my mother's and she's wearing a white tank-top dress and silver sandals. In the photo, I look like a miniature version of my mother. Behind us, there's a handsome man with brown hair and brown eyes. He's dressed in a short-sleeve polo and khaki pants and he's smiling as he watches us.

I take a few deep breaths and continue to sort through pictures. They're more of the same—until they're not. There's a batch of pictures of me running in a large plain of grass. Most are me by myself. Some are me and a boy. The boy from my dreams: Nathan. I squint my eyes to study him, but the pictures were taken from a far angle. After looking through those, I put everything away and beg sleep to take me when I lie back down. I wake up again at 8:00 and get ready for class.

"Hey," Aimee says when I walk into the kitchen.

She's been staying here a lot recently. I greet her and Bruce, my security guard, or shadow as he calls himself. Bruce is a kind, older man. We're only going to have him around until the deal for the land is signed on the other end. Then I want life to go back to normal—whatever that is.

Aimee and I arrive at school, and she's still talking to me about Thanksgiving. I tell her that I'm going to spend it with Cole at Maggie's this year. She tells me to invite Maggie to her house, but I refuse. I know how Maggie is—she won't want to burden Aimee's family. Aimee asks me to go with her to her parents' house after class so she can pick up some things that she needs. I'd been wanting her to invite me for a long time but only because I wanted more information about Mark. Now that I have access to him, I don't really care to go. I agree to go with her anyway. I'm curious to see the place and figure out why she hates going home so much.

Her father is the mayor, and I assume that he's personable, but who knows. Maybe he's so busy and stressed that he's an asshole. I also think her mom is probably one of those snobs that spends her husband's money and goes to charity events to show off her new wardrobe. I can't imagine why else she'd hate her parents so much if they were nice people.

Aimee's parents' house is in Winnetka, which is only a twenty-minute ride from school—in slight traffic. We drive through an affluent neighborhood, where the kids are outside riding bikes and older folk are watering their gardens—all without a care in the world. We pull up to a huge brick house, and my eyes widen at the sight of it. This is the most beautiful house I've ever seen in real life.

I turn in my seat to face Aimee. "*This* is your parents' house?"

"Yup," she draws out. "Trust me; it's as dead as it is lavish."

I purse my lips but continue to look around as she makes the drive toward it. There are topiaries on both sides, lining the long circular driveway. When I get out of the car, I look at the house across the street and do a triple-take as I slap my hand over my mouth.

"Wait a minute ... Is that ... Do you live in front of Kevin?" I ask shriek.

Aimee laughs loudly. "Kevin?" she asks in amusement.

"Yeah, is that the *Home Alone* house? It looks just like it," I squeal.

Home Alone is one of my favorite movies. I used to be obsessed with Kevin when I was little. When I moved in with Maggie, she rented it for me one night, and we all watched it together. I knew every line. Cole was so impressed that he bought it for me for Christmas that year.

Aimee laughs and shakes her head. "Yes, that is the house. But if you're looking for Kevin, you may find that his real name is George, and he's an eighty-year-old man who likes to wear his underwear when he fetches the newspaper."

I grimace at the mental image, before laughing along with her. When we walk into her house, I gape at my surroundings. It looks like a museum where you're not allowed to touch anything. It makes me feel like a child, and I hope she doesn't ask me to sit down because I wouldn't know where to sit. None of the couches have plastic over them, and they're all light colors. The first room we pass is red, the second room is blue, and the third is dark purple.

"Your mom has a thing for colors, huh?" I say, following her up the stairs. Our boots clink against the creaky hardwood floor with each step.

"You have no idea," she replies.

There are five doors upstairs. She leads me to the first one, which is her room. Her room is completely pink.

"Oh, I have some idea," I deadpan.

As Aimee goes to her walk-in closet, I look around her room; she has pictures of herself with her parents on a couple of frames. Her mom has short brown hair and sad green eyes and her dad has brown hair and dead brown eyes. I remember seeing him on television a couple of times and his looking animated. They look like a happy family in the pictures. They're both smiling at the camera, but their eyes say otherwise. As I look at the pictures, a thought strikes me like a thunderbolt embedding into my brain.

"Aimee, you're an only child?" I ask curiously.

I hear her rattle and drop some things in the closet. When she steps out, her eyes look pained.

"I am now," she says as she drops her sad gaze to the hardwood floor.

"Oh, sorry," I say with regret.

"No, it's okay. It was a long time ago. I guess you might as well know. It'll make more sense if you meet my family and you realize how crazy they are. Hell, maybe you can even warn Aubry before he meets them during Thanksgiving," she says as she sits down on the edge of the bed.

I sit on the other side and wait for her to continue.

"I had a brother—a twin. He looked nothing like me. He was older by two minutes. He died when we were little."

I give her an empathetic look. "I'm so sorry."

She shrugs. "I have some pictures of him in that album," she says, pointing to her desk. "I just can't bear to look at them. I looked at them every day for years, wishing he was alive. When I realized he wasn't, I stopped looking."

Aimee gets up and goes back to the closet, and I get up and sit in her chair to leaf through the album. Bu-bump. Bu-

bump. That's the noise I hear in my clogged ears. I clutch on to my heart with both hands, willing it to slow down. Willing it to be quiet.

"Oh, honey, I didn't mean to make you cry," Aimee coos when she walks out of the closet.

I shake my head vigorously and look at her through blurred eyes for a long moment.

"Aimee, what is your mother's maiden name?" I ask shakily.

She crinkles her eyebrows and looks at me like I'm crazy. "Murphy."

I gasp and shoot up out of the chair, hitting my knees against the desk and knocking over the cup of pencils. "Where's your bathroom?" I ask desperately.

She points at the next door down the hallway. I run to it, close and lock the door, and spew the tuna salad I had for lunch in the toilet.

"Are you okay?" Aimee calls from the other side of the door.

I grip on to the toilet seat. "Yes," I reply weakly. "I think the tuna I had for lunch was bad. Keep packing or whatever. I'll be fine."

"Okay," she calls out unconvinced.

When I'm sure she's left, I get off the floor, splash my face, rinse my mouth a few times, and open the door very quietly to look out. I can hear Aimee in her closet, so I tiptoe to the room next door and open it. It's a storage room. I open the one next to it—master bedroom. I open the one beside that—it's completely blue.

I step in and switch the light on. I feel my body shaking as I close the door quietly behind me and lean against it. I don't know if the tuna salad really upset my stomach or if it's my nerves. I'm going to have to go with the latter, though. I look around the room and see wooden shelves on both sides of the room that have baseball collectibles on them. There's also a lower shelf by the bed that has all kinds of G.I. Joes. I spot something peeking out from the closet and it's almost as if it's calling me to free it. I can't stop my wobbly legs from slowly walking toward it. The door creaks as I push it open slowly—as soon as I see it, I fall to my knees with a loud thump. I stare at it as water wells in my eyes and affliction courses through my veins. I grab it and stuff it in my oversized purse. I get up shakily, my heart still drumming in my ears, but and quickly walk back to Aimee's room. She comes out of her closet with a bag in her hand and looks at me with furrowed eyebrows.

"Are you okay?" she asks.

"No," I reply as I grab on to the strap of my purse to calm my shaky hands. *I'm not okay at all.*

On the ride back to my apartment, I debate whether or not I should ask her any questions. I decide not to. She tells me that her parents are in DC for the week. She explains that she thinks she remembers a time when they were a happy family—before her brother died—but it's been hell living with them most of her life. I listen quietly and send Aubry a text message, asking him to please stay at Aimee's house tonight. Cole's flight gets in at 8:00, and I want us to be alone for the night.

At 9:00, the door opens, and I hear Cole speaking to Bruce. He knocks on my bedroom door three times, and I open it. He leans in and gives me a big wet kiss on the lips before crushing me into his chest. I breathe in his scent—masculine Christmas tree mixed with Jean Paul Gaultier—and hug him tightly, bracing him and myself for what's to come.

"Cole, I found something out about my nightmares and my past and everything," I say, rushed as I shuffle from one foot to the other.

He frowns, narrows his eyes, and grabs my arms to pull me to the bed. He sits me between his legs and kisses my head.

"What'd you find, baby?" he asks softly.

I take a deep breath and look him straight in the eyes. There's no point in me blinking back my impending tears at this point. I weep for family, friends, love, and the existence of bastards who punish children for their parents' sins.

"Cole," I say before taking a deep breath. "Remember how I told you about that little boy? Nathan?" I ask brokenly as he wipes my tears from my face.

He furrows his eyebrows and nods. "Yeah ..."

I let out a strangled sob before standing and walking to my purse. I take a deep breath as I unzip it and take out the tattered Rainbow Brite doll. I see recognition flash across his eyes as he stares back at me, completely dumbfounded with his mouth hanging open.

"What the fuck?" he says horrified. His voice barely a whisper.

I fall to my knees and weep loudly with my face in my hands. I hear the bed creak when he gets up and walks over to me. He gets down on his knees in front of me and holds me. He grabs my tear-stricken face between his hands and examines me like he's looking at me for the first time. I look at him the same way. Then, after a minute, our bodies crash together again. I feel his body quaking beneath me as his own grief trembles through. We hold each other for minutes, hours, days. When we finally calm down, we sit next to each other.

"So … you're ... oh God. I'm ..." he says, breathing heavily and wiping tears from his own face. "Your nightmares?"

I nod. "They're about that night. Do you remember now?"

"No. I remember it was awful, but I don't remember it. I do remember you, though," he says, caressing my face with the back of his hand. "My princess."

I smile through my tears. "Your princess?"

"Yeah," he sighs. "I always thought you were a princess, but I never wanted to tell you that. I wanted you to act like a G.I. Joe with me."

"I know," I whisper, nodding my head. "I remember."

"How'd you get this?" he asks, lifting up the doll.

"I went to your parents' house."

His mouth pops open. "How? Did you know who they were?"

"No," I shake my head. "I think I had some suspicions for a while. Well, sort of ... You know my friend, Aimee?" I wait until he nods, but he looks horrified. "She does these things that remind me of you sometimes, but I just figured it was a coincidence. Anyway, she's ... your sister."

He gasps as if I've punched him in the stomach. "What?"

"I know. It's a lot to take in. Trust me, when I was at her house today, I thought I would leave in a gurney."

"Does she know?" he asks, still horrified.

"No," I shake my head rapidly. "I didn't want to tell her. I wanted to tell you first. I don't even know how I would tell her."

He raises his eyebrows and nods. "So my parents think I'm missing?"

"They think you're dead," I whisper.

"Oh, God," he says hoarsely as tears stream down his face. I hold his face to my chest and stroke his hair as he weeps quietly, the same way he's comforted me so often in the past.

We spend the rest of the night talking about what we remember and looking through my pictures.

"Do you think that's the same place you took me to that time?" I ask him as we look at a picture of us in the farm.

He looks at me as he contemplates the possibility. "It might be. It's completely destroyed now, so we would have never linked the two together. Let's go tomorrow."

"Okay, if you're up for it."

"I just don't understand why they would put it under my name. And if my parents are alive ... I don't know. This is so confusing." he says, shaking his head slowly.

"I know," I reply, idly twirling a strand of hair around my finger. "Do you want to meet Aimee?"

He lets out a breath and shrugs. "I guess."

"I can talk to her about it and explain what I remember. I know it's going to be hard for her to believe, but she's great and I know you'll love her."

"I just don't understand how I don't remember. I remember going to the farm. I remember wanting to play with you. I remember that stupid doll you used to bring along with you all the time. How can I not remember my own family?" he says in a wavering voice.

I give him a sad smile and hold him tighter, thankful that, as crazy as this is, we have each other to lean on.

"How old is she?" he whispers later on when we're lying in bed.

"She's your twin," I whisper back. He squeezes me tighter and buries his face in my neck.

I feel sunlight on my face and blink my eyes open slowly. I can't even remember falling asleep last night. I look over and find Cole looking through the pictures again. My heart hurts for him, but there isn't much I can do, other than help him and Aimee get to know each other again.

"Good morning," I say huskily.

He turns his face and smiles at me. "Hey, baby."

"How'd you sleep?"

"Good, actually. I always sleep well when you're beside me," he says as he lies down next to me and kisses my forehead. "I'm starting to remember things."

"Really?" I ask surprised.

"Yeah, I remember Aimee and my mom. They used to go to Aimee's piano lessons while I went with my dad to the farm. I guess that's why she never went with us. I remember the night they took me; she had a cold and was sleeping with my parents." I caress his face and feel my heart flutter as I look into his beautiful green eyes.

When Cole is in the shower, I hear Aubry get home and go to the living room. I see him and Aimee standing in the kitchen making themselves coffee and take a deep breath before greeting them. I ask them to sit down and start to tell them everything. Aubry already knew my story for the most part, so I'm mainly filling Aimee in on it, until I get to the part about Cole. I tell her how I got kidnapped as a child and there was a boy named Nathan with me. I tell her how I met Cole at Maggie's. She already knows a lot about our relationship because I've told her about him in the past. I told her that my freak out and throwing up at her house wasn't because of the tuna I ate—but because I figured out that Nathan was Cole.

"What are you talking about, Blake?" Aimee asks horrified as Aubry sits there with his mouth hanging open.

"Your brother, Nathan, is alive. It's ..." I take a deep breath. "It's Cole," I say softly and wait for the news to sink in.

A plethora of emotions pass her face as she looks at me while she fidgets with the napkin she has in her hand until she tears it in little pieces. "No," she sobs. "No. He's dead. He's dead. He was never found. Those people killed him."

I sigh and take her hand in mine, looking into her brown eyes with a sad smile. "No, babe, he's not dead. He's alive and he's here, and if you don't want to meet him today, it's totally fine. We just found out yesterday; he's still having a hard time with it himself."

"No," she says, shaking her head. "I want to meet him. I have to. Oh my God," she weeps as she launches herself into me for a hug. We hold each other tightly and Aubry gets up and holds us both in his arms. The three of us snap our heads up when we hear Cole approach us and Aubry lets us go and goes to him and goes him tightly.

"I'm so sorry, bro," Aubry cries as he hugs Cole. Their chests both heave as they talk quietly to each other. I smile through the flow of tears that fall down my face as I watch them together: the two boys that have known each other since they were children and were raised brothers. My heart doesn't hurt as I watch them, though. I know Aubry is glad that Cole is getting the answers he's been searching for his whole life. Cole separates himself from Aubry and winks at me as he walks over to dry my tears before he looks at Aimee.

"Hi, I'm Cole," he says, extending his hand. Aimee, who's not one for handshakes, wraps her arms around him and begins to sob loudly again. I try to stifle my own sobs with my hands as I look on. My heart swells for them because they found each other after living apart for so long, but I feel sad because I know I'll never have this with my own family. I feel Aubry's arms wrap around me and his head rest on my shoulder and the thought evaporates. *I have the family I need right here.*

"Aimee," she says when she lets go. "And I missed you so fucking much," she continues as she wipes the tears from her face again. Cole laughs but has tears running down his face. I crack a smile because I've never seen him this emotional and it makes me feel so good that these are happy tears. We all spend the rest of the night together, drinking wine and catching up. Cole asks Aimee not to tell their parents anything yet.

"Cole, really, do you think they'd believe me if I told them?" Aimee asks with a raised eyebrow.

"Good point," he says, scrunching his eyebrows together. "Do you think they'll ever believe it—when we decide to tell them?"

She puts her hand over his. "Honey, if I can believe it, they'll definitely believe it, with time. Especially Mom. She's been dreaming of this since that night. Trust me," she says sadly, and I can see the years of hurt that she's been put through over something that she had no control over.

CHAPTER FIFTEEN

Present

Our trip to the farm is a quiet one since we're both still processing this new information. Cole went from elated to pissed off for not remembering. Then he was sad for his family and for himself—until he settled on being relieved that we were both okay. He's been sneaking looks of wonder at me when he thinks I'm not watching. I don't blame him—I feel the same way. The man that I love and hope to spend the rest of my life with is the same boy who used to chase me around the farm and secretly thought of me as his princess. I smile at the thought and squeeze his hand a little tighter.

As we drive through the tall grass, Cole curses for not thinking to bring a mower. We spot a clear area, where the grass looks as if it has been burned, and we park there. We get out and stand on the bed of the truck for a better view. Now that we remember, this place is starting to look familiar, but it's still different from my dreams. Things looked more colorful as a child—I guess that's one of the many truths of life, though. We sit down next to each other with our legs crossed, and face the deserted plain.

"Do you remember why we used to come here?" he asks as he looks around.

"No, I just remember always looking forward to seeing you," I reply as a slow smile creeps up on my face.

He smiles and pulls me close to him. "I remember that, too."

"You used to come with your dad," I say.

"Yeah, and you used to come with yours."

I nod. "I think I used to call it my grandfather's farm, but that wouldn't make sense. If it were, why would it be under your name?"

He scratches his head. "I have no idea."

I sigh. "I'm going to go see Mark this week-again. I need him to give me more information. He must know more than he's telling me."

"I'll go with you," he suggests.

I purse my lips and think about it. I guess it would be okay. Mark hinted that he knew about Cole.

"Sure, why not?" I shrug.

Cole's first day of work in Chicago is Monday. He brought all his stuff with him on this trip and is moving in with Aubry and me. Aimee had asked—before this ordeal—if I thought it was too sudden. I replied, "I've lived with him all my life, how could it be too sudden?"

We know each other better than we know ourselves; there's no point in doing the whole "You get your own place, and I'll keep mine" thing. Besides, I live with Aubry. How weird would it be to tell Cole he can't move in with me? I snort at the thought—as if he'd be okay with that.

We stay on the farm for the better part of our afternoon before heading to see Maggie. We had promised her that we would have dinner at the house and stay the night if it got too late. I guess we were staying the night after all. We walk up the creaky porch steps, and Cole mumbles something about fixing it in the morning. I knock on the door when we reach it. We all still have a key, but I feel weird using it. Cole jams his key into the hole and turns it before I stop his hand and glare at him.

"What?" he shrugs.

"We don't live here anymore, Cole."

Maggie opens the door as we are about to argue and shakes her head at us.

"Blake, this will always be your house. Let the boy use his key."

I smile at Maggie. Her hair has gotten whiter and her face has creased with age, but her brown eyes still glow with gentle wisdom. She hugs me, and I put my arms around her wide hips. She and I are about the same height. Greg used to always call us "shorties"—but then again, he used to call anybody who had a vagina that. I follow her to the kitchen while Cole takes our bags upstairs. I wonder if he's going to put them in my room or his. This is the first time we've been back here as a couple. I know he's not even going to pretend that we're sleeping in separate rooms, though.

"So you and Cole finally getting along again?" Maggie asks, stirring the pot.

I smile. "You can say that."

"Hmmm," she badgers with a knowing smile. "Does that mean you'll be making babies soon?"

"Umm ... no, that's not what it means at all," I reply, resisting an eye roll. "We're taking it slow."

"Slow?" she laughs. "Since when have you known Cole to take anything slow?"

I laugh. "Okay, fine. He just moved in with me and Aubry."

She throws her head back in laughter. "That boy has been crazy about you since the minute you stepped foot in this house."

"Still am, Mags. Still am," Cole booms as he walks into the conversation. Our eyes lock, and he gives me his wide smile, showcasing the dimple on his right cheek.

"Boy, you better take care of her heart. That's all I'll tell you. She was so hurt all those years. I could hear her heart breaking from across the table during Christmas dinners," Maggie chides.

"Her own fault," Cole replies, sticking a piece of bread in his mouth. "She broke up with me, remember? And she never wanted to give me another chance."

I roll my eyes at his statement.

"Cole, stop talking with your mouth full. It's disgusting," I groan. "And please let's get off the topic of how I broke up with you and how you took advantage of that to sleep with every girl that acknowledged you. Let's drop it." I sigh. "Maggie, I have some things I need to ask you. Important things. Actually, we both do."

Maggie takes a deep breath. "I always knew you'd come back asking questions that I don't have answers to," she says sadly.

"I brought photos to show you. It's ... It's very complicated, and we can't tell many people about it," I explain.

Maggie turns off the stove and sits down. "Photos of what, exactly?" she asks while wiping her hands on her apron.

I ask Cole to run upstairs and get me the envelope I brought. When he comes back, he hands it to me with a kiss and sits beside me. My chair squeaks loudly on the hardwood floors as he pulls it closer to his.

"Photos of my childhood ... our childhood," I clarify, looking at Cole.

"Both of your childhoods?" Maggie asks with a frown. "Your Aunt Shelley didn't bring you here as a child."

"Maggie, that's why I said it's complicated," I interrupt as I hand her one of the photos of Cole and I standing next to each other by some chickens in the barn.

She gasps loudly and places her hands over her mouth, her brown eyes looking at us in complete shock.

"Holy mother of pearl, that's Cole," Maggie says as she gapes at me. "Is that you, Blake?"

"Yes, that's what we're trying to tell you. We knew each other before we met here," I start. "We need to know. Who brought Cole here? You said it was his father, but we're pretty sure it wasn't."

She sighs and closes her eyes. "I got a call from a man that said he knew me—or of me—I can't remember which. It was around 4:00 in the morning, maybe later, when he called. I thought it was a prank caller because I'd been getting a lot of calls from teenagers that used to mow the lawn here. Anyhow, I hung up twice before he called back again and begged me to listen to him. He sounded like he was crying, so I stayed on the line. He said he was a friend of Liam's ..." she pauses and gives me a pointed look that I don't understand. "And Cory's, so I stayed on the line. He told me that he was going to be dropping off a four-year-old boy. He said he'd explain everything to me when he got here. We hung up, and I still wasn't sure if it was a fib or not—until I heard knocking on the door. The young man was dressed in all black. He looked familiar, but I couldn't place him. He had the clearest blue eyes. I just couldn't get over how young he was. He looked so scared and terribly sad. When he saw me, he started to cry. Really cry. I held him for a bit.

"He told me that he didn't know where else to go. He'd gotten my phone number from his mother, and he needed to separate the two children. He didn't give me too much information. Really, he was just upset and rambling on about needing to keep them safe. He left Cole with me. He told me his name was Cole Murphy and that his parents left him for dead. I didn't think to call the police. Well, I did think of it, but the man told me that Cole would be in danger if I did that. He gave me information to a bank account and told me that he would deposit money in that account and in my own until Cole turned eighteen. That was it."

Cole and I look at each other for a long time, our mouths hanging open.

"Well, Cole is his middle name. Murphy is his mother's maiden name. You said the man was young. How young?" I ask.

"I don't think he could have been older than twenty. He was a baby himself. He looked so scared," she replies sadly.

"Is it this man?" I ask, pointing at a picture with my Uncle Michael in the background.

She shakes her head but wrinkles her forehead. "Where did you get these photos?"

"Shelley left them to me in a box. Why?"

"That kid—that's Mark," she says confused as she points at another one of the photos of a little boy—photos of Shelley's family, not mine.

"Really?" I ask shocked. "How do you know?"

"He's Shelley's son. I met him when he was about that age. That was the last time I saw him, too," she says sadly.

I know that Shelley knew Maggie, but I didn't know how well they knew each other.

I frown and look at Cole as he holds my hand tightly in his.

"Are you sure that's him?" I whisper.

"I'm positive," she says without doubt.

I let out a breath. *This shit is exhausting ... and confusing ... and crazy.*

Tuesday creeps up on us and I'm kind of freaking out about Mark seeing Cole and vice versa. I told Cole that Mark was the one who took us that night, mainly because I was scared of Cole remembering him and getting physical with him.

When we step into the building, I stop walking and hold on to his arm until he faces me. "I need you to behave," I say seriously.

He chuckles and dips his head to kiss me. "Baby, I'll be fine. Even if he is the guy, I'm fine. Right now, I don't care about any of it, Blake. If this wouldn't have happened, we might not be together," he murmurs against my lips.

"Cole," I say through gritted teeth. "My mother is dead. My father is dead. I'm going to pretend you didn't say that. Besides, we might have still ended up together."

He gives me a long, lingering kiss and a smack in the butt before we get in the elevator.

We arrive on Mark's floor and Office Barbie greets us with a real smile as she blatantly checks out my boyfriend. My mouth pops open in disbelief, and I turn my head to look at Cole, who's watching me—with a smile on his smug face. I narrow my eyes at him and dare him to say anything to her. He chuckles lightly, reading my expression correctly, and gives me a loud kiss on the lips. I look back at Office Barbie and tell her we're here to see Mark and watch as she calls him, never taking her eyes off Cole. It pisses me off, but I decide not to push it.

When Mark steps out to greet us, his eyes are nothing short of surprised. He frowns at me, and I shrug at him in response before he introduces himself to Cole and leads us to his office. I look at Cole, but his smooth expression doesn't give away what he's thinking. I'm not sure if he recognizes Mark or not.

Suddenly, he says, "So, Blake tells me she trusts you for whatever reason. I personally don't understand how she can—knowing who you are and what you did."

Mark shakes his head slowly, chastising. "You two really are meant for each other. I already told Blake that if I wanted to harm you, you wouldn't be here. What I did was help you. I know you don't see it that way, but that's the truth."

"Finally," I deadpan.

"Yeah, well, two against one," Mark says, cocking his head to one side. "Are you here because you remembered and wanted to drill me for answers? I told you that you're better off not searching for trouble."

"Maybe, but now I know who my parents are," Cole says in an even tone.

Mark's eyebrows shoot up, and he looks at me for an answer.

"I went to Aimee's house after I had gotten pictures from Shelley. Aimee let me look at pictures of her *dead brother*." I emphasize the last part. "You can imagine how I felt when I saw Cole ... or *Nathan* ... looking back at me."

"Does Aimee know?" Mark asks concerned.

"Yes, but she's not going to tell," I say.

He looks at Cole. "You better hope not. Your father is a very public figure, and you're popular in your own right. If people find out, it'll be a circus—and when the wrong people find out, it'll be a bloodbath."

I feel my eyes pop out of their sockets. "What?" I ask horrified. "What do you mean a bloodbath?"

Mark takes a deep breath and perches up on the corner of his desk. "Blake, everybody thinks Nathan and Catherine are dead. If people find out they're not, it's not going to end well."

"Who are we?" I ask horrified. "Oh my God, are we related?"

Mark laughs shortly. "No, not at all."

"Why did they want us, and why are we so important?" Cole asks.

"They wanted you as warnings and as bait. I can't tell you why you're so important," Mark states. "Trust me—you don't want that kind of information weighing on your shoulders."

"Was Shelley your mom?" I ask quietly.

Mark snickers. "You're quite the detective, Blake. Let me see those pictures. Our time's almost up."

I show Mark the pictures I brought and let him sort through them. I'm too preoccupied with his evasive answers to examine his face as he looks at them. He asks me to sign the deed of the land over to the buyers and tells me that my money will be wired by the end of the week.

Thinking about my parents, Cole's parents, and our kidnapping is exhausting. Cole and I decide to put it behind us unless something else comes up. We say this—but I know we'll both be silently brewing.

I put my focus on school, even though this year of law school seems much easier than the last two. Maybe it's because my life is a little more hectic and it makes school work seem stupid. I see Russell every day, and now that he's dating another student, we've become friends again. Cole doesn't mind that he's in my study groups as long as he "doesn't try anything"—his words, of course.

CHAPTER SIXTEEN

Past

I had been in the University of Chicago for a month before I started to get used to the ever-present knife that gutted my heart every day. I had spoken to Cole a handful of times after our breakup, and he sounded like his normal self. I knew better than to think he was fine though, and Aubry reminded me of it often.

"He feels like shit, Blake," Aubry said whenever he hung up the phone with Cole.

I knew Cole did—he had to if he felt half the pain that I was feeling.

"Aubry ..." I said one particularly gloomy morning.

"Yeah, Cowboy?" he replied as he poured our coffee.

"Do you think ... Do you think if I were to ..." I took a deep breath and buried my face in my hands.

"Spit it out!" he said exasperated.

"Okay, do you think if ... AH! What do you think would happen if I were to visit him?" I asked, cringing.

He stood there with a mug in one hand and the coffee pot in the other. He was totally frozen. "Do you mean if you asked him to get back with you?" he asked cautiously.

I looked down and started chipping my nails. "Yeah?"

He laughed once. "Fucking-A, Cowboy. What the fuck do you think would happen? He'd probably fucking propose to you on the spot!"

I looked up smiling. "You think so?" Not that I wanted Cole to propose to me or anything, but the fact that Aubry thought he'd want me back for sure spoke volumes.

"Do I think so?" he asked, rolling his eyes. "Let's go see him tonight."

Aubry had been dying for an excuse to visit Duke University, so of course he'd jump at this opportunity.

I smiled widely. "Alright, let's go!"

We booked our flight, but I begged Aubry to keep our trip a surprise. He somehow got Cole to tell him what party he'd be at that night, so we were going to go from the airport to the hotel and straight to the party. I was so excited—and nervous at the same time. I kept wringing my hands together and biting my lip as I paced the room while I waited for Aubry to get out of work so we could leave. I took a deep breath when I heard Aubry get home and off we went.

"Calm the fuck down, Cowboy! You're making *me* nervous," Aubry said as he stilled my bouncing leg when our cab was pulling up to the frat house where the party was taking place.

"Oh my God, I think I need a drink ... or five," I said as I clutched my stomach.

"I think if you drink now, you might puke," he said, looking amused.

"You're probably right. Let's just go inside," I said and plastered on my best smile.

My stomach was flip-flopping and my hands were shaking as we knocked on the door. A short guy with beautiful aqua-blue eyes opened the door for us and gave Aubry a confused look before he checked me out slowly.

"Who are you?" the guy asked Aubry a little rudely.

"I'm a friend of Cole's ... and Warren's," Aubry said confidently, and I smiled up at him. I'd heard of Cole's friend Warren, but I knew for a fact that Aubry didn't know who the hell he was.

"Oh, cool," the short guy said as he stepped out of the way. "And what's your name?" he asked me when I brushed past him.

"Blake," I said with a smile.

He checked me out again. "Blake, I'm David. If you need anything, I'm your man."

"Thanks," I replied while grabbing on to the back of Aubry's shirt so I wouldn't get lost in the crowd.

We walked around without spotting Cole, but we did see Sarah, a girl from our high school. She looked more than a little surprised to see us there. She was nervous as she greeted us, and I figured she probably felt bad for ganging up on me with Sasha-the-Slut one time after school. She looked like she wanted to tell me something—probably apologize—from the look in her eyes, but I smiled and waved at her as I walked away with Aubry.

"That was awkward," Aubry said, leaning down to my ear.

I shrugged. "Whatever. Old news. I'm gonna go use the bathroom. I'll be right back."

He laughed. "First of all, hell no. I'm not letting you run off by yourself at a *frat party in a frat house.* Second of all, how the fuck do you know where it is?"

I laughed back. "Umm ... there's a huge cardboard sign that reads 'bathroom' over there," I said, pointing. "But yeah, maybe you should stay close to it. Look, there's a keg right by it. I'll go to the bathroom, and you get us some beers."

We walked to the keg, and I left Aubry there to go to the bathroom. I passed two doors before I saw where it was. As I stood behind a ridiculously drunk girl, I heard a guy scream Cole's name, causing my head to snap up, and my insides to warm at the sound. I immediately got out of line and walked in that direction. I rounded the corner and found a group of guys and girls standing around a pool table. Butterflies danced in my stomach when I spotted him. His back was facing me, but I could see he was in the middle of an animated conversation. He was wearing a fitted navy T-shirt, and his brown hair was cut short. I frowned because he never told me he had cut it. My feet started making their way toward him but stopped about three feet away—when I saw female hands with red fingernails stroking his lower back. My heart was pumping so hard I couldn't even breathe. I wanted to turn away, but my feet were cemented to the floor. I couldn't peel my eyes away from them and the worst part was that I could *hear* them from where I was standing.

"Let's go to the back room," she said, giggling as she squeezed his ass.

I could recognize that fake voice anywhere. *What.The.Fuck?*

His head leaned down and kissed her neck, giving me a full view of her face. When she saw me, her eyes widened for a second before they slanted. She narrowed her blue eyes at me as if to tell me, "Yeah, he's mine now." I felt acid kill the butterflies that were in my stomach minutes ago. To drive her point home, Sasha held his body tighter to hers and bit his neck—all while looking right at me. She smirked and told him she was ready to go to the room. I saw him nod right before I turned around and shuffled my feet toward Aubry. When I found him standing by the keg, I grabbed the red cup from his hand and chugged it. The guys around us cheered as he looked at me in astonishment.

"Blake, what the fuck?" he asked.

"Let's go. NOW." I snapped.

"What the hell happened? Did you find Cole?"

"Fuck Cole," I said as I grabbed the other cup from his hand. I turned on my heel and started chugging that one, too.

"Holy shit! This girl is awesome!" one of the guys chanted as three others cheered.

"Cowboy, slow the fuck down," Aubry growled.

I angrily wiped my mouth with the back of my hand, took a deep breath and decided I would confront Cole right now. I told Aubry I was going to the bathroom, and I stomped (quite literally) to the "back room." I asked where it was, and when I found it, I held the doorknob for a while. My head was still swimming from the beers I had chugged when I turned the knob. Before I pushed the door open, I heard someone—who I assumed was Sasha—moan loudly with pleasure. My stomach twisted at the sound, and I unturned the doorknob keeping my grip on it. I wasn't sure if I could go through with it. If I barged in there, I would *see* them.

I covered my mouth with my free hand to keep my gag from escalating. I could hear her repeated moans and screams, the sound was like nails on a chalkboard—but I stayed there, nonetheless. I closed my eyes and tried to control my breathing. The longer I stood there, the more my heart broke, but I welcomed the pain. It was my fault this was going on. I clenched my jaw at the thought. *No.* We hadn't even been broken up two months, and there he was screwing her brains out. I gagged again before I heard him for the first time.

"Oh yes ... fuck ... yes ... *Blake* ..." My stomach dropped. *Did he really just say my name?* Blood rushed to my head as my heart beat frantically. No amount of oxygen would have been enough for me at that moment. I'd finally had enough and ran to the bathroom with tears in my eyes.

After I somewhat composed myself, I went back to where Aubry was playing beer pong. I chugged another beer as I stood there waiting for him to finish the game. When I thought we were finally leaving, the guys brought out Cuervo and convinced me to take some shots with them. By that point, I just wanted to drown my sorrows, so I drank everything in sight—it's not like I could taste it anyway. An hour later, Aubry and I were both drunkingly laughing, hanging over each other to keep from falling as we talked to Bobby, David, and Rob when one of them suggested body shots.

"Woohoo! Body shots!" I screamed, flinging my hands up in the air wildly.

They hooted and hollered. Before I knew it, somebody lifted me onto a table. I never thought in a million years that I would have done that, but there I was doing it. I lifted up my already short shirt and tucked it under my bra. Aubry laughed and made a joke about something before grabbing the brunette beside him and making out with her. I laughed at him and was about to make a comment when I felt cold liquid being poured over my bare belly.

"Aaahhhh," I shrieked. "That's cold."

"Sorry, babe, we keep it in the freezer," said Bobby. *Bobby was soooo cute.* Through my haze, he looked like Ryan Reynolds.

"Are you going to lick me?" I flirted.

"Hell yeah, none of these fuckers better even try it," he bellowed, making sure his friends heard. They all groaned, laughed, and clapped his back.

I felt Bobby's tongue lick around my belly button and make its way up, stopping right below my chest. When he was done, he stood above me where the lime was squeezed between my lips and licked around it, tasting me before he put the lime into his mouth. He hovered over my face, staring down at me for a while. He was leaning in, and even in my drunken state, I knew he was going to kiss me. I reached up behind his neck and pulled him in closer to meet his lips.

"What the fuck?" Cole screamed at the top of his lungs. I backed away from Bobby and propped myself up on my elbows, accidentally hitting my forehead with Bobby's. I rubbed it and looked at Cole who was standing with Sasha clinging on to his arm. She had a satisfied look on her face that I wanted to claw off.

"Cooooole," Aubry slurred beside me. "Dude, where the fuck have you been? Blake wanted to leave an hour ago, but I convinced her to stay and have some fun for once." I saw Cole's face fall before closed my eyes for a second and let my body fall back on the table.

"Bobby, can you help me up?" I asked drowsily.

I felt him lift me in his arms. I didn't expect him to carry me. I wanted him to just put me on my feet, not hold me like a freaking baby. I put my arms around his neck to keep myself from falling over.

"Put her down, Bobby," Cole spat angrily.

"Oh, you're the ex-boyfriend?" Bobby smirked. I looked up at him, but all I could see was his jaw from where I was. I knew I was smiling, though—why I had no idea. I couldn't remember what I'd said to him other than I was visiting my ex-boyfriend. I might have said that my ex-boyfriend was an asshole, but I didn't remember saying anything else.

"Bobby," Cole warned again. "Put her down. Now."

I cringed at the sound of his tone. "You ... have no right ... to tell him what to do ... with me ..." I slurred, pointing my finger at Cole. "I ... want *Bobby* ... to take me to the ... *back room*," I finished, narrowing my eyes between Cole and

Sasha. He looked like I'd just thrown a bowling ball at his testicles. *Good.*

"What ... Blake, what the fuck?" Cole asked quietly, his voice pained.

I shimmied out of Bobby's hold and stood with my back to him, facing Cole and Sasha. I placed my closed fists over my hips and suddenly felt like an ant amongst humans. *Everyone was so tall.* I looked down and hazily remembered taking off my heels earlier. I took a deep sobering breath and wobbled back a little and felt Bobby's hands on my shoulders steady me.

"Blake, let's go," Cole pleaded.

"No," I said, stomping my feet once, accidentally stepping on Bobby's sneaker. "Sorry," I said looking back and apologizing before turning back to Cole. "I will not go anywhere with you and that ..." I shouted, pointing at Sasha. "Skank."

I heard a couple of gasps and a guy scream "cat fight" somewhere, but they all sounded far away. Sasha's grin widened as she put her hand on Cole's forearm, and I saw him shrug her off angrily before I closed my eyes and sucked in a deep breath, trying to keep myself composed.

I turned to Aubry once I opened my eyes again. "Aub, let's go. We came, we *saw,*" I said, glaring at Cole. "We conquered," I finished, lifting Bobby's arm as if we'd won a race.

Aubry hesitated but stood beside me—and thankfully, took my side. "Alright. Guys, it's been real. Thanks for everything. Cole, can I talk to you?" Aubry asked quietly.

Cole agreed with a nod, never taking his eyes off of me. He was looking at me the way he did when he left Maggie's house a month and a half ago. Tears prickled my eyes at the memory, but I held them at bay. It'd been a month and a half since I felt his lips on mine. A month and a half of sleepless nights, wondering if he'd been thinking of me as much as I thought of him. A month and a half of wondering what could have been. A month and a half of kicking myself for being insecure about a long distance relationship.

By the time Aubry and Cole walked back to us, Bobby had given me his number, and I apologized to the guys for the scene I had caused. They all laughed it off and told me it had been fun. I was much more sober though, and quite frankly, very embarrassed. Sasha didn't say anything as she stood in the corner. She didn't have to. She had accomplished what she wanted and would forever be known as "that skank"—to me at least ... and to Becky, of course.

"Blake, please talk to me," Cole pleaded before I left the party.

"I have nothing to say to you," I replied quietly. "I'm sorry I came here."

He grabbed my elbow when I tried to walk away. "Please don't. Please don't be sorry you came here. I wish you would've told me you were coming," he said sadly as he dropped my arm from his hold.

I glared at him. "Why? So you wouldn't have fucked Sasha tonight? You would've waited until tomorrow night instead?" I spat. I knew I had no right; he wasn't mine anymore.

He cringed. "Blake—" he said as he grabbed my arm again.

I pulled my arm roughly away from him. "No. Just. Don't. I'm glad you're doing well. I really am. I won't be back—ever."

He gaped at me. "Baby, please don't say that. I don't want you to not come back. I'm sorry," he pleaded quickly.

"Don't call me that," I said through gritted teeth. "And I don't want you to be sorry. There's nothing to be sorry for."

I walked away and got into the waiting cab to find Aubry already passed out inside. Cole was still standing in the street with his hands tucked in the pockets of his jeans. He was looking somberly at me, his broken eyes matching my heart. As we started to drive away, I lowered my window.

"Have fun with your skank!" I said loudly. His eyes were glistening as he shook his head in defeat.

The next morning Aubry and I headed back to the airport, and I was glad to leave the sad memories behind me. I knew they would haunt me for a while—if not, forever. *Her hand on his ass. Her teeth on his neck. His wrapping her in his arms as he kissed her neck. The sounds they were making as they had sex.* I shuddered at the memory and brushed myself off disgustedly. The worst part was that out of all of the memories I wished I could erase, the most prominent one was the pain in his eyes as I left him. *Fucking Cole...*

The night we got back home, Aubry told me that Cole had given him a letter to give me. I told him to rip it up and throw it away. I didn't want to read it now—*or ever*. Months later I wondered whatever happened to that letter, but I never asked Aubry.

CHAPTER SEVENTEEN

Present

It's been a couple of months since our meeting with Mark, and Cole still hasn't met his parents or even let them know that he's alive. He and Aimee are taking time to get to know each other better, which has been great for them. If anybody were to see them in the street, they would never know that they hadn't seen each other in so many years. I'm not sure if it's because they're siblings, or the fact that they're twins that makes their bond so unique. It's almost as if they picked up where they left off twenty-one years ago; it's an incredible thing to witness.

Aimee moved in with us when the lease on her place was up, but she and Aubry are looking for another place. When she first moved in and realized just how paranoid I really was—between my locked doors, alarm system, and my three-knocks-on-the-door code—she thought I was a little crazy. Even after knowing what happened to me, she doesn't completely grasp *what happened to me*. I don't blame her. I don't think many people can understand it or fully believe it; it sounds like an episode of *NCIS* or something.

The recurring nightmare hasn't come to me in a while and I know I should be happy about it, but it's really bothering me. It's not that I want to remember my mother lying in blood, but I want to remember the faces. The faces of the killers. Cole keeps asking me to see a therapist. He promises it'll help to talk about what I remember. I went to a therapist for years, though. It only helped me because they gave me something to help me sleep. I just need to remember. When I remember, I'll be fine. When I remember, I'll move past it. I started keeping a box of memories. In it, I have the photos Shelley left me and her last letter. I also have a timeline that I've been working on and a diary that I'm using to write my memories in.

Recently, Cole and I have been discussing buying a house together. I know it's a big step, but I also know that it's not something we'll regret. He thought it was hilarious when Aimee told him that their parents live across the street from the house from *Home Alone*. He keeps telling me that it's a sign. I don't think I should remind him what the plot was in that movie. Every Sunday we go house hunting, which can be pretty fun sometimes. We've driven by a couple of adorable-looking town homes in the city, but he says the yards are too small, and they all have stairs. It's a big issue for me—the stairs.

"Remind me again why it is that you hate stairs?" Cole asks one afternoon as we're driving by some big two-story homes.

"I hate the build-up of emotions related to them," I say before I bite the inside of my cheek, waiting for him to start laughing at how stupid that sounds.

He chuckles and grabs my hand as we stop at a red light. "Baby, they're just stairs. They don't have emotions!" he says as his eyes twinkle at me.

I take a deep breath and shift my body to face him. "They're not *just* stairs. Have you ever seen a movie with a *one*-story house? Stairs are a big deal. They're such a big deal that you never have a scene of a girl walking toward her prom date without her walking down the stairs first. You never see a bride stroll through the hallway in her wedding dress. You always see her walk down the stairs. You never watch a scary movie where the main character doesn't run up the stairs to get away from her attacker. In my case—in *real life*—I walked straight into my attacker. After I walked down the stairs. There is no way I want to own a house with stairs. No way." The amused look in his eyes vanishes as he looks at me for a long moment before nodding his head once and continuing to drive. I let out a sigh of relief and turn to look out the window as one house catches my attention. It's a white colonial-style house with a pink front door and it's beautiful. *Too bad it's two stories.*

***

It's dead winter, and I swear I'll never get used to this weather, even though I've lived here my entire life. I think it's a little strange, until I look around and see herds of people bundled up like pigs in a blanket. I am on my way to meet Cole for lunch at a little Irish restaurant in Michigan Avenue. As I'm walking—and trying not to slip in the icy street as I curse myself for wearing heeled boots—I spot a man among the pack of hungry vultures that work in corporate America. He's looking right at me, and it makes me cross my arms over my chest. He has short blond hair, almost shaved bald and is very big. Something about the way he's sneering at me makes the hairs on my arms stand up. As I'm approaching where he's standing, I notice that he has two different color eyes. One is dark—black almost—the other is blue, I think.

I want to look away from this man—so bad because my stomach is in knots, but I cannot look away from his stare. As I get closer, I squint my eyes to get a better look at his face and feel the air swish out of my body when I notice his dark eye is a glass eye. My step falters, and I have to grab on to the wall beside me to keep my knees from giving out on me. I'm still looking at him when he leans away from the wall, still watching me intently. When I start to move again, I look down—breaking eye contact—to check if my bootie is stuck on something, and when I look back up he's gone.

I look around in a hurry, trying to spot the glass-eyed man. There are too many people walking to and fro, and I can't find him. My eyes can't focus on one specific person, but I know I didn't imagine him. I know he was right there. *How can somebody walk so quickly? It's impossible .. .right?* But in a place that can make anybody disappear—whether they want to or not—it is impossible to catch those who are looking to blend in.

When I walk into the restaurant, I find Cole talking to a group of young men that he quickly dismisses when he spots me. I look at the table and see that he already ordered wine and an appetizer.

"Am I late?" I ask as I bend over to kiss him. He wraps his arms around me and pulls me down to his lap to give me a kiss that leaves me light-headed.

"No, baby, you're right on time. I got here a little early."

While we're eating, he shows me new house listings he found in Glenn Ellyn, Glenview, Wilmette, and other expensive areas.

"Cole, don't you think it's better if we get a smaller, less-expensive home for now?"

"Why?" he asks, genuinely confused.

I laugh. "Because there're only two of us, and we don't need the space."

"There're only two of us *for now*," he replies, picking up my hands and kissing each finger lightly before nipping on the pads, making me squirm in my seat.

"You're giving me that look," he says, raising an eyebrow.

"What look?" I ask.

He tilts his head and shoots me a crooked grin. "Blake, I happen to know the owner of this restaurant, and trust me when I say that he won't mind me borrowing the back room for a little while," he replies in a low voice.

I bite my lip and shake my head. "That wouldn't be a good idea."

He shows me that dimple that I love and leans in to kiss my lips before going back to a specific listing that he's interested in. It's hard to resist going to see some of these homes, when Cole is talking about playing football with future babies and grilling on our deck. I know that as much as he wants that, we're not ready for kids yet, though.

Later that night, as we're lying in bed, he's watching the news and idly stroking my hair as I sort through Real Estate Law notes. The news reporter is talking about a familiar case, about some men with ties to organized crime. I sit up straighter when I see Mark addressing the media and ask Cole to turn up the volume. One of the men they're talking about is young; he can't be older than thirty. He's good looking; he has dirty-blond hair and gray—maybe blue—eyes.

> "Connor Benson, is said to be Reggie Isaac's accomplice in assaulting an employee outside city hall last fall. They are both linked to organized crime kingpin, Brian Benson. If charged, they could face up to three years in prison for assault of a city employee."

The camera cuts to a video of Connor Benson leaving the courthouse and then to Mark addressing reporters.

Cole and I shoot each other wide-eyed looks.

"Is it me or do they—" he says.

"Yeah. I thought the same thing," I reply nodding slowly.

I tune out when they start the sports segment and switch on my computer. I run my hands over my face before I type in my fourth birthday on Google. I've done this before, of course, but now I have more information—I think. As usual, my friend Google has a billion links. "Today in history: In California, a forty-one-year-old man named James opens fire in a McDonald's and kills twenty-one people." *Interesting.* "Beverly Burns becomes the first woman Boeing 747 captain in the world." *That's positive.* However, there is absolutely nothing on what happened in my home that morning. Nothing.

How could a shooting and two kidnappings not be reported? Then I find:

> "Camden and Colleen Wolf's four-year-old son, Nathan Cole Wolf, was taken from his bedroom in the middle of the night. Both parents say that their bedroom was barricaded by their intruders. Their daughter, Aimee, was sleeping in their bedroom at the time of the kidnapping. If you have any information, we urge you to contact this number."

As I scroll down, I see the search engine overflow with articles about Nathan's disappearance.

I cover my mouth with both hands to keep my sobs in before I feel my protective blanket shield me with his warmth.

"What's wrong, baby?" he coos in my ear.

With one shaky hand, I point to my screen. He turns my computer to get a better look, and I feel his body still as he reads. There are pictures of his parents in all of the articles. They look tired and distraught, both of them with dark circles under their eyes. My heart breaks for them. I can only imagine what they must have been feeling. They put a roof over their children's heads, taught them right from wrong, fed them and bathed them every night. They held their hands to cross the street, shielded them from the outside rain so they wouldn't get sick, and tucked them in every night at bedtime. I just can't imagine what they must have gone through when their child was taken from the safe haven they had created for him.

Cole snaps my laptop closed and puts it on his nightstand before he pulls me into his arms and cradles me tightly. I hide my head in the crook of his neck and breathe him in. I wish I could say something, but no words would take the pain away. I lift my face to his and kiss him softly before he deepens the kiss and devours my mouth in his. He begins to stroke small circles with his thumbs over my hips before making his way up to cup my bare breasts. His lips only leave mine when he shifts his body and pushes mine down, covering it with his. Urgent wet kisses down my neck make me throw my head back with a moan. I feel him groan against my chest as he continues to caress me, covering every inch of my entire body at once. The heat of his gaze when he looks into my eyes lets me know that every ounce of anguish has been forgotten—even if it's just for now.

He trails kisses up my calves, making me squirm from the five o'clock shadow that traces his face. He pins my thighs with his arms so I don't move away as he buries his face in between my legs, while he continues to tease my breasts and brings me to ecstasy. I'm still shivering when he kneels above me and thrusts into me, stretching every inch of me to welcome him as he growls out my name, and he circles his hips, making me raise my hips in response. I wrap my arms around his neck as he lifts me up by the waist and sits me up on top of him as he continues his sweet torture. He moves me until I convulse around him and fall limp against his chest.

"Thank you, baby," he says as he kisses my face gently before placing me back down on the bed and pulling my back against his chest. "I love you so, so much."

We hold each other tightly for a long time, neither of us saying a word. Despite the ways we've been wronged, we're thankful that we have one another.

"You're the best thing that's ever happened to me, Blake. I'm never letting you go," he whispers hoarsely.

I smile and reply by kissing the hand he has resting on my arm. My smile is sad, yet hopeful, when I go to sleep.

CHAPTER EIGHTEEN

Past

I didn't know how I was going to survive law school—if I ever got in. I hated reading and writing long papers. I looked at the time; it was only 8:00. I didn't know why I thought procrastinating homework was a good idea. My bed looked so warm and cozy. I glared at Zack, who looked too comfortable sleeping on my pillow. If he weren't Aubry's swimming mate and my boyfriend, I'd totally kick him out right now. I thought I heard someone knocking on my front door, so I got up and unlocked my bedroom door. I looked around at our tiny living room and across to Aubry's bedroom. His door was closed and the light was on, so he must have been there. Maybe he was expecting Megan. I rolled my eyes at the thought of his annoying girlfriend. I felt the blood drain from my face when I looked through the peephole. The last person on earth that I expected or wanted to see was looking back at me.

I opened the door slowly.

"What are you doing here?" I asked as I played with the hem of my shirt.

"Visiting," he said abruptly. "Aubry home?"

"Yes," I replied as I moved out of the way to let him in.

He stepped in and looked around. I wondered how his place looked. I'd never been; I'd stayed away like I said I would. The amount of times I'd seen him could be counted on one hand. I saw him for Christmas every year at Maggie's, and that was about it. He still looked weird to me with his short hair. He strode over to Aubry's room and knocked on the door, making it obvious that he'd been here before. That was news to me. I turned on my heels to go back to my own room.

"You look different," he said, making me halt mid step.

I turned back around and found him examining me—or undressing me. The look he was giving me made me run my hands up and down my crossed arms, even though the heater was on.

"Thanks, I guess," I replied with a shrug. "I liked your hair long."

He gave me a smile, and even though it was a sad smile, it melted my heart. That was the first real smile he'd given me since ... well, in a long time. His smile fell suddenly as he looked over my shoulder. Zack threw his arm around me and looked at Cole.

"Zack," he said, introducing himself with a nod, before he nuzzled into my neck.

"Cole," he returned, narrowing his eyes at Zack, and clenching his fists at his sides.

I closed my eyes and took a deep breath. Thankfully, Aubry opened the door and greeted Cole with a hug, asking him if he had met his teammate, Zack. Cole replied that he had, his green eyes never leaving mine. I could tell by the smirk he gave me that his eyes were still undressing me. I shivered in response to his smolder and shot him a warning look that he shrugged off. I turned back to Zack and looked up to see his face and found him glaring at Cole. *Great.*

"Zack, I have to finish my paper, so I can't go anywhere tonight. I'll call you tomorrow after class," I said quietly as I turned my body into his embrace.

He turned his attention to me and ran the back of his palm down the side of my face. "Or I can just stay here," he said in a suggestive tone.

I shook my head. "I have to turn in this paper *tomorrow*," I emphasized.

He pulled my body into his and leaned down to give me a very long goodbye kiss, leaving me breathless. I knew he was putting on a show for Cole, but I went along with it. *He doesn't even know the half of it.* He stepped away from me and gave Cole a smug smile before saying goodbye to Aubry. The minute Zack left, I walked back to the living room to find Aubry laughing while Cole looked like he wanted to murder somebody.

"Oh man," Aubry said in between fits of laughter. "That was so wrong, yet so right."

"Karma's a bitch," I smirked as I walked into my room, shutting the door behind me.

Four years ago, after our first semester of college—and after that dreadful visit to Duke University—we all went home for the holidays. I was at the mall, Christmas shopping with Becky, when we saw Cole and Sasha making out. Making. Out. I could see her tongue invading his mouth, in the middle of the mall. In plain daylight. I gagged, like literally, I gagged at the sight of them. I couldn't believe that he would hook up with her *again*. That wasn't the best part though—of course, it couldn't just end there. As we passed them, they stopped kissing, and Sasha looked at me. A slow, sly grin spread on her face that I wanted to claw off—better yet, I wanted to shove a grenade in between her teeth.

"Hey, Blake," she said, her voice dripping mirth. "Thanks for putting Cole back on the market. He totally rocked my world when I visited him at Duke. Oh, that's right, you were there."

I felt like I got punched in the chest and kicked in the gut simultaneously. I glared back and forth between her and Cole, who was missing the color from his face, and looked like he wanted the earth to swallow him. Becky grabbed my arm and said something to Sasha about being a loose slut, and we walked away. We left the mall right after the incident. I didn't even cry. I was so mad and sad—overall, just feeling a whole mix of emotions. He wasn't mine anymore. He could do whatever he wanted. *Why Sasha, though? Why her? Why couldn't he just turn her down and pick someone else?* Then I remembered how she was all over him at the lake that day and at Duke, and I clutched my stomach. The rest of our trip Cole tried to get me alone to talk, but Becky intervened. Thank God for girl power and solidarity. We drank to that a couple of times during that break. At least I had my girl time with Becky to smile about.

After that, I made it impossible for Cole to contact me directly. Well, not really. We text messaged each other back and forth once in a while, even though I hated his guts. The loud knock on my door snapped me back to the present.

"What?" I called out.

"Open the door, please," Cole said in a pleading tone.

"Cole, go away. I have too much homework to do, and I'm not up for your bullshit."

"Just let me in. I won't bother you."

"You're bothering me now. Go. Away."

"Please, Blake."

"Why don't you walk around the building? You might find a girl willing to keep you company. Actually, I'm quite positive that you will find one."

"Blake ... please."

I ignored his begging, plugged in my earbuds, and blasted my music mix as loud as I could. I was rubbing my tired eyes as I looked back at the time; it was past midnight and I could barely keep my eyes open. When Alicia Keys started blaring in my ear, I groaned as I pulled the earbuds out, and tossed them on the desk. I loved Alicia Keys—I really did—but every song made me think of him. After I finished printing the paper, I got up to stretch and get water. I unlocked my door and idly wondered if Cole and Aubry were still here. When I opened my door, I found Cole sprawled across the floor directly in front of my room. I stepped over his body and tilted my head to look at him. He was sleeping. He fell asleep outside of my room. *What the hell?* I tiptoed to Aubry's room and opened the door slowly.

"Aubry?" I whispered.

"Yeah?" he said.

He was sitting by his desk on the other side of the room, so I walked over to him.

"Cole is sleeping on the floor by my door," I said, crossing my arms over my chest.

"Yeah, I know. He told me he was tired, so I told him to take the couch, but he told me he was sleeping with you." I rolled my eyes, and he continued. "I told him there was no way in hell you were going to share a bed with him. He said he couldn't sleep under the same roof as you on separate beds. I reminded him that he did it all the time during Christmas, and he said it was hell for him."

I felt an uncomfortable pain in my chest. "What do I do? I can't just leave him there."

Aubry shrugged. "I don't know. If you wake him up, he's going to your bed though."

I exhaled. "Damn it."

I turned back to my room and sighed when I looked at Cole's sleeping body. I took a couple of deep breaths before getting on my knees beside him. I shook him as hard as I could. Shaking Cole was like moving a big bag of bricks; he barely moved, and I was using all of my body weight to wake him.

"Cole," I started to shout as I shook him. *How can he be such a heavy sleeper?*

His green eyes popped open, and he sat up swiftly, banging his head against mine. We both cringed and rubbed our heads before I rolled my eyes, stood up, and walked into my room. I got into bed and watched Cole as he followed, closing and locking the door behind him. I averted my eyes as he stripped down to his boxers and settled down beside me.

"Stay on your side," I warned as I leaned over and turned off the lamp.

His low chuckle vibrated the mattress, and I moved over as far away from him as I physically could without falling out of bed.

My ringing phone woke me up the next morning. I slowly opened my eyes and looked down at the arm draped across my stomach. I gritted my teeth together a couple of times to control my temper. He thought he could just come barging into my life and flip it upside down. I threw his heavy arm off of me and got out of bed.

"Hey," he said softly behind me.

"Hey," I replied shortly. "I have to go. I don't think Aubry has class until this afternoon, though."

I walked to the bathroom with the clothes that I took out last night. Cole stepped in as soon as I finished changing. I gritted my teeth but didn't even acknowledge him as he stood behind me when I was applying my makeup. I was in the kitchen making coffee when Zack knocked on the door to pick me up. He and I had class at the same time some days, so we carpooled. I asked him to make our bagels as I finished doing the dishes. I sat down and tried not to make a disgusted face as I watched him overload his bagel with cream cheese. I always hated when he did that. We were talking nonsense when Cole appeared in the kitchen, glaring at Zack and me. I smiled brightly at his pissed-off face.

"Why are you so happy this morning, Princess? Did you miss me sleeping next to you?" Cole smirked.

I thought you could hear my jaw hit the floor. It was that bad. I bit my lip and grabbed my bagel as I narrowed my eyes at him.

"Let's go, Z," I said as I pulled his arm to stand up.

"Hc slept with you?" Zack asked with a look of confusion painted all over his face.

"He didn't sleep *with* me. He just slept in my room," I said, trying to save this morning from turning into a drama-filled battle. I hated Cole at that moment.

"You let him sleep in your bed with you?" Zack asked in a serious tone.

I threw my head back and let out a breath. "Z, are you serious right now?"

"Yes. I am dead serious right now," he said, crossing his arms.

"Yes, he slept in the same bed as me. Nothing happened though. He slept on one side, and I slept on the other," I said as I rubbed my forehead and Cole made a single cackling sound. *Asshole.*

"Hm," Zack replied before turning to the door. He shot Cole a death glare over his shoulder. "Let's go, babe. We're going to be late."

I looked at Cole and noticed his jaw tighten at Zack's endearment. I flipped him off as I walked out and closed the door behind us. On our way to school, Zack wanted to quiz me about Cole and our history. He told me that he didn't want Cole anywhere around me—least of all, sleeping in my apartment. He went on for a while, and I could only hear that noise the teacher in *Charlie Brown* made. I stared out the window while I thought about how I was going to break up with Zack on our way home from school.

When I walked through the door later that day, I spotted Cole and Aubry in the living room, playing a video game.

"Aubry, can I talk to you for a minute ... please?" I asked after I put my books in my room.

"Sure, Cowboy, can you wait 3 minutes? We're almost done with this game," he replied, never taking his eyes off the television.

"Why can't you just talk to him here? I don't mind," Cole said as he pressed down on the controller repeatedly with his thumb.

"This is an A-B conversation, Cole," I said with an eye roll before turning toward the kitchen.

When they were done, Aubry met me in the kitchen, and I quietly told him that I broke up with Zack but asked him not to tell Cole anything. I only wanted to warn Aubry since Zack was his friend and teammate. As for Cole, I wanted him to think I was happy with my boyfriend when he headed back to North Carolina. He didn't need to know that I ran off yet another guy—because I couldn't connect with any of them the way I did with him. I kept trying to tell myself that I just hadn't found the right guy. The worst part was that I had the right guy—before I drove him away, too.

The following night, the guys went to a party. They tried to convince me to go, but I told them that Zack hated parties, and I couldn't go without him. Aubry gave me a look, but

Zack wasn't the party type, so he wouldn't be there. Really, it would have been a great plan—if it wasn't for my sucky luck.

At 11:00, I heard them rush through the door and I sat up in my bed, putting my book down. Cole started shouting my name and pounding on my door shortly after. I got up and slowly shuffled my feet toward the door, praying that he wasn't drunk. I found his green eyes glaring at me as he leaned his forearm against the doorframe. Behind him, I saw Aubry with his arms crossed over his chest with a similar flushed look on his face. *Oh, shit.*

"How'd it go?" I squeaked. I hoped this had nothing to do with me, even though I knew it had everything to do with me.

"Why didn't you tell me that you broke up with Zack?" Cole demanded, narrowing his eyes.

I sighed. "Cole, that's none of your business. What happened? Did you hurt him?"

"No. I wanted to. I was going to. If it weren't for Aub, I might have killed that jerk."

I ran my hands down my face before I sighed and looked at him again. "What happened?"

"He was at the party, talking to some girl. She had her hands all over him, and he was loving that shit. I confronted him about it, and he told me you broke up. I didn't believe him. I thought he was just talking shit in front of the girl."

"They shoved each other back and forth, knocking over everything. When I noticed, I ran up to them right before Cole swung at Zack. I told him it was true, and we got out of there," Aubry finished in an annoyed tone.

I shook my head. *Unbelievable.* "You were going to punch *my* boyfriend for letting a girl touch him while they were talking? Are you hearing yourself? Doesn't it remind you of someone?"

"That was different, damn it. When are you going to let that go?" Cole pleaded angrily.

"Maybe when I forget how you rocked her world when she visited you a couple of weeks after we broke up. Maybe when I get the image of you two together at that fucking party out of my head. Maybe when I stop seeing her tongue down your throat months AFTER THAT," I snapped. He paled and took a deep breath. "You can sleep on the couch or on the floor or on Aubry's bed. I don't care where you sleep, but you are not sleeping in my bed tonight," I continued.

Cole nodded his head slowly. "I'll take the floor ... next to your bed."

I let out a sarcastic laugh. "When are you going to get over that? Why don't you call Sasha and see if her bed is unoccupied?"

"Are you fucking kidding me, Blake? I made a mistake. I was hurt. Can you stop rehashing that? I'm sorry. I'll be sorry for the rest of my life. Fuck," he muttered.

I turned on my heels and walked back to bed. Before I reached it, I heard a thump behind me. My heart started beating rapidly, and I looked back startled, not knowing what to expect. I definitely didn't expect to find Cole on his knees, right behind me. When I turned my body, he hugged my lower half tightly, crushing his head against my abdomen.

"What the hell are you doing?" I asked as I tried to pry his arms off of me.

"Please forgive me, Blake. Please. I swear it only happened that one time. Then at the mall she kind of—"

"Kind of what?" I interrupted. "Kind of plunged her tongue into your mouth without you noticing?"

He groaned and squeezed me tighter. "Blake, please. I was desperate for you. That was the first time I was going to see you after a while, and the last time I'd seen you, you gutted my heart for the second time. I'm sorry if I made bad calls, but I was so fucking lonely and depressed and sick without you," he pleaded.

I sighed. "It's fine, Cole. I forgive you. Please get off of me. You're still sleeping on the floor though." He let go and settled himself down next to my bed while I tucked myself in and turned off the light.

"Blake?" he whispered later when I thought he was asleep.

"What?"

"I love you ... more than you'll ever know," he said hoarsely.

I felt tears sting my eyes. "Go to sleep, Cole."

CHAPTER NINETEEN

Present

"Aunt Shelley," I call out. "There's a man here to see you."

"Be right there," she shouts back.

She's been in the kitchen all morning, baking bread and cookies for tonight's bingo guests. I can tell she's exhausted today. The chemo has been dragging her down more than usual lately. Other than bingo, she hasn't had the energy for many things. She hardly has the neighbor, Phoebe, over anymore. I think she's embarrassed by her hair loss. If I were Aunt Shelley's age and looked the way she did, not much would embarrass me. She's never told me her age, but I know Phoebe and most of the bingo players are in their sixties, so I'm guessing she's around that age. I've also come to that conclusion based on the music she listens to, which isn't saying much because I listen to the same music—and I'm thirteen.

She doesn't seem to know many people outside of the bingo realm, and those people are mostly Phoebe's friends. The man that's here to visit is younger than the others. I can't tell how old, but he doesn't have wrinkles. He's looking at me really funny, and it's making me feel a little uncomfortable. I ask him to come in, but he says it's best if he waits on the porch. I tell him I'm going to get Aunt Shelley for him since she still hasn't come out. He takes a seat on the rocking chair out on the porch.

"Aunt Shelley, the man is still out there waiting," I say when I walk into the kitchen.

"Oh, honey, I forgot all about that. Who is it? Is it Bob?" she asks.

Bob is one of the Bingonians—as I call them.

"Nope, this is a young guy," I reply.

She furrows her eyebrows and looks a little panicked. "I'll be right back," she says, throwing down her apron in a rush. "Watch the oven."

I'm curious to know who the guy is, so I wait until I hear the screen door shut and tiptoe to the living room, hoping to hear something.

"Oh, baby," I hear her cry.

"I know I shouldn't be here, but I needed to see you," he says, his voice choked up.

"I'm glad you came," she replies quietly.

"She's gotten so big. She looks just like her," he says hoarsely.

"I know," Aunt Shelley whispers. "It's so hard sometimes," she sobs.

"I'm sorry, Ma," he says. "I know it is."

I run back to the kitchen when I hear the sound of the timer go off. I put on a mitten and take the bread out to cool. I really want to hear more, but I don't want to go back. I know Aunt Shelley heard the timer; it was really loud. I wonder why he called her "Ma." I wonder how he knows me. He said I've gotten big, so he must have seen me small. I don't remember seeing him though. And who do I look like?

The worst part is that anytime I ask Aunt Shelley anything, she gives me the run around. I wonder if she'll invite him to stay for dinner. Maybe if he stays, I'll find out who he is. I doubt he will though. He sounds like he isn't supposed to be here. I sit down on one of the stools and prop my elbows on the wooden table and watch the bread cool. Aunt Shelley makes the best bread. She taught me how, but I don't have the patience for it. She tells me that I need to learn to have patience. She also keeps preparing me for the day that she's no longer here.

I hate to hear her say those words. I don't want her to leave me. She's the only person that I really have. I have my friends from school and dance, but I only see them in those two places. Our neighbors are all old and we live miles apart from most of them, except for Phoebe. She lives down the street and is only thirty-three steps away from us. I know because I count the steps whenever I go over to her house. It's always the longest and shortest walk that I take around here. I used to go over to Thelma's house, two miles down, when her grandkids used to visit. They stopped coming last year though. Now that they're teenagers, they're too cool to hang out with their grandma. Either way, Aunt Shelley is the only family I have. This is the only home I have.

"Is the bread done?" Aunt Shelley asks when she steps back in to the kitchen.

When I look at her, I can tell she's been crying. Her blue eyes are glossy, and her face is puffy.

"Are you okay?" I ask concerned.

She gives me a sad smile. "I am. I just haven't seen my friend in a long time. He's very dear to me."

I frown. "Why hasn't he come before?"

"He has, but work keeps him away sometimes."

I nod even though I don't understand.

The rest of the night is spent with the Bingonians cackling away at memories they have together. Aunt Shelley laughs along, and it makes me smile. She doesn't smile too often. Well, she does, but it's usually a sad smile as if she's missing something—or someone. None of her friends bring up any family Aunt Shelley may have had. She doesn't have any photos around her house—other than the ones of me and some of her when she was younger.

I ask her if she'd ever been in love, and she smiles brightly and says that she had been.

"What happened?" I ask.

She gives me a small smile and caresses my cheek. "Sometimes you need to do things that hurt in order to protect the ones you love." I frown and ponder her answer but don't question her about it, even though it doesn't make any sense to me.

I've never asked if she had kids. Surely, if she did, I would have met them in the almost ten years I'd been living here. As the weeks pass, Aunt Shelley becomes weaker. Every day, she rambles on about things that don't make much sense. She tells me that one day I'll understand my life. She tells me that if I ever find a good man that puts others before himself, I should hold on to him.

"Find a man that will watch over you. Don't settle for men who only have one thing in mind. If he doesn't like to eat, something is wrong with him," she says, which makes me laugh. "He needs to put you before himself—always," she would tell me. "He needs to love you more than you love him." That one confuses me a bit, but I don't ask.

The rambling goes on for a week before the live-in nurse we had tells me that the medication is making her a little spacey. One night Aunt Shelley asks me to lie in bed with her. With tired, shaky hands, she strokes my long hair and caresses my face.

"You mustn't be afraid of love, Blake. No matter what you go through in life, don't be afraid to love. Loving is the only thing that keeps us sane. If it weren't for love, the suffering we experience wouldn't be worth it. If it weren't for the suffering, we wouldn't cherish the good things life gives us. Sometimes it'll seem as though life only knocks you down, but you have to learn to pick yourself up and fight back. I love you, Blake. I will always love you even when I'm no longer here to tell you," Aunt Shelley breathes weakly.

"I love you, too, Aunt Shelley," I whisper as tears run down my face.

Her hand stills in my hair, and I look up to see her smiling at me. A happy smile. I sleep in her bed that night. The next morning I get up to shower, careful not to wake her, and when I get back to her room after drying my hair and changing, the nurse tells me that Shelley is gone.

Phoebe comes over within ten minutes. I lock myself in my room for a couple of hours before Phoebe tells me that I have to go stay with her for a couple of days. Aunt Shelley has left preparations for her funeral and burial. I don't remember any of it. Those days are a blur to me. I feel dozens of hands on my shoulders. I hear hundreds of "I'm sorry for your loss" sentiments. The only thing I remember is the empty feeling in my heart and thinking that I was alone, again.

When Phoebe asks me to pack up because she's going to drive me to Mrs. Parker's house, I am still empty. When I get to Mrs. Parker's house and meet the other kids, I feel at home and my heart starts to refuel with love—little by little.

I'm thankful to Shelley for the advice she gave me that week and I'm thankful that I still remember it. Thinking of her happy smile that night still makes me smile even though it was bittersweet. In retrospect, I wish I would have been more aware during the funeral and burial. I wish I could remember the faces of those who went. I wonder if that man that called her "Ma" was there. I wonder if Mark was there. I think back to the letter she left me—the one I decided to burn. She wrote that she was not my aunt. I figure that to be my aunt she would have had to be younger—but you never know. I don't know who she could have been. Unless—

My thoughts are interrupted by my ringing house phone. I groan and reach over to pick it up. Cole left for work a while ago, and Aubry and Aimee are away this week. I wonder which one of them is calling—or maybe it's Becky. I look at the caller ID, and it says *Private*. I consider letting the machine pick it up, but curiosity gets the best of me—as usual.

"Hello?" I say.

"Is this Blake?" a harsh male voice asks.

"Who's calling?"

"An old friend of her pops," he replies, giving me chills.

What the fuck?

"Blake doesn't have a father," I reply as evenly as I can.

He laughs and coughs heavily. I can tell he's a smoker. "Everybody has a father, Cupcake. Let me speak to Blake."

"Blake's father is dead, sir. Please don't call here again," I say before hanging up.

I feel my face heat from the blood rushing to my head before the phone rings again. *Private caller.* I grab my cell phone with my shaky hands and call the first person I think of-Mark. I rapidly explain the call I received and what the man said to me. He tells me that he's sending Bruce—my old security guy—to pick me up in five minutes. I agree and start getting dressed rapidly. When I'm in the closet, I hear the machine beep, and the same man's voice flows through the room.

"Blake, pick up the phone," the rough voice says. "Your father's not dead. He just doesn't want to be found ... but I can take you to him." My stomach drops and I hold on to the doorframe as I try to catch my breath.

Why are these people bothering me? How did he get my information?

"Blake, what happened to the boy? Catherine?"

I can't breathe. I try, but I can't. Only gasps escape me. My legs finally begin to function, and I run to the phone.

"Hello?" I shout. "Hello?" But the line is silent.

A loud knock on my front door makes me jump. I take a couple of deep breaths and walk out of my room. I look through the peephole and see Bruce standing on the other side, his full-grown beard bleeding into his scruffy salt-and-pepper hair. I open the door and see him eye me curiously. I look down and see my disheveled wardrobe. I grab my long black pea coat and put it on. It'll have to do.

I ask Bruce to give me a minute and run back to my room to grab the answering machine. I have to play the message for Mark. When I get to his office, I don't even bother to check in with Skipper. I just barge right into Mark's office. He looks up annoyed but stands when he sees it's me. I take a seat before he reaches me, because the adrenaline I'm running on is fading, making my knees weak again.

"Are you alright? Give me the machine," he says, grabbing it from my hands. "Let me get you some water."

As he serves me the water, I explain to him again what my conversation with the man was like. He plugs in the machine, and when I hear the voice, I cover my ears and look down. I can't bear to hear the man's words again. I look at Mark and his face has completely gone pale.

"Who is it?" I ask, my voice barely a whisper.

He clutches on to his shoulder as if he's been hit by a bullet and sinks into his seat. He doesn't answer me. He just stares blankly into my face.

"Is it true? Is my father alive?"

He exhales. "Your father … I can't talk about him right now," he says as he looks around his office, conveying a secret message to me. *Oh shit. This is bad.* "He's been dead a long time though," he says, but his eyes are telling me a different tale—a tale he needs me to know now.

I nod. "Yeah, you told me," I say, playing along. "Anyway, I just needed you to hear this. Do you know who it is?"

He nods but doesn't say a word. I know we're being taped or recorded, so I don't ask anymore.

"Mark ..." I whisper. "Cole ..." I say, taking a breath between my words, willing my tears to stay in my eyes. "If anything happens to me …" I choke through a sob. "Will you please take care of him?" I cry.

Mark looks at me with sad eyes for a long time before he nods his head.

"Blake," he says softly. "I'll always watch over both of you."

"Promise me, Mark. If anything happens to me, please promise me," I whimper, no longer in control of my sobbing. "Promise me that no matter what he says, you'll have two security guards on him. Promise me," I scream.

"I promise, I promise. Nothing is going to happen," he says sadly.

"It already has, though," I reply weakly. "It already has."

He doesn't correct me. He knows as well as I do that things we cannot control—and things I do not understand—are happening.

"Do you want to go out for lunch?" he asks.

I don't hesitate. I'm dying to get out of this office. Maybe we'll go somewhere we can speak more freely. I send Cole a text message, saying that I'm out to lunch with Mark. I can't tell him what it's about over text, or he'll leave work early. I ask Bruce to please get two of his guys to watch Cole without him noticing.

Mark and I arrive at a Lou Malnati's Pizzeria, home of the best deep-dish pizza—in my opinion anyway. We sit at a small table in the back of the restaurant and order one large cheese pizza and a pop each.

"So is this the part that you tell me how you and I are connected?" I ask.

Mark laughs. "You never give up, huh?"

"Nah," I say, smiling sadly and shaking my head.

"Blake, does it matter who I am? You know I'm taking care of you guys."

"I also know you helped take us," I retort, raising an eyebrow.

"Touché."

"Mark, be serious. Why were you involved?" I ask.

He lets out a breath and closes his eyes for a second before he answers.

"I was young—too young. I guess you could say that I was in the wrong place at the wrong time. I was at a point in my life where I was trying to do the right thing but still wanted to be cool. My brother was always walking on the wrong side of the law; I wasn't. The guys that took you—were involved in horrible things. Hell, my entire family was. They came to our house that night looking for him. Since he wasn't there, they took me. At first, I thought it was cool because I was going to live my brother's life for a little while. Then, they held me at gunpoint and asked me where Camden lived. I thought it was a joke. Everyone knew where Camden lived. I took them there, thinking they would let me go. They didn't. They got Nathan and threw him in the back of the truck with me. The leader of the two drove to your house," he paused and took a sip of pop, his eyes watering. I wasn't sure if it was from the sizzling pop or from the memory. "They—" he started in a hoarse voice before he cleared his throat. "Nathan cried the entire ride over. He was screaming for his parents. He kept looking at me as if I should help him, but I didn't know how I could. I didn't want to get us both killed. When we got to your house, they wouldn't let me out of the van. They were talking about it in the car. They said they were going to take your dad as ransom. I knew they wouldn't kill anybody there. I didn't think they could have possibly been *that* stupid.

"When I heard the gunshots coming from inside, I got out of the van and ran to the house. The main guy stopped me and told me that if I did anything stupid, he'd put a bullet in ... in your head. I told him I wouldn't, and he gave me two needles with a tranquilizer in them. Nathan had followed me out and was sticking by me when I looked in the kitchen. The other guy, whom I'd never seen before, was carrying your dad on his shoulder. I thought he was dead. When I looked at the floor and saw ... I had to step back out. One of the guys grabbed Nathan and took him back to the truck while I went to the side of the house to compose myself. I put on a brave face for you—or I tried to. I had only seen you a couple of times before that. I went in and gave you the tranquilizer, hoping to numb you from your pain and rid you of that awful memory. I'm so sorry, Blake," he said, tears streaming down his face.

My shoulders are shaking in quiet sobs as I listen to him. We're getting looks from the people around us, but we don't care.

"I'm so, so sorry. I didn't know what they were doing. I did what I could for you and Nathan. The head guy took off in another car with your father and left us behind with the other guy. I tried to pay him off. I promised him things. I knew who he worked for, and I knew that he wasn't happy about the predicament he was put in. He agreed to leave and never come back. I had you guys to deal with, and they wanted you dead, so I took Nathan to Maggie's because I'd heard of her from my mother, and I took you to Shelley's," he says, taking a deep breath and meeting my gaze, "because she was my mother."

I feel the air constrict in my lungs as I sit there, completely dumbfounded. I was looking for the truth, and now I had it. After a couple of minutes of pulling ourselves together quietly, the pizza arrived. We had both lost our appetites, and even though we both agreed that this was our favorite pie, we couldn't finish it. We could barely eat the slices we had on our plates.

"Do you know the guy with the glass eye?" I ask as I play with the melted cheese on my plate.

He sighs loudly, making me look up and see his mournful eyes. "I did. I knew him well, once upon a time."

I nod in response. "It's a lot to take in. I guess it's different, hearing it from your perspective, since you were older than us and actually remember it."

"I remember it every day, and every day, I wish I didn't," he replies solemnly.

CHAPTER TWENTY

Present

5 months later

Everything is blooming outside of the full-length windows of the two-bedroom apartment Cole and I bought together a couple of months ago. We decided that we'd look for a bigger place later—when we really need one. Our place is close to Soldier Field and to any job that I'll get once I pass the bar this summer. (Knock on wood.) Aimee and I have been studying for a couple of months now. We're both excited to put the killer that is law school behind us and get on with our lives.

As I rummage through the kitchen drawers, looking for a spatula to decorate a cake for Cole's birthday—which is today—I stumble across the Christmas card we sent out months back and smile. It's a picture of Cole and me standing in front of the tree in Rockefeller Center in New York, as we do our best Home Alone "scream face" expressions. I tuck the picture back in the drawer when I hear the shower turn off. I go back to icing the cake and turn around when I hear the bedroom door open. I turn and find Cole dripping wet, with a towel wrapped around his waist. His wet long hair is flicking up and down every time he blinks, and his crooked grin tells me he's up to no good.

"Why are you wet?" I ask, crinkling my nose.

"I thought you were going to sneak up on me in the shower," he says with a fake pout.

I laugh. "Aww, poor baby. Get back in the shower; maybe I'll make an appearance in a couple of minutes." He smiles, flashing one dimple and winks at me before turning around—fully aware that I'm gawking him—and lets his towel fall to give me a view of his perfectly sculpted ass. I gasp loudly, which makes him laugh before facing me to show off his very hard—all over—body. I toss the spatula aside, throw off my While-I'm-Wearing-This:-I'm-The-Boss" apron, and run to jump on him, wrapping my legs around him as he squeezes my bottom and walks us into our room.

That night, Aimee, Aubry, and Mark come over for cake and ice cream. We all settle down around the living room, talking about anything and everything. Cole, Mark, and Aubry get into a heated conversation about street lights—yes, really, street lights.

"Why it is that you didn't go into law school, Cole?" Mark asks with a laugh.

Cole smirks. "Because I don't like bullshitters."

I slap Cole playfully on the shoulder. "Hey! I'm not a bullshitter!"

He grabs my hand and pulls me into his lap. "You are, and I love you anyway," he says before stopping my reply with a searing kiss. I'm breathless when I pull away. "Asshole," I mutter against his lips before smearing his face with the piece of cake I had left on my plate. We spent the rest of the night, throwing cake all over each other. When Aubry shoves a blob of ice cream down the back of my shirt, I decide play time is over. After we clean up and everybody leaves, Cole and I shower and lie in bed grinning at each other.

My heart is overflowing with love for him, for us, for our life together. As I look into his loving green eyes, I think of all the years I've known him and all the years that I will continue to know him, and it makes me smile brightly. I am so thankful for him. He's never given up on me, no matter how crazy and impossible I get. And I do get crazy and impossible—often.

I lean into his face, and just as I'm about to kiss him, I whisper, "I love you, Cole." He doesn't return my kiss, and his face is priceless when I back away. He looks at me in awe before leaning up on his forearm to look at the time.

"Eleven fifty," he announces when he looks back in to my eyes. "That was the best birthday present I have ever gotten," he replies, brushing my lips with his. "Say it again," he murmurs before sucking my bottom lip into his mouth and letting go.

"I love you," I say with a smile.

His eyes are glistening as he positions his body over mine. "I love you, Blake. More than you'll ever know," he says softly before he captures my lips in his again.

The next morning, I wake up smiling, until I recall telling Cole that I loved him. I take a breath and look over, expecting for him to be missing half his face. I literally put my hand over his heart to make sure it's still beating. *Ugh, I am so paranoid.* I lay my head over his chest, and wrap my arms around him tightly, as I silently pray that nothing bad happens. During breakfast, he makes me tell him I love him about a hundred times and kisses me each time I say it. Aimee picks me up for school later, and Cole goes off to work. He's working at a local news station today, talking about whatever sport is on this time of year. Probably baseball—it seems like baseball is always on ... or soccer.

The day goes by and that night is similar to the one before—minus the guests and the cake fight. I have never been so happy in my life, and find that I can't stop smiling. Cole has had the same goofy grin on his face since I told him I love him. It sort of makes me wish I would have said it to him years ago. *I'm as superstitious as a baseball player.* I roll my eyes as I think that, but it's true.

A couple of weeks later, Cole mentions that he has to fly out to New York, and will be coming home late because he couldn't get an earlier flight. We kiss goodbye before he heads to the airport and I get ready for class. Aimee isn't going to pick me up for today because she has to go to an event with Aubry tonight. We agree to get together at our usual Starbucks for coffee, and walk together from there. I've come to love Aimee like a sister, and I'm glad she and Aubry are doing well together. They moved into an apartment nearby ours shortly after we moved. I'm glad they didn't stay at our old place. After the break-in situation, I'd been wanting us to get out of there.

I feel eyes on me as I walk to Starbucks and look around anxiously. To my left, I find a man staring at me while he smokes a cigarette. The way he's leaning against the wall with his legs crossed at the ankles, as if he owns the place, makes me frown. His brown hair is gelled back, and he's wearing black boots, dark jeans, and a black cashmere sweater. He reminds me of a modern-day James Dean with his rugged good looks. I look away from his intense gaze quickly, because I don't want him to think I'm interested in him or anything. I can still feel his eyes on my back when I stroll by him.

I continue down two more blocks, shaking away the oddness of that situation, and arrive at Starbucks. Aimee is still not here, so I get our usual drinks and grab a table by the window. My heart drops as I'm rummaging through my messenger bag, looking for my phone, and hear a loud machine gun go off. I look around frantically, knocking over my cup of coffee in the process, and spot Derek as he walks behind me. *Damn it.* Derek is a heavy-set guy in his thirties that comes in here every day, playing his machine gun app as he strolls in and out of the coffee shop. The first time I heard it, I cringed and yelped loudly. After the third time, I decided to talk to him. I figure that if he comes in here one day with a real machine gun, he may spare my life for being nice to him. I put my phone on the table and pick up the cup. Thankfully, it was mine and already half empty.

"Hey, Blake," Derek calls out as he walks by again.

"Hey, Derek," I smile.

I look back outside and jump in my seat when I see the same guy that was watching me earlier. He's standing across the street, staring at me, with a cigarette in his hand—again. I feel my knee begin to bounce under the table as I bite my finger nails. *Why is he staring at me like that? Is he following me? Where's Bruce?* I look around anxiously for him and spot him on my side of the street. I let out a slight sigh of relief.

Once again, I think of movies—the ones where the unsuspecting girl gets abducted in broad daylight—and I get paranoid. I call Aimee; she tells me she's almost here, but I quickly tell her to go to school instead. I don't want her to be spotted with me, just in case. Mark said once that the people involved in mine and Cole's kidnapping start stripping off your loved ones first, and I can't let that happen. Aimee is confused but agrees to meet me at school. I don't know what to do. Should I call the cops or Bruce? *What is standard protocol for a situation where a good-looking guy is creeping you the hell out by watching you?* That's all he's done—watch me—but it's the way he's watching me. He's looking at me as if there's nothing going on around him. This guy could seriously be mental. He could be a killer or worse: a killer and a rapist. Well, I'm not sure if that's worse, but right now I can't think straight. Derek passes by me with his stupid app on full blast, and I jump in my seat again and let out a growl of frustration. *Damn it.*

I take a few deep breaths and finish silently freaking out before I decide that I'm going to ask him why he's looking at me. *What the hell?* I mean, it's 9:30 in the morning. We're on a busy street, so he can't do anything stupid. Besides, I need to know what I'm dealing with here. I'll see what I'll do after I get my answer. I take a deep breath and step outside, idly wondering if I should download the machine gun app, just in case. The weather has been marvelous lately. It's sunny and windy, not too cool and not too hot. Absolute perfection.

I make my way across the street and look around to see if I spot Bruce. I see him on the other side of the street and give him a nod, letting him know that I'm still okay. Bruce and I have an agreement. He can shadow me, but I don't want anybody to know he's watching me, so he keeps his distance. He's only allowed to step in if he sees me in real danger. The mystery guy is still standing in the same spot. His straight lips curve into a slow smile as I approach, and it makes me want to slap it off him. It's almost as if he were expecting me to go up to him—or worse, he wanted to corner me into doing it. I look across the street one more time and see Bruce making his way across the street as well. I stand in front of mystery guy and awkwardly cross my arms in front of my chest while holding Aimee's cup of coffee in my right hand.

"Why are you following me?" I ask in a clipped tone.

His smile broadens and he lets out a single laugh. "You got guts, girl." His voice has a different timbre to it. *Maybe he's from Boston?*

"Girl?" I repeat, narrowing my eyes at him. He doesn't give me a creepy vibe up close—well, not a *completely* creepy vibe. His eyes are hazel, they're light up close, and they're completely laughing at me.

"You are a girl, right?" he asks as he slowly studies the length of my body, with his hand under his chin.

"Stop looking at me like that. Stop following me. I don't have time to waste," I growl as I roll my eyes before turning around and walking away.

Bruce is standing on my side of the street now, but I wave him off dismissively.

"Hey, girl, what's your name?" the guy calls out from behind, and I can hear the smile in his voice.

I don't turn around. I just flip him off over my shoulder as I continue looking forward. I hear him laugh loudly behind me, and it makes me shuffle my feet faster. His cocky attitude reminds me of Cole's, but his words don't match his actions. It's confusing and unnerving, and it pisses me off. A guy like him shouldn't be wasting his time on a random girl in the middle of the street.

He obviously has money, judging from the way he's dressed. Even though it's not a suit, I know he paid a lot to look casually chic. He's also wearing a Rolex, which he may or may not have stolen. If he's an expert pocket-picker, he probably stole all of my belongings in the two minutes I was standing in front of him.

I stop walking and turn around to reply, because I really don't need another shadow following me around. "There are a lot of fish in the sea," I call out and stomp back around.

"That's true," he replies. His deep voice is so close to my ear that it stops me dead in my tracks. My heart is racing wildly, and I have to use both hands to steady the cup of coffee so that I won't drop it. He totally snuck up on me—ninja style. Now I'm freaked. "But they're only paying me to catch *one*."

My mouth drops and I turn to face him, but I can only see his back as he walks the opposite direction. I run up to Bruce and tell him what the guy told me. He assures me that he'll keep his eye on him. He took a photo with his phone while the guy was speaking to me. By the time I get to school, I feel like I've just finished running a marathon. I speed walk through campus and hand Aimee her now ice-cold coffee before running to the bathroom. I lock myself in a stall and take a deep breath as I lean against the door. *What do I do now? What do you do when the people you love may be in danger?* I call Mark and leave a message. I know I can't tell Cole about what happened to me today. I want to, but I can't. I don't want him more involved than he has to be. His life was already shattered once because of these people, and he's finally starting to pick up the pieces. I can't let them harm him again. There's only one thing I can do to protect him, and the thought of it brings my soul to its knees.

Cole gets home as I'm serving our shrimp stir-fry with white rice. He looks exhausted, and my mind is running a mile a minute. I'm thankful that I turned in my last assignments today, but now I keep thinking that maybe everything I did was for nothing. I haven't gotten a call back from Mark—maybe I should have left specific information in my message.

"Baby, what's wrong?" Cole asks, snapping me out of my thoughts.

"Cole, we need to talk," I say shakily.

He puts down his utensils and props his elbows on the table and arches an eyebrow.

"I've been having second thoughts about all of this," I say as I wave my hand around the apartment, before taking a deep breath to steady my voice. "I think maybe we need to take a break." I close my eyes when I finish because I don't want to see the pained look in his eyes that I expect to see.

I hear the legs of his chair screech against the hardwood floor, and I pop my eyes open. His jaw is tensed, and he looks livid as he corners the table, walking toward me. *Not what I was expecting.* He runs his hand through his long hair—the hair he grew out for me again—before he starts pacing in front of me.

He stops and looks at me. "Why? What brought this on?" he asks tensely.

"It's a lot of things. I just think maybe we should take a break and make sure that we want to spend the rest of our lives together," I say quietly. *This isn't going well.*

He laughs once and waves both hands in the air. "We just bought this place together. What the fuck made you think of this now?" he growls.

"Cole, I just need time. Please. Give me time," I say quietly and focus my eyes on the plate of food in front of me.

"What?" he screams, making me cringe. "Are you ... Oh my God, Blake. I swear to God if you even *try* to break up with me right now, I'm going to fucking lose it." He's shouting so loud that I can see the veins in his neck bulging.

"No, just a break," I clarify weakly.

He sits back down in the chair next to mine and puts his face in his hands, taking deep breaths.

"Blake," he says calmly. "Correct me if I'm wrong, but you already did this to me once before. I didn't want to break up with you, but I let you go anyway. I was young, and I was stupid. I'm not that kid anymore. You're going to need a better reason this time. A *real* reason. And just to be clear, I don't give a fuck what it is because I am not letting you go. Period," he says watching me intently.

I let out a deep breath. "Someone's watching me," I say as tears form in my eyes. "And if they're watching me, they're watching everyone around me. I can't let them take the people I love. Cole, they already killed my family. They were supposed to kill me. They got you once before. I can't let them kill you," I whisper brokenly.

He gets up and kneels down between my legs, before crushing my body to his. I feel his body shaking lightly under mine, and I realize he's crying.

"I'm sorry," I whisper.

"Don't," he says gruffly. "Just don't. Don't fucking say anything. Don't *ever* try to leave me again. I can't take it, Blake. I'll die before I let something happen to you, but don't fucking leave me. Please," he pleads.

I start to cry with him, and I replay what happened to me as he listens quietly. He calls Greg and tells him to get someone to watch him and Becky and does the same for Aubry and Aimee. I let Cole do this. He needs to feel as if he's in control, and I know this helps him. I let him take care of me—the way I always do—because I crave it as much as he needs to show me he can do it.

CHAPTER TWENTY-ONE

Present

They say we're all just one phone call away from our knees, and today, I learned the truth in that. I got a phone call at five in the morning that startled me enough to jump out of bed to answer it. Any phone call before six in the morning brings a dreadful feeling with it. I know something is wrong as I stare at the screen, but I'm not sure I even want to answer it and face reality. I look over, and Cole is still in an undisturbed slumber.

"Hello?" I manage to croak out.

"Cowboy ..." Aubry says in a hoarse voice, and I can hear him trying to control his sobs. "Maggie's dead."

"What? What do you mean?" I sputter.

"She's dead," he wails loudly. "She's dead! They shot her!"

My knees give out from under me and I start to scream. I scream so loud—all of my pain and agony pouring out of my lungs—that I'm sure I woke up my entire floor. Cole shoots out of bed, runs over to me, and grabs the phone from my shaky hands. I double over and vomit all over our hardwood floor, and stay on my hands and knees shaking furiously. When I look back at Cole, he's staring at me blankly with his mouth hanging open, as if he can't believe what he just heard.

I give myself ten minutes to pour out my angst and cry as hard as I can. When I look back at the clock, it is 5:27. I get up, concentrate on breathing, and take the phone from Cole, who's clutching it tightly, clearly still in shock from the news. I try to sooth Aubry and tell him that I will take care of everything and that we'll be over there soon. After I clean up after myself, I call and wake up Becky to give her the horrific news.

I make a note in my head of flowers, caskets, and burial sites that I've seen and wondered about along the years. I start to cry again—silently—as I speak to the mortician. *Maggie Parker was found shot dead from a bullet to the head.* Maggie Parker—the most selfless woman I've ever met. The woman who took us in—no questions asked. The woman who taught us to cook, clean, do laundry, and treat others the way we want to be treated. The woman who rooted for us when nobody else cared to. The woman who drove us to parties and movies and picked us up late at night and never complained about it. The woman who kept us safe and out of trouble. Maggie Parker—the only mother three of us had ever known. Shot. Dead. Shot dead in her own home. *Our home.* The neighbors called the police when they heard the gunshot.

When Cole and I get to Aubry and Aimee's apartment, Aimee greets us at the door and gives us each a long hug, expressing her sympathy. Cole runs in and holds Aubry in a tight hug as they both grieve the loss of the wonderful woman who raised them. She may not have legally adopted Cole, but she was his mother as well. I place my hands over my throat and cry as I watch them comfort each other. When

I fall to my knees, Aimee kneels down beside me and holds me in her arms, shedding her own silent tears beside me as she strokes my hair. I sit up on my knees and sob into her shoulder, and let her hold me tighter, until Cole and Aubry walk over to us and the four of us hold each other for a while. Once we compose ourselves enough, we head out to make the somber drive to Maggie's house.

When we get there, police tape is all over the place. The house is turned over, papers everywhere, furniture scattered. It looks like a botched robbery, but nothing was taken. The guys start fixing the furniture and Aimee leaves to get us food. I walk in the kitchen and am transported back twenty-two years, when I see the red stains on the floor. I grab on to the edge of the counter to keep me from falling, and close my eyes to cast my feelings aside. A strangled sob escapes me when I open my eyes back up and head to the sink to get a pair of gloves. Once I put them on, I get a bucket of water and a scrubber, and get down on my knees. The more I scrub, the less I can see the floor, but it's not because the blood stains are coming off, it's because my vision is so blurred, because my tears are making it impossible to see anything.

"Baby," Cole says in a pained voice. "Let me help you." He gets down on his knees beside me and tries to take the scrub away from me, but I yank my arms away from him.

"No!" I yell. "I have to do it. I have to clean it! This is my fault!" I wail as my body shakes violently.

He grabs me by the shoulders and shakes me roughly one time. "Look at me!" he shouts. I do and all I see is the sorrow in his bloodshot eyes, so I close my eyes. "Look at me, dammit!" My eyes remain closed as I shake my head stubbornly. "Look. At. Me. Blake," he repeats again.

"I can't," I say, my voice barely a whisper.

"Please. Please look at me," he pleads brokenly as he lets go of my arms. I open my eyes and feel my face twist in agony as I start to cry again. I throw my arms around his neck and sob uncontrollably as I squeeze him.

"I'm so sorry," I say in between sobs. "I'm so, so sorry."

He wraps his arms around me tightly. "Baby, it's not your fault. None of this is your fault. Please don't blame yourself. I know your heart is as broken as ours. She was a mother to you too."

"Oh God," I say as my chest heaves. "Why? Why? Why her? WHY DOES THIS KEEP HAPPENING?" Our bodies tremble as we hold each other, sitting over our loved one's spilled blood, tasting the smell of iron and Clorox that now lingers around the kitchen.

He pushes away and wipes his face with the back of his long sleeved shirt before wiping mine with his thumbs and kissing my forehead.

"We're going to be okay, baby. Leave this, let's call a cleaning company to do this," he says softly.

I shake my head. "No. I have to do it. Let me do it, please." He takes a deep breath and nods slowly.

"Okay," he agrees, "but let me help you."

I don't want his help. I want to do it on my own, but he insists on helping me—as he always does. So we scrub together. We scrub until the skin is peeling from our knuckles.

Becky and Greg get in later that night and we all comfort each other by looking at photos of all of us together and telling stories about Maggie.

"You know she told Cole to stay away from you, right?" Aubry says, smiling sadly.

"What do you mean? When?" I ask confused. I'd never heard that before.

"When you got here from Shelley's. She sat us both down, and she said she wasn't worried about me because she didn't see me ogle you. But Cole, she told him ... What was it that she told you, dude?" Aubry asks turning his face to look at Cole.

Cole lets out a laugh. "She told me that if I knew what was good for me, I would stay away from Blake. That she saw the way I kept looking at her and she wasn't sure she could deal with a pregnant teenager in her house," he says smiling. "She even said if I tried to chase after you, she'd find you another home to live in."

"What?" I shriek. "I can't believe that!"

Aubry chuckles at my reaction. "Obviously she was kidding! She just didn't want Cole to be trying to have sex with you."

"But still! She never said anything to me at all," I say, frowning. "I can't believe that. She seemed so happy when we finally started dating."

Cole smiles brightly. "That's because I asked her blessing the night of that Halloween party."

I laugh and crinkle my nose. "You asked for her blessing to drag me out of a party because you saw me making out with another guy and practically forced me to start dating you?"

Aubry, Aimee, Becky, and Greg laugh collectively as Cole snickers and gets up to sit on the floor beside me. He sits so close to me, that I'm forced to turn my body to meet his ardent gaze.

He grabs both sides of my face as he softly strokes my cheeks with his thumbs. "First of all, that *guy* you were kissing was a douche. Second of all, I didn't *force* you to do anything. You wanted me from the moment you stepped into this house. You think I didn't notice your catty looks every time I brought a girl over?" he asks with a raised eyebrow. "Why do you think I kept doing it?" he smirks when my mouth drops open. "I knew you wanted me, but I also knew you were scared of getting involved, so I left you alone until

I couldn't take being without you anymore." He leans in and nibbles on my bottom lip before he coaxes it open and caresses my tongue with his. For a moment we're lost in a world where only he and I exist. Where nobody can harm us or tear us apart. We're in heaven, until Aubry clears his throat loudly, and we're brought back to reality.

"You really brought all of those whores over to get a reaction out of me?" I ask, scrutinizing his face.

He shrugs in response. "Well, that's not the entire reason, but it was definitely a perk."

"You're such a jerk," I say, narrowing my eyes at him and pushing him off as he laughs and hugs my body close to his.

Days after the shooting, we have to deal with sentiments from the neighborhood. We're told what a good person Maggie was, what a big heart she had, what an amazing job she did with us, and how much she would be missed. We have blank stares through all of it. We stare at nothing as we watch her casket go into the ground. I feel so much of nothing it feels like my body is going to blow up. Even though Cole has taken every opportunity he could to make sure I know that I'm not the problem, I can't stop blaming myself. Cole and I had just visited Maggie and asked her about our past. We went to see her after those people started contacting me, and I'm thinking they probably followed us there. Guilt is eating at me little by little, and I'm not sure how much more it'll take from me before its belly is full.

CHAPTER TWENTY-TWO

Present

One Month Later

I decide to drop my issues on living with Cole, as long as he promises to have two bodyguards with him at all times. I can't stand the thought of him being taken from me. The police still have no leads on who killed Maggie. They keep saying it might be gang members in the area. They're full of shit, and they know it as much as we do. I've called Mark to harass him for information that he swears he doesn't have—and for once, I don't think he's hiding anything from me. I've decided to accept my fate and tell those I love that I love them. Because what the hell? If I'm going to die today, they might as well know it.

Every day, I call Becky and Greg and let them know that I miss them and love them. When I hug Aubry and Aimee goodbye, I tell them the same. I'm sick of living in fear. And if I'm going to live in fear, then I'm going to do it right, dammit. Since they've decided not to let me shut them out,

I'm going to let them know how I feel. I just hope my love doesn't kill them, too. I know those three words are not at fault, though. It's me—my presence. I'm tainted.

Every day since Maggie died, I've made it a point to take the long route home. I want to enjoy the buildings, the trees, the faces, the colorful flowers that are blooming, and the sun hitting my face. I want to enjoy the air that I'm fortunate enough to breathe and cherish the people that I have in my life. I haven't decided to stop searching for answers, but I've put it on hold. I'm focusing on the bar exam that I'm taking in a couple of weeks, which is more important to me—for now. I have a timeline of my life's events at home in my box. So far, I have a couple of things filled out, but no concrete answers. I walk around aware of my surroundings, but some days, like today, I let myself go and just focus on walking. Bruce watches me from afar, and I'm grateful for him.

When I get home, I find Cole packing for his trip to New York. I love that he loves his job, but I hate that he has to travel so much for it. His trips are usually one-day trips; he rarely even stays anywhere overnight, which makes it silly for me to even care about him going. I go to the kitchen and make him a sandwich and coffee for his ride to the airport. He sits on the barstool in front of me and watches me as I'm putting everything away.

"Marry me," he says behind me, making me drop the packs of cold cuts in my hand. I whip around and gape at him. He laughs and gets up to walk over to me. He bends down and picks up the packs of roast beef and cheese that I dropped, and puts them away for me before turning back to face me again. He holds both of my hands in his and kisses the tip of my nose.

"Marry me, Blake Brennan," he says as he looks at me with hopeful wide eyes. I bite down on my lip to keep from smiling.

"Aren't you going to get down on one knee?" I ask quietly, raising an eyebrow. We've talked about marriage before, and he swore he was going to orchestrate the most "epic" proposal-his words. *This* was definitely not "epic," not that I needed that. With the way my heart felt as if it were about to pop out of my chest, I clearly didn't need anything fancier than this.

He tilts his head and smiles. "You're right. I did promise you epic."

I shake my head slowly and laugh. "I'm kidding! Don't take it back!"

"Oh, I'm not taking it back, but I definitely want to do it over. I want you to remember it forever. I'll come up with something…" he says, his words trailing off as he ponders.

"No! I loved it this time!"

He laughs. "I know you did, baby, but I don't even have a ring yet," he says before he kisses me softly. "And technically you never said yes, so I still get another try. I'll see you tonight."

"See you. I love you," I reply with a smile and a loud kiss.

He beams at me. "I love you, too."

A couple of hours after he leaves, Aubry drops by. He's still unpacking boxes, which is absurd. He finds the funniest things from our teenage years and brings them over. I open the door for him, and we sit in the living room talking about Maggie for a while. Her death has taken a toll on him, and he's now swimming twice a day, instead of his regular one hour in the mornings. He says being in the water gives him a numb feeling, which is all he wants sometimes.

"It sucks to lose your mother," he says as he lets his head fall back on the couch.

"Sucks is a bad word for that loss. I don't think a strong enough word exists," I reply sadly as I squeeze his hand in mine. "I'm so sorry."

He sighs and looks at me. "Will you please stop saying you're sorry? You lost her too, Cowboy. If you keep blaming yourself, I'm going to disown you as my best friend," he huffs.

I sputter in laughter. "Really? Is that even possible?"

He smiles and shakes his head. "Nah, probably not."

"So what'd you find this time?" I ask him as I cross one leg under the other.

"Well, other than these," he says, smiling and handing me our old Jax sets. "I found this," he gives me a ratty-looking envelope.

"What is it?" I ask with wide eyes. "Oh my God, Aubry. Don't tell me you had a crush on me all this time!" I squeal.

He throws his head back and laughs loudly. "Fuck, Cowboy, it took you *this* long to notice?" he asks amused. "I gotta step up my game!"

I laugh and roll my eyes. "Really, though, what is it?" I ask examining the envelope in my hand.

"It's the letter that Cole gave me that time, you know, after we went to see him? At Duke?"

He sees the realization cross my face and nods along with me. "Oh," is all I can reply. I'm not sure if I want to read this—ever.

"Well, I figured you're together now. You won't die if you read it. Or you can just throw it away. I didn't want to make the decision for you."

"You didn't read it?" I ask surprised.

He tilts his head and gives me a look. "Of course I fucking read it. Have you met me?"

I laugh loudly, because Aubry is seriously one of the nosiest people I know.

After he leaves, I throw on a light jacket and decide to go to the park for a while. After walking around and lounging for a bit, I look at my phone and see that it's only 3:10. I smile and type a quick text message to Cole.

I love you.

I do this sometimes in the middle of the day—in hopes of getting him through a rough day. I'm not sure that it helps him, but I like to imagine his smiling face when he reads them. I press Send and lie back down on the grass. I hear a crunch in my back pocket and remember the letter. I sit back up and take it out. The envelope is unmarked. It looks as if it's been through hell and back—and in a sense, it has. I hear my phone beep Cole's reply:

I love you to the moon and back. Sitting in a meeting, scheming our epic engagement.

I laugh out loud at that before I put my phone beside me and take the letter out of the envelope. I raise my eyebrows at the sight of Cole's messy handwriting. His penmanship has definitely gotten better over the years. I don't know why my hands are shaking. It's not as if this letter will change anything now. The thought doesn't stop my heart from skipping a beat, though.

Baby,

I hope by the time you get this letter, it's not too late. I hope that I never have to give this to you at all. I hope that tomorrow morning you come downstairs and have chocolate chip pancakes with me, as you do every morning, and tell me that breaking up with me was the stupidest thing you've ever done. I hope you ask me to get back together with you, because I'd do it. I'd forget about the hole that you made in my heart when you said your goodbye. I know that won't happen though. You're stuck in your ways—as usual. You seem to think I would be missing out on some awesome college experience if we stayed together. I fucking love you. When will you understand that? I don't wanna see other people. There is nobody out there that will ever be what you are to me. Nobody will ever be pretty enough, smart enough, funny enough, or as big of a pain in my ass as you are. You're the only one I want. You're the only one I've ever wanted.

I hope by the time you get this you haven't moved on—but if you have, know that I haven't, because I'm not moving on. Ever. I don't know how to be without you anymore. I don't know how to wake up without your good mornings or go to sleep without your good nights. I don't want to know what that's like. I don't want to not touch you when I see you during holidays. I don't want to know what it's like to share you with someone else. The thought of that makes me sick. I can't share you, Blake. Please don't make me. I hope that when you read this, you'll be sitting next to me, rolling your beautiful big gray eyes at me. I hope that you lean over and call me out on how sappy I am for even writing this shit.

I hope you tell me that you know we can make it through four years of college, even if we are apart, because you know I wouldn't do anything to hurt you. I hope you ask me to give up my scholarship to Duke and go to UC with you and Aubry—I'd do it in a heartbeat.

These next four years without you are going to be fucking hell for me. Please don't make me go through them without you. Please say you'll take me back. I love you. I love you more than anything else in this world. It'll always be you.

I love you to the moon and back.

Cole

Through my tears, I can barely make out the last few lines. I wipe my nose with the back of my hand and look at the date on the top-right corner. *August 3, 2005.* My eyes widen. That was *before* we went to see him at Duke. That was ... oh my God. My stomach turns once more. That was the day I broke up with him before we left for college. *Why didn't he tell me any of this?* I close my eyes and let more tears spill out of them. I wish I could go back to that night when Aubry tried to give this to me. I shake my head. *No, I don't.* Everything would have been different. Yes, we wasted a lot of time, but it was for the better. We're together now, and nothing can break our bond. I smile at the thought while I wipe the last tears from my face and pull my hair into a ponytail.

I get up and shake off the grass stuck on my jeans before I start to walk out of the park. As I scroll through my phone to call Cole, I hear a loud sound and screams that startle me. I have the ringing phone up to my ear as I look in the direction of the screams. I feel a strong tug on my arm that causes me to lose my balance. I'm expecting it to be a rude homeless man or a drunk, anything but what I'm faced with. He's so close, and he's holding on to my arm. I open my mouth—

about to scream, and I hear Cole answer the phone. The man covers my mouth roughly with one glove-covered hand and it feels like sandpaper.

Through my muffled screams, I can taste the mix of gasoline and metal in my mouth. I'm kicking and pulling down on his strong arms, and accidentally let my phone slip out of my hands. My frantic eyes widen as I'm dragged away from my only source of communication. I look around for Bruce. *Where's Bruce?* My chest is heaving in panting breaths and I'm sweating profusely, but it has nothing to do with the sunlight that's hitting my body. He turns my body and grips me tighter in his hold, crushing my ribs.

A carnival of dread washes over me when I see that he's dragging me to an unmarked van. This is suddenly too familiar. Too real. Too much. He puts a gag in my mouth, and I am finally able to take a good look at him. He's a big man; I would never stand a chance against him. He has short blond hair and one blue eye and one brown eye—made of glass. I narrow my eyes at him and curse him for being so evil. Through his glass eye, I can see the reflection of my own. My eyes look stormy, surely a reflection of what's to come.

His eyes are filled with hatred that I don't understand, and I want to ask him what I did to deserve it. I whimper when he throws me into the van and pulls up the sleeve of my shirt to inject me with something—a tranquilizer, I'm guessing. I try to squirm away from the needle, but he pins my body down with his legs, making it impossible for me to move. He ties me up tightly with rope and closes the doors with a bang. I try to twist my aching body, but cannot move anywhere. My eyes droop heavily, and I feel them beginning to close. The sunlight is fading through the tinted windows; it's getting dark again. I will my eyes not to close on me. I try to force them open. I think of Cole and try to push through the tranquilizer's effects. It's no use though: my breathing is beginning to relax, and my chest is no longer heaving. My eyes begin to shut heavily—once, twice, then a third time. I open them one last time as I try to search for light, but I know I'll never find it, because *there is no light in darkness.*

###

Dear Reader,

If your TBR list is as long as mine, I'm sure you had a hard time choosing what to read next. Thank you for choosing this one. I hope it was worth your time. :)

I have a confession to make: I hate cliffhangers. I always want to strangle the author when they leave me hanging. So, if you're like me, I'm sorry about that. I wrote the ending to this story before anything else, so yeah, I'll try to have book 2 ready as soon as I can. I promise.

In the meantime, I would love to hear your thoughts on this one!

Love,

Claire

P.S. Thank you, thank you, thank you for reading. Contact me about whatever your heart desires:

CContrerasBooks@Gmail.com

Facebook.com/CContrerasBooks—teasers will be posted here

GoodReads me: Claire Contreras

Tweet me: @ClariCon

ACKNOWLEDGEMENTS

This is going to be VERY long, so bear with me. It really took an army for me to get this done.

Christian: Thank you for putting up with my craziness, never giving up on me, and treating me like a queen (even when I don't think I deserve it). Thank you for putting up with my snarky attitude and laughing at my sick sense of humor. Thank you for being an amazing father to our boys and for believing in me and my writing. Most of all, thank you for loving me. I love you.

MJ Abraham: I'm so glad we have each other to lean on during this crazy ride. Thank you for believing in me as much as I believe in you. One day, we'll move to a world where reading and writing are the only things we need to do to survive. Love you! Write on! Happenstances is coming!

A.L. Zaun: The original Colette. I feel like I don't have enough room on this page to thank you. You read,

read, re-read, and read again, and read again after that. Thank you for not being scared to tell me to re-arrange and change things that needed it. Thank you for spending so much of your time on this when you had your own writing to worry about and for pushing me to be a better writer. I can't wait for the world to read your triangle! ;)

Angie D. McKeon: Words cannot express how thankful I am for you. Thank you for: believing in this story, pushing me when I wanted to give up, finding me beta readers, being my friend, personal assistant, publicist, beta reader, and giving me the guidance I needed.

Taryn Cellucci: I'm SO glad that I got to know you during this incredible journey. You're so much like me it's scary (& pretty damn awesome, of course, lol), I feel like I've known you forever. Thank you for being HONEST, not sugar coating shit, being real, bantering with me about nonsense ... and for just being you. Thank you for reading, reviewing, and sending me picture messages (LOL). I really wanted to write Taryn "The Asshole" Cellucci, but I thought it would look tacky, so I'm writing it in here since not everybody will read this LOL. <3 <3 <3

The girls who have stuck by me from the very beginning and read all of my stories, no questions asked: Frances Molina, Megan Burgin, Mari Mendez & Nat Rodriguez, Andrenella Dielingen, Brigitte Aleman, Carla Crespo ... I appreciate you more than you'll ever know. Your feedback and support means the world to me.

My WWM Girls: Luisa Hansen, Lisa Harley, Crysti Perry, Lisa Chamberlin, Laura Benson, Sarah Lowe. Thank you for your support. I'm always rooting for you.

Michelle Finkle, Dyann Tufts, Barbie Bohrman, Sandra Cortez, Kimberly Shackleford, Ciara Martinez, Megan Hand: Thank you SO freaking much for reading this story, reviewing it, and for your support.

Jessica Carnes: You thought you got off the hook, huh? LOL THANK.YOU.SO.MUCH. for kicking my ass with your feedback on my first draft. Honestly, because of your feedback, this story ended up the way it is now (which is good, I hope, because if it sucks, then you have to take some blame too, lol). Thank you for being honest:).

Eli Salom, Alexandra Jorge, Yvette Huerta, Fred LeBaron (my book guru!), Christine Estevez: Your support means the world to me.

Mami, Jay, & Barbara- Thank you for your help and support. I love you more than words can say.

Stepha, Blanca, Diana, Anabelle, & Lidia: Thank you for always supporting me. Love you!

Sarah Hansen: Best cover artist ever. You're such a pleasure to work with. Thank you for going back and forth with me a gazillion times & for making such an amazing cover.

Jovana Shirley: Seriously, editor extraordinaire. No words for you, lady. You. Are. Amazing.

Keri Wilson: You ROCK! Thank you so much for the work you put into this.

Katja Millay & Kyla Linde: Thank you for answering ALL of my questions! I appreciate you more than you'll ever know!

Theresa Wegand: Thank you for going beyond just formatting.

My Secret Romance Book Reviews, Angie's Dreamy Reads, Shh Mommy's Reading, Books, Babes & Cabernet, Kindle Buddies, Book Broads, Book Lovers & More.

ABOUT THE AUTHOR

Claire Contreras graduated with her BA in Psychology from Florida International University. She lives in Miami, Florida with her husband, two little boys, and three dogs. Her favorite pastimes are daydreaming, writing, and reading. She has been described as a random, sarcastic, crazy girl with no filter.

Life is short, and it's more bitter than sweet, so she tries to smile as often as her face allows. She enjoys stories with happy endings, because life is full of way too many unhappy ones.

She is currently working on the second novel in her series.

Made in the USA
Charleston, SC
13 March 2014